Deadly
Ever
After

Also available by Eva Gates

Lighthouse Library Mysteries

Death By Beach Read
Deadly Ever After
A Death Long Overdue
Read and Buried
Something Read Something Dead
The Spook in the Stacks
Reading Up A Storm
Booked for Trouble
By Book or By Crook

Writing as Vicki Delany

Sherlock Holmes Bookshop Mysteries

A Three Book Problem
A Curious Incident
There's a Murder Afoot
A Scandal in Scarlet
The Cat of Baskervilles
Body on Baker Street
Elementary, She Read

Year Round Christmas Mysteries

Dying in a Winter Wonderland
Silent Night, Deadly Night
Hark the Herald Angels Slay
We Wish you a Murderous Christmas
Rest Ye Murdered Gentlemen

Ashley Grant Mysteries

Coral Reef Views
Blue Water Hues
White Sand Blues

Constable Molly Smith Mysteries

Unreasonable Doubt
Under Cold Stone
A Cold White Sun
Among the Departed
Negative Image
Winter of Secrets
Valley of the Lost
In the Shadow of the Glacier

Klondike Gold Rush Mysteries

Gold Web
Gold Mountain
Gold Fever
Gold Digger

Tea by the Sea Mysteries

Tea & Treachery

Also Available by Vicki Delany

More than Sorrow
Murder at Lost Dog Lake
Burden of Memory
Scare the Light Away
Whiteout

Deadly Ever After

A LIGHTHOUSE LIBRARY MYSTERY

Eva Gates

NEW YORK

Copyright © 2022 by Vicki Delany

Published in the United States by Crooked Lane Books, an imprint of The Quick Brown Fox & Company LLC.

Crooked Lane Books and its logo are trademarks of The Quick Brown Fox & Company LLC.

Library of Congress Catalog-in-Publication data available upon request.

ISBN (paperback): 978-1-64385-922-4
ISBN (hardcover): 978-1-64385-588-2
ISBN (ebook): 978-1-64385-588-2

Cover illustration by Joe Burleson

Printed in the United States.

www.crookedlanebooks.com

Crooked Lane Books
34 West 27th St., 10th Floor
New York, NY 10001

Trade Paperback Edition: May 2022
First Edition: May 2021

10 9 8 7 6 5 4 3 2 1

For my daughters, Caroline,
Julia, and Alexandra

Chapter One

Is there anything more perfect than a day at the beach? Sun, sand, water. The stuff of life, and time to enjoy it.

I love the beach the most when I'm alone, walking for miles through the surf thinking about nothing much at all, relishing the feel of the salt-filled wind in my hair and the cool ocean waters on my feet, watching sandpipers dart through the surf and pelicans soar overhead. I also love the beach when Connor and I have the chance to grab some quality time together, to talk about our lives and our friends and our jobs or to simply enjoy being in each other's company.

I love the beach in the summer when the sand's so hot you have to do a mad dance to get across it to reach the water. I love the beach in winter when the tourists are gone and the waves are high and rimes of blue ice edge the shore.

I live in the Outer Banks of North Carolina, near Coquina Beach, part of the Cape Hatteras National Seashore, an endless stretch of pristine oceanside wilderness facing east to the wilds of the Atlantic Ocean, and I'm so lucky to be here.

The beach is my happy place.

Particularly today.

I don't usually like the beach as much when it's crowded with people, but today I made an exception. Because these people were all here for me.

For me and for Connor.

My cousin Josie and her mom had wanted to throw us an engagement party, but in true Josie fashion, she decided to put a twist on it, and here we were at Coquina Beach.

Gripping hands tightly, Connor and I made our way through the sea oats and tough grasses and over the high dunes, following Josie and Aunt Ellen. This wasn't a surprise party—I knew about it—but I was excited to see what Josie had arranged and whom she'd invited.

We crested the final ridge, and I let out a gasp of pleasure. Beside me I heard Connor's deep chuckle. In front of us a wide swath of beach was dotted with umbrellas in joyful shades of primary colors. A stack of blankets were laid out beneath each one, with a scattering of chairs to provide seating for elderly guests. A larger umbrella shaded a table loaded with plates, cutlery, pretty paper napkins, and acrylic glasses. Next to it sat a galvanized steel bucket overflowing with ice and bottles. Two big chairs, one covered in pink cloth and one in blue, secured with color-coordinated bows, had been set up on the wet sand, and the table next to them was piled high with brightly wrapped parcels.

"I hope one of those chairs isn't for me," Connor said.

"No." Josie punched his arm. "I put it there in case some other recently engaged gentleman wandered down the beach this afternoon. Come on, you two." She grabbed my free hand and pulled me down the sand to the cheering, clapping crowd. I stumbled after her, laughing, feeling my cheeks flushing and my already curly hair curling even more in the damp breeze.

About fifty people applauded as we ran across the sand. Everyone was dressed in beachwear—sandals or flip-flops, shorts and T-shirts or light summer dresses. I recognized my closest friends, my coworkers from the Bodie Island Lighthouse Library, library board members and faithful patrons, Connor's coworkers from town hall, his close friends, and his parents.

And—I blinked in surprise—my own parents, Suzanne and Millar Richardson. I wrapped my mom in a hug while my dad shook Connor's hand.

"This is a surprise," I said. "Although a good one," I added quickly.

"We wouldn't miss it, Lucy," Mom said. "Even if I wanted to, Ellen wouldn't have let me."

"Darn right," Aunt Ellen, Mom's sister, said.

It was nice to see them. My parents live in Boston, and they don't get to North Carolina often. Mom had visited a couple of weeks ago, shortly after Connor and I announced our engagement, to congratulate us and throw us a small dinner party, but I hadn't seen my dad for several months.

They both looked good, I thought. Of course, Mom always looks good. She makes sure of that. She's always been an exceptionally beautiful woman, and she still is, even with traces of fine lines gathering around her eyes and mouth. I suspect she's had a bit of a nip and tuck here and there. She's the same height as me—a measly five foot three—and unlike me, she's as skinny as the legs of the sandpipers darting around on the beach, with wide hazel eyes in a thin face, sharp cheekbones, and light-brown hair highlighted in shades of caramel that turns under at her slightly pointed chin. I have her eyes, but aside from our height, that's about it for the resemblance between us. My face is round and my cheeks chubby, and my black curls can always be counted on to be some degree of out of control.

Her outfit, as could be expected, had probably been chosen directly from a Ralph Lauren catalog listing under "Beach Party": tight orange capris patterned with green leaves and blue flowers paired with a high-collared, three-quarter-length-sleeved, buttoned white shirt with the tails knotted at her thin waist.

"You've got a good day for an outdoor party," Dad said as he pecked my cheek in what for my father was an expressive gesture. He also looked good, I thought. His color was better, he'd lost a bit of weight, and his smile was broader than it had been for many years. My parents' marriage had almost ended a year ago, but they'd worked hard to keep it together. I hoped he was finally letting go of some of the workload at his law firm, passing the burden on to his younger partners.

"Would I have arranged anything else, Millar?" Aunt Ellen said.

"I can almost believe you control the weather, Ellen." Dad gave her a grin that I was pleased to see. Aunt Ellen and my father had never exactly gotten on. In all the years of my parents' marriage, my dad had been to the Outer Banks exactly once before, earlier this year for Josie's wedding. Mom and Dad met when she, daughter of an Outer Banks fishing family, was still in high school and he, scion of one of New England's oldest, proudest, and richest families, was on vacation from his law studies. They married far too quickly, without the approval of either of their families. Dad returned to law school and later joined his father's firm. Mom eagerly took up the life of a Boston socialite, which wasn't always as easy a life as you might think.

As for me, I was raised in Boston in the social whirl of my parents' circle, but I escaped every summer to the Outer Banks and the loving arms of Aunt Ellen and Uncle Amos. When my life in Boston imploded, where else would I go but to my favorite place in all the world?

I haven't regretted that decision for a minute.

I caught Connor's eye and gave him a smile.

He smiled back.

Our friends gathered around us, exchanging hugs and kisses, slapping backs and shaking hands. Someone pressed a beer into Connor's hand, and I accepted a glass of champagne. The flawless two-carat diamond set into my engagement ring caught the light of the sun and flashed as though it were sending a signal to ships at sea. Connor had had the ring designed for me, but he hadn't bought the center diamond; that had been a gift from a library patron whose long-lost family heirloom I'd found.

* * *

It was a great party. Laughing and protesting, Connor and I were led to our chairs and told to sit. My dad and Connor's mom, Marie, toasted the happy couple, and several guests said a few words that had me giggling and Connor actually blushing. Connor's the mayor of our town, so he's used to being surrounded by people and being the center of attention, yet I was pleased to see how boyishly embarrassed he was today. This was personal, not political, and he knew the difference.

At Josie and Ellen's insistence, the gifts were small and inexpensive. Some were practical—a stack of tea towels; some were frivolous—a plastic Halloween pumpkin to stand by the front door; and some were touching—a second-edition copy of

Pride and Prejudice in recognition of the opening-night reception for the Jane Austen exhibit at the library at which Connor and I had reconnected for the first time since our teenage years.

Once the presents were opened and words said, the food arrived. Josie owns Josie's Cozy Bakery, a popular spot in Nags Head, and she'd (as usual) done the catering herself. Not wanting to have the food sitting out in the hot sun, she'd arranged the timing of the party so her staff could bring it after the bakery closed at four. A huge tureen of cold leek-and-potato soup and another of chilled gazpacho were laid out beside platters piled high with a variety of cold meats, cheeses, pickles, sliced vegetables, and condiments, next to Josie's fabulous mini baguettes and freshly baked rolls. Dessert was a thickly iced hummingbird cake decorated with yellow flowers and two intertwined doves made of fondant.

Cradling my cake and a glass of iced tea (I didn't want to have more champagne than was good for me), I dropped onto a blanket under the umbrella where the library gang had gathered.

"Great party, Lucy," Charlene Clayton said.

"Thank Josie, not me," I said. "I didn't do anything but show up."

"Which is all you had to do," Bertie James, our library director, said. Bertie looked great curled up on a blanket surrounded by the yards of blue fabric of her dress, the long gray hair she wore in a tight bun to work pinned loosely back from her face and allowed to flow in a silver river down her back.

"I like your hair like that," I said. "I like yours too," I said to her date, Professor Edward McClanahan. He blinked and touched his tousled mop in confusion. Perhaps I had consumed more champagne than was good for me.

"We'll all so happy for you, Lucy," Charlene said. "You and Connor."

"Of course," Louise Jane McKaughnan, enthusiastic library volunteer, said. "I could have told you months ago to stop fussing about and get on with it."

"Of course." Charlene rolled her eyes at me, and I smothered a laugh.

"I agree with Louise Jane. And that doesn't happen very often," Theodore Kowalski said in a flawless English accent. "I don't think I've ever known a couple so perfectly suited to each other." He straightened the paisley cravat at his throat and peered at me through the round rimless glasses perched on his nose.

"Thanks, Teddy." I knew Theodore didn't have a wealth of experience in dealing with people and relationships. He was a rare-book dealer, and he thought the English accent, which he'd learned by watching *Downton Abbey*, and the old-fashioned clothes made him seem more respectable than the thirtysomething Nags Head native he was. He didn't even need the spectacles; they contained nothing but clear glass.

"Do you know," I said, feeling tears welling behind my eyes, "that I love you guys?" Definitely, I'd had more champagne than I should have.

We all leaned in for a spontaneous hug.

"You're not going anywhere, Lucy," Theodore said. "You're staying at the library, aren't you?"

"Oh yes. I've no plans on that score. Except . . ." I cleared my throat. "I guess this is as good a time as any to tell you, Bertie. Connor and I are looking for a house to buy together."

Bertie nodded. "I expected that would happen. Sooner or later."

A spark of interest flashed in Louise Jane's eyes. She glanced quickly between Bertie and me and then took a deep swallow of her beer.

I live on the fourth floor of the lighthouse, in a tiny perfect apartment I call my Lighthouse Aerie, which comes with the job. The commute can't be beat and neither can the view, but it's a long way from town, and it's barely large enough to accommodate one person without a lot of stuff.

Charlene let out a long sigh and pushed herself to her feet. "This has been great fun, but I'd better be off. Josie promised to save me some treats to take home to Mom."

"How's your mother doing?" I asked.

"She's doing great, Lucy. Thanks for asking. I see a small improvement every day, and her doctor's extremely pleased with her progress. She would have loved to come out today, but"—Charlene nodded toward our surroundings—"she can't manage the dunes and the soft sand."

"Tell her I say hi."

"Not to talk about work," Ronald said, "but . . ."

"Not to talk about work," Bertie said to Eddie, "means they're about to talk about work. In order that my staff can complain about me without me listening in, let's join Ellen and Amos." She gathered her skirts in her hand and started to stand. Theodore leapt to his feet like the true southern gentleman he is and gave her his arm. Once Bertie was standing, Eddie struggled to push himself off the ground, and Theodore gallantly extended a hand to the older man.

"Believe me, Bertie," Ronald said, "We have no complaints about you. I want to ask Charlene how things are going with those researchers she's working with."

"Good," Charlene said. "Although they scarcely need my help. They're both so totally competent. James in particular." Perhaps only I noticed a touch of color creep into Charlene's cheeks.

"What are they working on?" Eddie asked.

"Immigration patterns between Britain and the Carolinas in the sixteenth and seventeenth centuries."

"Interesting stuff," he said.

"And," Louise Jane said proudly, "because so much of immigration has to do with ancestors and family stories, I've been helping them."

"Louise Jane," Bertie said. "Please don't tell me you've told a pair of researchers from Oxford University that you can speak to the ghosts of these immigrants."

"Give me some credit, Bertie," Louise Jane sniffed. As though Louise Jane wasn't constantly trying to contact what she called the spirits. That she failed every time never seemed to dampen her enthusiasm. "No, I simply told them that my grandmother and great-grandmother might be able to help them sort through the wheat to get to the chaff, so to speak."

"Louise Jane is being helpful," Charlene said. "For once. She does have a wealth of contacts, and James and Daisy are interested in hearing the local legends and family stories. Legends, as we all know, often have a basis in fact."

Louise Jane threw Bertie a smug look that said *so there*.

"James and Daisy?" Theodore said. "Two of them?"

"James and Daisy Dalrymple," Bertie said. "Both are professors of North American history at Oxford University in England."

"James and Daisy Dalrymple." Theodore chuckled. "You can't find a more English name than those."

The color in Charlene's cheeks deepened, and she ducked her head. I hadn't been working the day Professors Dalrymple first arrived and were shown around the library, but I had subsequently been introduced and had greeted them on several occasions as they passed through the main room of the library heading for Charlene's office or the rare-books-and-maps room. Daisy was cheerful and friendly and sometimes stopped briefly to chat about the weather or ask my advice on where to go for dinner, but James's focus on his work never wavered. He greeted me with a grunt and didn't slow his march directly for the stairs. Or, I now thought, was he eager to see Charlene? If so, that would not turn out well.

None of my business.

"We're off, dear, and wanted to say our good-byes." Marie and Fred McNeil appeared at the edge of the umbrella. I leapt to my feet and gave my future in-laws big hugs. "Thanks so much for coming."

"Don't thank us," Fred said. "I never need to be forced into eating Josie's food."

Marie gave her husband a light slap on the arm. "Oh, you," she said in a tone that carried years of fond teasing.

I gave them both a smile. I liked Connor's parents a lot, and they'd been delighted to hear of our engagement. Connor clearly took after his mom, adding a masculine strength to the beautiful wide blue eyes, thick dark hair (in her case, touched up every three weeks at the hairdresser's) with a slight curl, prominent cheekbones, and strong jaw. Both of Connor's parents were tall and slim, and all three of them towered over me. I'd been pleased to see Mr. and Mrs. McNeil chatting with my parents and Aunt Ellen and Uncle Amos. It mattered to me that all the members of my family—the old and the new—got on well.

"I can't believe I haven't given you a hug yet, Lucy." Stephanie Stanton wrapped her arms round me. For once, I was being hugged by someone shorter than me. I liked the feeling. The next person to envelop me in an embrace almost forced the breath out of me. Steph's boyfriend, Butch Greenblatt, was not—to put it mildly—short.

"I'd stay to help clean up," Butch said, "but my shift starts soon."

"Any excuse to get out of the dishes," Steph said.

"Got that right," he said.

"I heard that," Josie interrupted, "but it's not necessary. Your brother ordered me to relax and enjoy this party and to pretend my own staff aren't catering it." Josie held a half-full glass of champagne in her hand, and I smiled to see it. I hadn't believed she'd be capable of letting other people do all the work. Maybe marriage to Butch's brother Jake was helping my cousin let go, if only a fraction. Then again, Josie's Cozy Bakery was a huge success; she shouldn't have to work so hard anymore. To make things even better, Jake had come to the party. He owned his own restaurant, where he was also the head chef, and he usually missed family events because of his schedule.

"Remind me again, Lucy, what book we're supposed to be reading for book club," Butch said.

Mrs. Fitzgerald, chair of our library board and enthusiastic member of the Bodie Island Lighthouse Library Classic Novel Reading Club, had made this month's recommendation: *The Hound of the Baskervilles* by Sir Arthur Conan Doyle.

I told Butch, and Stephanie clapped her hands together. "I love that story. So spooky: the moor, the demon dog, the family curse."

"And Sherlock Holmes," Butch said. "You might even get Sam Watson out to talk about that one."

* * *

The sun was dipping rapidly in the west, and people were saying their good-byes before heading for their cars. Connor came to stand beside me, and we exchanged more hugs and accepted more congratulations. Soon only my family were left on the beach as Josie's staff began clearing up the few leftovers.

"Now that," Dad said, "was a good party."

"It was nice. Have you thought about a beach wedding, dear?" Mom asked.

I glanced at Connor. "Thought about, yes. We've thought about a lot of things. We don't want to be too weather dependent."

"You don't want to go overboard," ever-frugal Dad said.

"But you want something suitable," never-frugal Mom said.

"Don't worry, Mom. You'll be involved in the preparations."

"You can count on that," Aunt Ellen said.

Mom sniffed but said nothing. The relationship between the sisters had always been fraught, but they tried to get on for the sake of their children.

Truth be told, Connor and I had done nothing about wedding plans. We'd tentatively decided on next August, a year from now, and that was as far as planning had gone. I'd been told, more than once, that the best facilities booked up years ahead. This party had been so perfect that right now I *was* thinking of a beach wedding. Although August was the beginning of hurricane season. Always something to bear in mind along the coast. Maybe a spring or early-summer date the year after next would be better?

As though he was thinking the same thing I was, Connor put his arm loosely around my shoulders. "Whatever Lucy wants is good enough for me."

"Glad to hear it," Mom said. "The groom has one job and one job only at a wedding. And that's to show up. On time, suitably dressed, and reasonably sober."

"I was sober at our wedding," Dad said. "Wasn't I?"

I was about to give Mom a wink, but the teasing expression died when I saw her face. The blood drained out of it, her eyes widened, and her mouth formed a shocked O. She was facing inland, and I was looking past her toward the beach and the open ocean. I whirled around to see what had caught her attention.

I suspect all the blood drained from my own face. I was certainly shocked.

"What's the matter?" Connor turned quickly. "Do you know those people?"

A young man and an older woman were picking their way carefully down the path through the dunes, a little white dog straining at the leash the woman held. The man was dressed as though he were about to set out for a day's sailing on his private yacht, in white trousers and polo shirt under a navy-blue blazer. The woman's high heels and snug yellow skirt threatened to topple her over. The dog was a bichon frise, all tight white fur, bushy arching tail, round black eyes and nose, pink tongue, rhinestone-studded pink collar, and pink leash.

"I know them," Mom said. "But I can assure you they were not invited. Not by me, at any rate. Millar, are you responsible for this?"

"I might have mentioned something about it to Rich," my father said, referring to his law partner. "But I didn't invite anyone."

The new arrivals saw us watching. The woman yelled, "Yoohoo! Hope we're not too late." The young man lifted a hand in a lazy greeting. The dog broke into a chorus of barking and lunged at us.

"Who are those people?" Connor repeated.

"Richard Eric Lewiston the Third," I said, "and his mother, the formidable Evangeline. The dog, I don't know."

"Not—"

"Yup. Ricky himself. The last time I saw Ricky, he was on bended knee proposing marriage to me."

Chapter Two

That was embarrassing.

Ricky and Evangeline exchanged air kisses with Mom, Dad, and me. Ricky grunted at Connor and stared out to sea, while Evangeline oozed false charm at meeting my fiancé and her dog sniffed at everyone's ankles. Uncle Amos, Aunt Ellen, Josie, and Jake simply looked confused.

"*Sooo* sorry we're late," Evangeline cooed. "It looks like we've missed all the fun. Pooh. Our plane was delayed leaving Boston. I told you, Ricky, we should have chartered a jet. I never like to fly commercial," she said to Aunt Ellen. "So dreadfully unreliable."

"I totally agree," Aunt Ellen said. "Don't I always say that, Amos?"

"What?" Uncle Amos said.

"It wouldn't have helped, Mother," Ricky said. "A private jet can't fly in a thunderstorm either. Everything was grounded."

She waved that trifle away. "And then we had to rent a car in Norfolk and drive all this way rather than conveniently land in a local airport. Such a bother. The check-in at the hotel took so long, and I had to bathe and change, of course." She glanced up the beach to where Josie's helpers were packing up the last

15

of the picnic. "Is that a wine bottle I see? Do get me something, will you, Ricky? Lucy, you help him."

I gave Connor an apologetic shrug and followed Ricky.

"Did you have to bring Fluffy?" my mother said. I assumed she was referring to the dog.

"Of course I brought Fluffy, Suzanne. She can't be left alone at home, and you know how busy Rich is these days. Now, I hope you're not totally full. We'll want to go out to dinner, of course. If you'd care to join us, Eileen, you'd be welcome."

"Okay. And it's Ellen."

"Perhaps not tonight," my mom said. "We've just finished a huge—and marvelous—picnic, so we are, as you put it, full."

"Congratulations, Lucy," Ricky said to me in a low voice as we walked across the sand. "Mom told me you're engaged. I'm happy for you."

"Thanks," I said. "Connor's a fabulous man."

"He has to be. To land you. I mean it, Lucy."

I stopped walking and turned to face him. "Why are you here, Ricky?"

"Why? For the same reason Mom sent me to get her a glass of wine she doesn't want. She doesn't want to congratulate you on your upcoming nuptials either. She wants you and me to get back together."

"Is that what you want, Ricky?"

He studied my face. He was a handsome man, in that New England preppy way, the look accented by the outfit he was wearing. I hadn't seen him for a long time, but he looked the same as I remembered, although perhaps he had a bit less hair and had put on some weight, all of it around the middle. If he wasn't careful, he'd end up with a stomach like a basketball by the time he turned forty. He was losing his hair quickly, and I knew he was self-conscious about it, but he didn't go to great lengths to try to cover up the bald spots. Ricky and I had dated for a long time. A very long time. When he finally proposed to me, I realized that the only reason we were still together was because our parents expected it of us. The Lewiston and Richardson families go back a long way; Ricky's grandfather founded a law firm with my grandfather. Both our fathers were partners there, and Ricky had joined the firm straight out of law school.

"I've thought about a lot of things over the past year, Lucy. You most of all." He rubbed at his chin. "I was about to call several times, but . . ."

"But you didn't really care, Ricky. That's okay. I understand. That's why I left. Because I understood that neither you nor I much cared if we got married."

"Things change."

"Some things change. Some things don't."

"If you want to get that glass of wine"—Connor slipped his arm around my shoulders but he kept his eyes on Ricky—"you'd better hurry. They're packing up the bar."

I glanced over to see Blair, who worked for Josie, standing by the nearly empty table, watching me with a question on his face. One bottle of white wine and several acrylic glasses were all that remained of our feast.

"Nah," Ricky said. "We'll go for drinks before dinner."

"Sounds like fun," Connor said. He didn't add *Not*, but it was implied.

Ricky looked at me one more time and then headed back toward the group.

"Everything okay?" Connor asked.

"Yeah." I wrapped my arms around his waist. "You've got nothing to worry about."

"Worry? I wasn't worried."

*   *   *

Curse good manners, whether southern or Boston Brahmin. Evangeline and Ricky had come all this way to toast my engagement, and Mom wouldn't let me back out of having dinner with them at least once. We'd been able to get out of it on Sunday on the grounds that we'd all had so much to eat and drink at the party, but somehow I got talked into joining them on Monday evening.

As I should have expected, Evangeline couldn't let an entire day pass without reminding me of all I would be missing if I didn't marry her son, and Monday morning she sailed into the library on a scented cloud of Elizabeth Taylor's White Diamonds, tottering on sandals with killer heels and draped in the latest summer wear from Dolce & Gabbana, not long after we opened for the day.

"Goodness," she said to me, after passing her lips a few inches off my right cheek. "This library is . . . small. When I drove up, I thought I must be at the wrong place, but then I saw people walking out with books."

"It is small," I said, "but perfect. Somehow the Bodie Island Lighthouse Library seems to be able to stretch at the seams when necessary. Would you like a tour?"

"Another time, perhaps. That's not why I'm here. Now, Lucille, we've known each other for a long time. I remember the day your mother brought you home from the hospital. She was so delighted to have a darling little girl at last. Of course, your father was delighted too. I—"

"This is the main level, with our fiction collection and pop-ular-interest nonfiction. The children's library's on the second floor; the rare-books room is accessed by the back staircase. Our academic librarian, Charlene Clayton, is available to assist—"

She waved her hand in the air. "That's all well and good, dear, but I would have thought a librarian as qualified, as pro-fessional, as experienced as you would get tired in this little . . . public space." Evangeline glanced around, taking in the shelves groaning under the weight of popular fiction, books for cook-ing and gardening enthusiasts, general history; the line of com-puters for use by our patrons; the cardboard cutout of Benedict Cumberbatch and Martin Freeman as Sherlock Holmes and Dr. John Watson in the alcove next to the table on which rested a deerstalker hat and pipe and a selection of modern Holmes pastiche novels. The display had been arranged as supplemental material for this month's classic novel book club reading of *The Hound of the Baskervilles*. "And Sherlock Holmes. Could this place get more . . . pedestrian?"

At that moment, another one of the library employees awoke from his nap in the comfortable wingback chair next to the magazine rack. Charles yawned mightily and stretched.

Evangeline noticed him for the first time and let out a frightened squeak. "And a . . . cat. You allow a cat in the library? Really, Lucy. What's next? A horse?"

"That's an idea," I said. "But I don't think even this library can stretch that much. Where's your dog?"

"Fluffy's waiting in the car. I don't bring her with me *every-where*, dear. Don't worry; I left the engine running to keep the air conditioning on." Charles leapt off the chair and wound himself around Evangeline's legs. She took a step back. He took a step forward. Like most cats, Charles knows when people don't like cats. And, like most cats, he makes the most of it.

I bent over and scooped him up. I tapped his little black nose. "Enough of that, you. Off you go; preschool story time will be starting soon." I put him down. I swear he winked one blue eye at me before slowly and lazily crossing the room in the direction of the spiral iron stairs leading to the children's library on the second floor.

"That was Charles," I said. "Named after Mr. Dickens. He's enormously popular with our patrons, particularly children and the lonely elderly. We welcome dogs also, provided they're leashed and well behaved. Libraries today are much more than a place to take out books. A public library's the center of the community, one of the last public spaces where people can gather without having to pay to get in." I nodded to the cardboard cutout. "The American public likes Sherlock Holmes. I like Sherlock Holmes."

Evangeline lifted her arms and held them out as though encompassing the whole of the library. "I merely meant that, as delightfully charming as this is, it isn't exactly Harvard, now, is it? You were doing such important work at Harvard. Helping some of the most prominent men in the world with their research."

"They have women professors at Harvard now, I've heard."

Her eyes narrowed as she bit back a retort. And I realized that I was no longer afraid of Evangeline Lewiston. She had no power over me: I genuinely didn't care what she thought of me. She gave me a tight smile. "You know what I mean, dear. You must miss it terribly."

"Actually, Evangeline, I don't miss it one bit. It's nice of you to drop by, but I have work to do. If you'd like to look around, you're welcome to." I lifted my left hand to point toward the stairs.

Evangeline grabbed my hand. She studied my engagement ring so closely, I was surprised she didn't dig a jeweler's loupe out of her purse and put it to her eye. "That's a lovely diamond, dear. And quite . . . large. It looks real. I'm surprised your fiancé could afford such an excellent ring on what he makes as mayor of a small town."

I snatched my hand away. I wasn't going to explain the gift to her. "You can bring your dog in, if you like. The view from the top is magnificent, and it's only two hundred and seventeen steps. If you want to go up, I'll unlock the gate for you."

She shifted on her heels. Not exactly practical daytime wear for the Outer Banks. I suspected she'd worn them in an attempt to intimidate me. In that, as in other things, she'd failed. "That won't be necessary," she said. "Another time perhaps." She coughed lightly. "You do seem . . . fond of this tiny place, but a few of us in the know have heard that the head librarian at the J. D. Rockenheimer the Fourth collection is retiring and they will be looking for a fresh young face to take it over."

Now we were on to bribery. The Rockenheimer Library is one of the largest private libraries in the United States, and people say its collection of letters from and to our country's founding fathers is unparalleled. Running it would once have been my dream job. But I have my dream job now: assistant director at the Bodie Island Lighthouse Library, "tiny" though it might be. I'd met my dream man here. I wasn't going anywhere. "I'm not—"

My protest was cut off as the front door opened and a cluster of people fell in. Daisy Dalrymple came first, followed by

James Dalrymple and Theodore Kowalski, laughing over a shared joke. Charlene brought up the rear, her eyes fixed on James's slim back.

"Oh yes," Theodore was saying. "The Lake Country. Wordsworth, Samuel Taylor Coleridge. Always wanted to visit the Lake Country, old chap."

Evangeline let out a small gasp, and I turned quickly to check that she was okay. She blinked rapidly, visibly struggled to control her emotions, and turned to me with a smile so fake it would embarrass a crocodile. "You do what you have to do, dear, and I'll show myself out. Mustn't leave Fluffy alone much longer." She laughed a sort of strangled laugh. "Goodness knows what she's capable of getting up to if she gets bored, and it is a rental car."

I wondered what had caused her to so suddenly call off her charm offensive, but I had no doubt it would be back. Charm and bribery. Maybe guilt would fall into the mix next.

If it did, and if she persisted, I'd have to simply tell Evangeline that arranged marriages had gone out with Jane Austen's era. I didn't want to marry her son, which was fine, because he didn't particularly want to marry me.

"Hey, Lucy," Daisy said. "Thanks for suggesting the drive to Ocracoke. We went on Saturday and had the best day ever."

"I haven't been down there for years," Charlene said, "not since I finished college. It was great fun. Teddy was nice enough to ask his mom to sit with my mother for a few hours so I could go with James. James and Daisy, that is," she added quickly.

Theodore grinned. "Mom enjoyed it. She said she needs to catch up with her school friends more often. Did you know my mom and Mrs. Clayton went to school together, Lucy?"

"I didn't, but I'm not surprised. Outer Banks links are long and deep and complex."

"As we're finding out, to our advantage," Daisy said.

"Can I help you with something, ma'am?" James asked Evangeline.

Her entire body almost shook, and she blinked rapidly. "No. Nothing. I'm . . . noticing your English accents. All of your accents, I mean. Are you on vacation in America?"

"Daisy and I are here to do research," James said.

"I'm a proud resident of Nags Head," Theodore said, his accent a reflection of James's. "And a proud patron of this library."

"Time to get at it," James said. "Coming, Charlene?"

"Be right with you. I'll check to see if Blacklock College has gotten around to sending us the map book I requested. They're not being entirely helpful."

"Imagine that," I said. We'd had contact with the professors of North Carolina history at Blacklock College before. It had never gone well.

Charlene laughed. "Miserable lot, they are." She gave James a warm smile, all dancing eyes, fluttering lashes, and dimples.

He grinned back at her. It was as though the rest of us had suddenly vanished into thin air. *Oh dear*, I thought.

Daisy hadn't seemed to notice the interaction between James and Charlene. She spoke to Evangeline. "Nice meeting you."

James and Daisy were both in their midthirties. He was tall and slim, with a large nose that didn't do anything to spoil his good looks, skin indicating Greek or Italian forebears, and thick dark hair brushing his shoulders. She wasn't much taller than me, softly rounded with sparkling blue eyes, chubby pink cheeks, and silky straight hair the color of the sand at Coquina Beach. Colored tattoos of intertwined branches, leaves, and flowers ran up her right arm to disappear into the sleeve of her T-shirt, and a silver ring pierced her right nostril. A thick gold wedding band carved with an intricate pattern of oak leaves surrounded the ring finger of her left hand.

Theodore gave Daisy a small bow. "I'll keep an eye out for anything that might help you in your work coming onto the market."

"We'd appreciate that," she said. Her smile at him was nothing more than casually friendly.

"That's a striking ring you're wearing," he said. "Most unusual."

"Daisy," James said, "doesn't go for the usual."

She gave him a fond smile. "And you love me for it."

James and Charlene headed for the stairs. "Hey," he said, "I forgot to mention. One of my mates back in the UK sent me a link to this hot new artist everyone's saying is the next big thing."

"I can't wait to hear it," Charlene said. "Why don't you come up to my office before starting work and help me download it?"

The corners of Daisy's mouth twisted in a grimace. "James and that awful stuff he calls music. Makes the man a nightmare to live and work with. I'm so glad they invented earphones." She ran after them. "Don't you dare play that racket around me, James Dalrymple."

"I'm sure you'll love it, Daisy," Charlene called over her shoulder, "if it's as good as James thinks."

"That," Daisy said, "is a matter of taste. I have good taste. James has none."

Charlene laughed and led the way up the spiral iron stairs. Charlene loved rap and hip-hop music with a passion, and she firmly believed that if everyone else was only exposed to it enough, they'd also come to love it.

So far, that wasn't happening to me.

"Lucy," Theodore said, "you called me on Saturday to say my copy of the book club book is in?"

"It's on the holds shelf."

"I'm looking forward to diving in," he said. "I haven't read Sir Arthur for a long time. Are you a Holmes aficionado, Mrs. Lewiston?"

Evangeline started. "What? I mean, no. Sherlock Holmes? Not at all. Dreadfully pedestrian. All those ridiculous television shows. I'll see you at dinner this evening, Lucy. I've made a reservation for seven o'clock at your cousin-in-law's restaurant because your mother mentioned how marvelous the food was at your cousin's wedding." She practically ran out of the library, her heels tapping on the tiled floor.

"That was odd," Theodore said.

"She is odd," I said. Yes, Evangeline could be "odd," but she was never rude. Seeing James had shaken her, but I didn't bother to wonder why. He clearly didn't know her. Maybe he reminded her of something or someone in her past. Did Evangeline have a secret past?

I chuckled to myself and answered the ringing desk phone.

Chapter Three

I told Connor I'd meet him at the restaurant at the assigned time of seven o'clock, and as soon as the library closed for the day, I ran upstairs to change into something suitable to wear for dinner with the family, and then I drove to Uncle Amos and Aunt Ellen's house. Mom and Dad were staying there, which showed how things were changing between my mother and her sister. In the past Mom had always stayed at a hotel, saying she didn't want to "inconvenience" her sister. Aunt Ellen had been more than happy not to have her, not wanting to wait on Mom hand and foot.

"Your father," Mom said, giving Dad a poisonous glare, "told Rich about the engagement party."

"I didn't know it was a secret, Suzanne!" he protested.

"Not a secret, but you should have known he'd tell Evangeline."

"What does it matter? I thought you and Evangeline were friends."

"We have never been *friends*, Millar. We are wives of business partners. There is a considerable difference."

My dad threw me a panicked look.

"It doesn't matter," I said. "I'm not going to dump Connor and run back to Boston with Ricky. Having him here is mildly embarrassing, that's all."

"I'm sure all they're here for is to wish Lucy well," Dad said. "After all, Evangeline's known Lucy since she was a baby."

"You can be so naïve," Mom said. "It's a good thing you never became a trial lawyer. You'd believe everything the witnesses told you."

Dad wisely said nothing.

"Mom's right," I said. "Evangeline still wants me to marry Ricky. Ricky came right out and admitted it."

"He did?" Mom said.

"Yes, he did. I have to ask: are you on my side in this, Mom?"

"Side in what?" Dad asked.

Mom ignored him. "I hope there aren't going to be any sides, dear. I admit, I was disappointed when you and Ricky broke off your engagement—"

"We were never actually engaged. I ran out of the restaurant before he finished the proposal."

"Creating quite the scene, which my friends dined out on for months after, to my intense embarrassment." She patted her hair. "However, that's in the past. I will admit, now and publicly, that I was wrong. You're clearly so delightfully happy here in Nags Head, and Connor is head over heels in love with you. And you with him."

"It doesn't hurt that he's a doctor," Dad said.

"And so dreadfully handsome," Mom added.

"Connor's a dentist," I said. "These days he's only a part-time dentist, while he's serving as mayor."

"He's still Dr. McNeil," Mom said. The sparkle in her eyes told me she was teasing. "You would not have been happy with Ricky, and I can see that now."

I decided not to tell my parents about the apparent bribe of a job at the Rockenheimer Library. My mom might say she's come around to accepting my new life in the Outer Banks and my relationship with Connor, but she's a social climber to the core. Having me in that prestigious position would be a notch in her belt.

"Why are we talking about Lucy marrying Ricky anyway?" Dad said.

Mom didn't bother to answer him. She often didn't. "As for why she's here, you're right, I fear. Evangeline has not come around to my way of thinking. She wants to see you and Ricky married."

"Lucy is getting married," Dad said. "Isn't that why we're here? To celebrate that?"

"Do try to keep up, dear," Mom said. "Evangeline wants Lucy and Ricky married to each other."

"Oh." Dad checked his watch. "What time are we leaving for dinner?"

"Why does it matter to her?" I asked.

"Because you're a sensible young woman from a good family with a proper ladylike profession," Mom said.

"Ladylike?"

"In her eyes, yes. You are, Lucy, in a word, respectable. Ricky has been, shall we say, up to some shenanigans with unsuitable—in Evangeline's eyes—women over the past year."

"More than a year. Mom, I guessed at the time he was fooling around on me."

"What your mother's trying to say," Dad said, "is that the Lewiston family is facing financial ruin. Rich has made some bad—very bad—investments, and his gambling habit isn't helping. We all know Evangeline's trying to exert some control over their finances, but it is Rich's family money he's squandering, plus his income from the firm, and she doesn't have the control she'd like. Evangeline needs an influx of cash to turn things around. And fast."

"But I don't have any money," I said. "Other than what I earn at the library."

"Evangeline doesn't know that," Mom said. "Your father and I don't discuss our private financial arrangements with anyone. Even Rich and Evangeline. Particularly Rich and Evangeline. You'll get your inheritance when your father and I are gone and not a minute before."

I've always known that. My parents ensured that I received an excellent education, finished college with no student loans hanging over my head, and had a good start in my career. They helped with my rent for the first year after I graduated from college, and since then I've managed for myself. I have three older brothers and they all have wives and children, so I'm not expecting to inherit a lot when my parents are gone.

Which, I hoped, would be many years from now.

"What are you smiling at?" Mom asked.

"Nothing. This dinner's going to be mighty awkward. If Evangeline says anything, I'll have to come flat out and tell her I'm not marrying her son."

"I feel a headache coming on," Dad said.

"No, you do not," Mom said. "It's time we were going."

*   *   *

Dinner began as a dreary affair. I don't mean the food. The food is never dreary at Jake's Seafood Bar. Nor is the atmosphere. It was a beautiful, clear warm night, and our group occupied a big table on the deck overlooking Roanoke Sound and the lights of the island beyond. In the distance, the fourth-order Fresnel lens of the reproduction Roanoke Marshes Lighthouse flashed its regular pattern and boats bobbed gently on the waves. I find the lights of a lighthouse, any lighthouse, comforting in their reliability and regularity. And tonight, even though I was sitting next to Connor with my hand held tightly in his under the table, I needed that comfort.

Aunt Ellen, Uncle Amos, Josie, my parents, and Connor and I had joined Ricky and his mother for dinner. Jake was in the kitchen, cooking up marvelous things.

I was confident in my love for Connor and confident in the strength of his love for me. But . . . Evangeline Lewiston was a force to be reckoned with, and always had been. My mom was a southern upstart, and Evangeline never let her forget it. Whereas Evangeline's family had—according to her—come over on the Mayflower and immediately set about rising to their proper place at the pinnacle of society.

I reminded myself that Evangeline was facing financial ruin, and in the circles in which she moved, financial ruin meant social ruin.

Although you wouldn't know it by looking at her. Small diamonds glistened in her ears, and a larger one hung from a gold chain around her neck. She wore a slim-fitting black knit dress under a gold lamé jacket with elbow-length sleeves that sparkled in the lights of the bar, and gold sandals, again with the dangerously high heels. A small clutch purse, also golden, rested on the table beside her. This morning her nail polish had been a deep red; this evening it was a light pink. She'd been to the spa.

Ricky, on the other hand, had spent the day at the beach or lounging around the hotel pool. His nose was badly sunburned and his cheeks were pink, a sharp contract to the white skin where his sunglasses had been placed. He turned quickly and caught me looking at him. He winked, and I felt myself color as I dipped my head to read the menu.

Not that I need to read the menu at Jakes. I know it, and love it, by heart.

Drink orders were taken. Evangeline asked for a martini and Ricky for a double Scotch. Connor and Amos had beer, and Mom, Josie, and I ordered a glass of wine each. My dad asked for a club soda with a slice of lime. I glanced at my mom, and she avoided my eyes.

"Is this your first visit to Nags Head, Mrs. Lewiston?" Josie asked Evangeline.

"Please call me Evangeline, dear. After all, we're almost like family."

Not if I can help it. I gave Connor's hand a squeeze.

"I've never been to your lovely town," Evangeline said. "Such a delightful place, but we're not exactly short of seafront pleasures in Massachusetts."

"How about you?" Josie asked Ricky.

He grinned at her. He'd been looking at my cousin a lot. Then again, men tend to do that. Josie's a beautiful woman and looked particularly so tonight, dressed in slim-fitting jeans and a frilly white off-the-shoulder blouse, with her long golden hair pulled back in a high ponytail and just a hint of pink on her lips. She and Jake had been married over the winter, and that newlywed glow still bounced off her.

"I might be persuaded to come again, given the right reason," Ricky said in a low, slow voice.

"Josie's married to the owner of this restaurant," Evangeline snapped at her son.

"Then I'm sure we'll get a good meal." He gave me a crooked grin. "In answer to your question, Josie—no, I've never been. My dad comes for the fishing most years, but fishing isn't how I prefer to spend my time."

No one asked him how he preferred to spend his time.

"Your dad fishes?" Amos said. "What's he after?" My uncle's a keen sport fisherman, and now that he was leaving more and more of his law practice to his partner, my friend Stephanie Stanton, he was looking forward to opportunities to get out on the open water.

Ricky shrugged. "The biggest fish, of course. What else would Dad want? It's a working vacation for him. He has clients with summer homes down here, and he takes them fishing once a year."

"You're not interested in fishing, Evangeline?" Connor asked.

My mom smothered a snort.

Evangeline shuddered. "I tried it once when we were first married. Worst experience of my life. Not to mention the most boring. But that doesn't matter. I have always maintained that it's healthy for a long-term, stable marriage when a husband and wife have separate interests. As you'll find out, Ricky and Lucy."

Ricky waved to the waiter to bring him another double Scotch.

"Shopping in Paris is one of Evangeline's interests," my mom said.

"As you well know, *dear*," Evangeline replied through gritted teeth, "I go to Paris for the art."

I took a deep breath and opened my mouth to remind Evangeline that I was engaged to Connor, not to Ricky, but Josie beat me to it. "Jake and I not only have the same interests, we work together sometimes. He helps out in the bakery, and I come here a lot to give him a hand with dinner prep. We believe closeness makes a good marriage. It will be up to Connor and Lucy to find what works best for them."

"Hear, hear." Uncle Amos raised his glass. "To Connor and Lucy."

"I'll drink to that," Ricky said.

His mother glowered at him, but she lifted her glass along with the others.

Connor and I smiled at each other. I felt tears behind my eyes.

"Compliments of the chef." The waiter placed a platter overflowing with crispy brown hush puppies in the center of the table.

"Thank him for us," I said. Jake knows hush puppies are my favorite, and no one makes them as good as he does.

My mom leaned over and whispered something into my dad's ear. He nodded, and then he got to his feet. "As the father of the bride-to-be, I'd like to welcome Connor to our family." Dad lifted his glass of soda to Connor.

"They're not married yet, Millar," Evangeline growled.

"What was that, dear?" Mom said. "I missed it."

"Nothing."

Connor was next to stand up. "My thanks to you and Suzanne for creating this marvelous woman who has been kind enough, or foolish enough, to want to spend the rest of her life with me."

"I'll drink to that," Ricky said again, and again he did so. Evangeline looked as though she was considering knocking the glass out of his hand.

"Speaking of dinner prep," Josie said. "I was in the kitchen before y'all arrived, and bluefish is the special tonight. Bought straight off one of those fishing boats you want to go out on, Dad."

"Sounds delightful," Mom said. "I think I'll have that. We've kept the staff waiting long enough; I'm ready to order. Josie, I'm going to have the bluefish. What would you recommend for a starter?"

The menu was discussed at great length, and finally the waiter went around the table taking our orders.

He left, and a man approached our table. "I thought I recognized you, Mrs. Lewiston. And Ricky. What brings you folks here?"

Ricky leapt to his feet and took the man's extended hand. Evangeline's face twisted, and she might have been considering spitting on the floor. Connor didn't look entirely pleased either, but he pasted on his politician's smile and stood up. "Gordon."

"Mayor McNeil." Gordon pumped Connor's hand enthusiastically.

He was a big man, tall and round bellied with pale skin, greasy gray hair, a bushy gray moustache that could use a trim, jowls that bounced when he spoke, and small but intense dark eyes behind thick glasses.

"My mother and I are visiting friends," Ricky said. "Everyone, this is Gordon Frankland. Mr. Frankland's an important client of my father and me."

Connor stared at Ricky in surprise. "You're his lawyers?"

Ricky nodded.

"I recognize the name." Dad stood and extended his hand. "Although we've never met. Millar Richardson."

"Pleased to meet you at last, Millar," Gordon said.

Evangeline picked up her napkin. She twisted it in her freshly manicured fingers. Her face was stiff, her lips tight with what might have been suppressed rage. My mom gave her a worried glance.

"Your dad not here?" Gordon said to Ricky.

"He couldn't get away," Ricky said. "You know what the law's like. I should be back in the office too, but I wanted to escort my mother."

"I know what the business of the law's like. I also know when a well-compensated lawyer's falling down on the job. I planned to give you a call later in the week, Millar, after you've had time to consider my latest offer. I'm glad I had the opportunity to put a face to the name first."

"Call me about what?" Dad asked. "What offer?"

"You'll find out. Once you're back in the office after enjoying your little vacation."

"I don't think this is the time or the place," Uncle Amos said.

"We're here to celebrate an engagement," Josie said.

"Yes, I heard the good news. Congratulations, Mr. Mayor." Gordon leered at me. "Shall I assume this radiant beauty is the lucky lady?"

He meant the comment as a compliment, but my skin crawled. There was something very creepy about Mr. Gordon Frankland. He winked at me.

Yup. A creep. He knew it and he reveled in it.

He reached into his pocket, pulled out a business card, and slapped it into Connor's hand. "See you around, Mr. Mayor. We still have matters outstanding."

"You can make an appointment by calling my office during business hours." Connor's voice was cool.

"I'll do that. If I can get my lawyer's attention for once. You might want to see to that, Millar. Have a nice dinner. Ladies." He walked back to his table, where he appeared to be dining alone.

The waiter brought our starters out of the kitchen and placed a steaming bowl of Outer Banks clam chowder, clear and full of clams, bacon, and potatoes, in front of me.

"What did he mean with those cracks about his lawyer?" Dad asked Ricky. "Is something wrong?"

"We're not here to discuss work." Evangeline took a vicious stab at the innocent lettuce on her plate. "Or that odious man. Ricky, what is he doing here? He didn't follow us, did he?"

"I doubt it," Ricky said. "Frankland has a vacation home in Nags Head. Divides his time between here and Boston. He keeps a place in New York City too, I've been told."

"To the detriment of the citizens of all those places, I'm sure," Connor muttered.

Evangeline and Mom soon drifted into conversation about mutual friends and wives of their husbands' partners, but I could tell that Gordon Frankland had upset Evangeline. She turned her chair slightly so she wasn't facing directly toward his table, drank steadily, ate her salad without pleasure, chattered with forced cheerfulness, and when she wasn't eating, talking, or drinking, chewed the lipstick off her lower lip. Uncle Amos and Connor discussed a proposed development that was splitting the town council, and Aunt Ellen wasn't shy about expressing her opinion on the matter. Josie asked me about wedding plans, and I confessed we hadn't made any yet.

"You're lucky my grandma Gloria isn't on your side of the family," Josie said. "Or she'd be here right quick, telling you what your plans are."

"She told me I'm now an honorary granddaughter of hers. You don't think—"

"Be afraid, Lucy, be very afraid."

"What's Lucy to be afraid of?" Connor asked.

"Interfering relatives," Josie said.

My mom was an excellent hostess, and invitations to her dinner parties were highly prized among her social set. She was able to engage fully in conversation with one person while listening to everything being said around the table. Her head whipped around now. "I am hardly interfering. I'm the mother of the bride, let me remind you. The second-most-important person at a wedding."

Evangeline stood up and left the table without a word.

"What about me?" Connor asked. "Where do I rank?"

Mom didn't bother to answer. "I will, of course, let Lucy make all the decisions, but—"

"We're not talking about you, Mom. Josie's grandma Gloria is the potentially interfering relative. I'm looking forward to hearing your suggestions."

"I liked Gloria," my dad said. "She sure could get herself through a bottle of bourbon, and she knows the good stuff when she sees it."

"I thought her absolutely delightful," Mom said. "Such charm. A true southern lady."

"As she reminds me at every opportunity," Aunt Ellen said.

I pushed my chair back. "If you'll excuse me." I headed for the ladies' room. Several minutes ago, Ricky had risen from the table and gone to the bar inside the building, saying he didn't want to bother the waiter. The sudden bout of thoughtfulness might have had something to do with the fact that the bartender tonight was young and female and very pretty.

He wasn't at the bar, and I headed down the hall. I was about to turn the corner into the corridor leading to the restrooms when Evangeline's voice, low and angry, had me stopping in my tracks.

"You're not even trying to woo Lucy back."

Chapter Four

"Give it up, will you, Mom," Ricky said. "She's not interested. She's made her life here, and I say good for her. Lucy's no fool."

"Maybe not, but you are. We need her now, more than ever. When Millar hears about—"

"He won't. We'll fix it."

"He will, and you won't fix it in time, Richard. Particularly not now that Millar's cut back on his drinking and transferred that so-called secretary of his in an attempt to save his marriage. Blasted Suzanne."

"Now it's Suzanne's fault?"

"It's not my fault, and I'm not going to see this family go down because of it. Once you and Lucy are married and you're Millar Richardson's son-in-law, he'll be reluctant to move against your father."

"You're not listening to me, Mother."

"No, Richard, you are not listening to me!"

I took two steps backward. The hostess was watching me. Her name's Ruth, and I know her well because I eat at this restaurant all the time. I gave her a wink and said in a good loud voice, "Where's the ladies' room?"

"Down that hall and on your right," she bellowed.

"Thanks," I said.

When I turned the corner, Ricky had disappeared and Evangeline was walking toward me with steps angry enough to shake the walls. When she saw me, she plastered on a smile that might have been formed out of concrete. "Such a delightful evening," she cooed. "It reminds me of when you and my Ricky came to the club on your first dates. Such good times, weren't they?"

Like every girl wants to go to her parents' county club with a new boyfriend. "Oh, yes. I remember. Do you remember the New Year's Eve party where I couldn't find Ricky at midnight for a kiss because he was in the kitchen with that waitress from Northeastern?"

The concrete smile cracked. "That was a total misunderstanding. That so-called friend of yours who delighted in spreading that nasty rumor wanted Ricky for herself."

"She got him eventually, didn't she? Although it didn't last long, I hear." I took a deep breath and spoke quickly before my courage failed me. "Evangeline, please go home. You and your family have been close to my family for many years, and I'm sorry it's come to this, but you're not wanted here."

A floorboard creaked behind the men's room door. Ricky was listening. If I'd been at all inclined to consider going back to him, the fact that he wasn't brave enough to come out and stand with me in defiance of his mother would have been enough to tell me he wasn't the man for me.

A footstep sounded behind me. "My daughter's correct." My mother had worked hard to get the Outer Banks out of her accent and speak as though she also had ancestors who came over on the Mayflower. At this moment her years of practice

40

worked. Evangeline's a good deal taller than Mom and I, but Mom peered down her nose at the other woman. "It would be for the best if you and Ricky left first thing in the morning."

Evangeline's eyes flashed. "It's what you want too, Suzanne—don't try to deny it. We always intended our children would marry."

"So we did. I hoped they'd fall in love. That didn't happen. It isn't going to happen. My daughter will marry for love." My mother put her arm around my waist.

"Like Elizabeth Bennet," I said.

"Do I know her?" Evangeline said.

"Apparently not," I said.

Evangeline looked at me. She looked at my mom. "You don't want to make an enemy of me, Suzanne."

"No, I don't. It's up to you how this ends."

Evangeline gave us a final glare and walked down the hallway, her head high, her heels tapping on the floor.

"Thanks, Mom," I said when Evangeline had disappeared.

My mother sighed. "I feel sorry for her, in a way. Her world is changing and she doesn't know how to cope."

"She can cope without me."

The men's room door opened, and Ricky came out. He ducked his head and slithered past us.

When he'd gone, I said, "Mom, is Evangeline closely involved in the business of the firm? I wouldn't have thought . . . "

"She's always been more involved than I have. Which isn't difficult, considering I know nothing that goes on there and I want to know nothing. But if Rich is in trouble and he's dragging Ricky down with him, then I can easily assume Evangeline has made it her mission to know precisely what's going on. She doesn't care for surprises. Why do you ask?"

"Just something she said to Ricky."

Mom and I waited a few minutes and then went back to our table, passing Ricky at the bar, where he was leaning toward the bartender. "What time do you get off work?" he asked as she handed him a fresh Scotch.

Evangeline's chair was empty.

"Did something happen?" Dad asked. "You two were gone for a long time. Evangeline said she'd taken ill and would drive herself back to the hotel."

"Happen?" Mom said. "Nothing at all." Our first-course plates had been cleared away and the main courses served. Mom picked up her fork. "This fish does look delicious."

Ricky didn't rejoin us, and now that the Lewistons had left, the mood at our table lifted considerably, and I enjoyed the rest of my meal.

"I thought this dinner was on Evangeline," Dad said as he scraped the last of his key lime pie off his plate. "Just like her to take off, sticking me with the bill."

Connor and Uncle Amos both reached for their wallets. Dad waved them away. "Just kidding. It's my pleasure to toast my beautiful daughter. Leaving suddenly isn't like Evangeline at all, truth be told, but it's certainly like her husband. And her son." He glanced through the windows into the main room of the restaurant. Ricky had gone. "There are going to be some changes at Richardson Lewiston soon, Amos. My offer stands."

Uncle Amos chuckled. "You're asking me to leave being the biggest fish in my two-person law firm to become a minnow swimming among the multiple sharp-toothed partners in the big tank that's your corporate offices? I turned you down forty years ago, Millar. Nothing's changed. Except us. Thinking of retirement yourself?"

"I'd like to," Dad said. "Think of it, I mean. Right now, the time's not good."

"Anyone for a nightcap back at the hotel?" Mom asked.

"Dad's never been to the library," I said. "Let's go there for a drink. It's lovely at night."

"Not for me," Josie said. "Morning comes early."

For her, it sure did. Josie got up at four every morning to get started on the day's baking. "I'm popping into the kitchen to say good-night to Jake." My cousin rounded the table to give everyone hugs in turn. " 'Night, all. I hope you come again soon, Aunt Suzanne, Uncle Millar."

"I believe we will," Mom said.

We gathered handbags and wraps and prepared to take our leave.

"It's been a long day for me too," Uncle Amos said. "So I'll pass on the drink. See you in the morning, before you leave?"

"Sure," Dad said.

"I'll get a lift with Connor," I said. "I shouldn't be driving tonight, and I can pick my car up in the morning before work."

"I came with Amos and Ellen," Dad said, "and Suzanne with Lucy. Connor can drop us at the beach house on his way home."

My mother gave him a sharp jab to the ribs. "That won't be necessary, Millar. Connor might not be going our way."

"Nags Head's not that big," Dad said. "Amos's house isn't far from the highway."

"We'll call a cab," Mom said.

Dad looked as though he was about to argue, but then his face flushed and he avoided my eyes. "A cab. Right. We'll call a cab. Good idea, Suzanne. We wouldn't want to put anyone out."

Laughing, I linked one arm in Connor's and one in Mom's, and we led the way through the building. Aunt Ellen followed, and Dad and Amos brought up the rear. "Retirement's starting to sound mighty good," Dad said. "But it's hard to get out of the saddle."

"Easier if you find a successor you can trust, like I did," Amos said. "Then you can ease into it at your own pace."

"That's my problem right there. Only one of my sons became a lawyer, and he's wasting his time, as I keep telling him, teaching at law school. As for that Ricky . . ."

"Speaking of Ricky," Mom said. "Where do you suppose he got to?"

No one was at the bar, and the bartender was idly polishing already sparkling glasses. The restaurant was almost empty.

"Don't know," Dad said. "Don't care. The boy can look after himself."

We passed the vacant hostess station and stepped out into the warm, humid air. Vehicles passed on the highway; an airplane flew high above. It was late, and only a handful of cars were parked under the strong lights of the restaurant's big lot. Connor pulled his keys out of his pocket and pressed the fob, and the lights of his BMW flashed in greeting.

Aunt Ellen gave Connor and me hugs good-night, and we all started to go our separate ways.

A scream pierced the quiet of the night, stopping us in our tracks. "What the heck?" Connor said. We looked around, trying to figure out what direction the sound had come from. We heard it again. "Help!" a woman yelled. "Someone help!"

Connor moved first, and I was right behind him. The screams were coming from the side of the restaurant in the direction of the kitchen door.

"Ellen," Uncle Amos yelled. "You and Suzanne stay here. Call nine-one-one."

The lights over the restaurant's main entrance and the parking lot faded the moment we rounded the building. A single weak lamp above the kitchen door cast a warm pool in the encroaching darkness. Ahead of us the waters of the Sound lapped at the shore, and the lights in the distance were not enough to see by.

I fumbled in my bag for my phone and hit the flashlight app. Connor had done the same, and we threw a circle of white light onto the shapes huddled near the kitchen door.

Ruth, the hostess, her tight skirt riding high on her thin legs, was kneeling on the ground next to a body that was lying very still. She looked up, fixing her round, frightened eyes on mine. "He's . . ." Her voice broke. "I found him like this. I think he's dead."

"Help's on the way," Aunt Ellen said. Into her phone she added, "We need an ambulance here. Quickly."

"I told you to stay behind," Uncle Amos said.

Ellen didn't reply, but my mom did. "We're not standing out there all by ourselves. Suppose that cry had been a diversion?"

Connor dropped to his haunches beside Ruth and reached for the body next to her. I held my flashlight high so he could see. Ruth started to stagger to her feet, and Uncle Amos helped her. When she was upright, my mom and Aunt Ellen surrounded her with soft murmurs. The kitchen door flew open and Jake's tousled head popped out. "What's going on out here? Amos, is that you? Connor?"

"A man's been hurt. We've called for help," I said.

"Mom? Dad?" Josie peered over Jake's shoulder. "What are you doing?"

"Trying to be of some help, honey," Amos said.

"Is he okay?" Jake asked.

"No," Connor said. "No, he's not. Tell them to hurry up, Ellen."

"Come with me, dear," my mom said to the weeping hostess. "Let's go inside and sit down. A cup of hot tea would be nice, Josie. With lots of sugar."

"I'll get it," my cousin said.

"Add a splash of brandy," Jake said.

"We'll go around by the front," Mom said, in a voice that reminded me of the time I'd fallen out of the apple tree at my grandparents' and broken my elbow. I never did tell Mom and Dad that I hadn't fallen: my eldest brother pushed me, saying girls didn't belong in trees.

He and I never did get on.

Mom and Aunt Ellen supported Ruth between them and walked slowly away, the two older women whispering softly.

I turned my attention back to Connor and the body on the ground. It was that of a man, dressed in dark pressed trousers, a blue button-down shirt, and brown loafers. He lay on his back, staring up into the darkness, unblinking and unmoving. Something dark and wet covered the ground under his back, and I tried not to think of what that might be.

Connor touched the side of the man's neck, and I focused my light on the face. He was in late middle age, silver hair expensively cut, cheeks flabby, prominent nose crisscrossed with red lines of rosacea.

There is something . . .

My dad sucked in a breath and swore.

"Millar?" Uncle Amos asked.

"It's Rich," Dad said. "Richard Eric Lewiston Junior. My law partner."

Chapter Five

D etective Sam Watson's eyebrows rose when he saw me sitting at the big round table in the center of the main room in Jake's restaurant, cradling a cup of excessively sugary tea in my hands. "When I got the call and it was not directing me to the Lighthouse Library, I dared hope you wouldn't be involved, Lucy."

I shrugged. What could I say? Not only was I involved, but my family was also.

"What does that mean?" Dad sputtered. "My daughter does not associate with common criminals."

"It's okay, dear." Mom patted his arm. "Lucy's acquainted with Detective Watson. As am I."

Watson nodded. "Mrs. Richardson."

"Detective, so nice to see you again." My mom is an accomplished liar. "Would you care for a cup of tea?"

The edges of his mouth might have turned up fractionally, but he hid it well and said, "Not at the moment, thank you."

"I don't believe you've met my husband. Detective Sam Watson, Millar Richardson."

Dad got to his feet, and the two men shook hands as they eyed each other warily.

My mom was "acquainted," as she put it, with Detective Watson. Not long after I arrived, Mom came down to the Outer Banks to try to talk me into going home to Boston and found herself accused of killing a high school rival.

Officer Butch Greenblatt had come in with Detective Watson. He didn't say anything but gave us all nods of greeting. Butch is Jake's brother as well as the boyfriend of Uncle Amos's law partner, Stephanie Stanton.

"Connor," Watson said as my dad sat down. "I see the gang's all here."

In answer to Aunt Ellen's call, the ambulance had soon arrived, sirens screaming and lights flashing, along with several police cars. We'd been bundled into the restaurant and ordered to wait for the detective. I hadn't heard the ambulance tearing out of the parking lot, which told me they'd been in no hurry to leave. Richard Lewiston Junior, Dad's business partner, Evangeline's husband, and Ricky's father, was dead.

Jake had closed the kitchen and hustled the remaining patrons out the door, many of them clutching hastily assembled takeout containers in confusion. Jake and Josie and the staff now huddled around the bar, waiting their turn to be questioned.

"Who found the body?" Watson asked.

I exchanged glances with Connor. So, as I suspected, it was now a body.

Ruth lifted a quivering hand. Her makeup had carved black rivers through her cheeks. "I . . . I did. I took my break and went out for a smoke."

"What door did you leave by?"

"The kitchen door. I stepped outside and started to light my cigarette. I . . . I . . ." She shuddered.

"Take your time," Mom said.

She gave my mother a grateful, although weak, smile. "I kicked something. I knew it wasn't a rock because it wasn't hard. I don't know what I thought it was. I looked down and saw . . . him. He was just lying there, staring up at me. Not moving."

"What did you do then?" Watson would have been anxious for her to spit it out so he could get to questioning the potential witnesses, maybe even the killer, but he spoke patiently, applied no pressure, and let the hostess compose herself. If she collapsed into a weeping puddle, it would do no one any good.

Aggression, as I well know, isn't Detective Watson's style. It wouldn't help him in this case anyway. Mom and Aunt Ellen formed a solid wall of matriarchal support around Ruth.

"I . . . I kicked him, and he didn't react. I thought, at first, he was a drunk who'd passed out on his way home. I gave him a nudge with my foot. He didn't move, so I leaned over to shake him. Then I saw the . . . the blood. And the knife. I guess I screamed, and then all these nice people were with me."

"Did you touch him?" Watson asked. "Did you try to help?"

"I . . . I don't remember. I think so."

"You were crouched beside him when I arrived," Connor said.

"Yeah. I guess."

"Did you touch the knife?" Watson asked.

"No. I'm sure I didn't."

"Have you ever seen that man before?"

"No. He didn't come in tonight or any other time when I was here."

"Are you sure?"

"I can't be positive about other nights. We get a lot of people in here. But definitely not tonight. It's Monday. We're never that busy on Mondays, even in the summer, so I'd remember if he'd been in. He couldn't have come in when I wasn't at the door. I only left my post a minute or two before. I walked through the kitchen to tell Jake I'd be outside. It was almost closing time anyway."

Watson glanced at Jake, still dressed in his chef's uniform of white jacket and gray checked pants. He'd left the group of his employees to stand protectively behind Ruth. "I've never seen him before, but you should ask the bartenders and the waitstaff. I don't come out front much. Some nights not at all."

"You have no idea who he might be and what might have brought him here tonight?" Watson asked them.

Jake and Ruth shook their heads.

"About that," my dad said. "I know him."

"You do?"

"He's my law partner of more than forty years—Richard Lewiston Junior, normally called Rich. Our fathers were partners before us. We're from Boston, and I'm here with my wife to congratulate my daughter and Dr. McNeil on their engagement. I had no idea Rich was anywhere in the vicinity, and I have absolutely no idea what would have brought him not only to the Outer Banks but to this restaurant."

Like a pair of ghosts, ever present but unacknowledged, the names *Evangeline* and *Ricky* hung over the table. Mom cleared her throat. "Someone has to say it."

"Say what?" Watson asked.

Dad sighed, but he gave Mom an almost unnoticeable nod.

"Rich must have decided at the last minute to join his wife and son," she said. "They were part of our dinner party earlier this evening."

"Is that so? Where are this wife and son now?"

"Evangeline—Mrs. Lewiston—wasn't feeling well, so she excused herself before we finished dinner, saying she'd drive herself back to their hotel. They're at the Ocean Side. As for her son, Richard the Third . . ."

"He's not actually called that, is he?" Connor whispered to me.

"'Fraid so," I said. "As I recall, he was suspended from school for fighting when his English class was studying Shakespeare's historical plays." Richard's a perfectly normal, modern American name, but teenage boys can make fun of anything. Never mind when we started going together and some people thought *Lucy and Ricky* dreadfully funny. I didn't even know why until someone told me about *I Love Lucy*, the old Lucille Ball TV show.

"Lucy," my dad warned.

"Sorry. Off topic. You might want to ask the bartender if she knows where Ricky got to. He was talking to her earlier."

All heads swiveled to the young woman perched on a barstool among her colleagues. She saw us staring and blinked in confusion. "What?" she said.

"Wait here, all of you." Watson took the few steps across the room to the bar to talk to her.

I edged ever so slightly toward them. If I could have pricked up my ears, I would have.

"I've been told," Watson said, "you were talking to a young man from those people's party earlier tonight?"

"Yeah. He said his name was Ricky. He'd been at Mr. and Mrs. O'Malley's table with Lucy and Connor and the others, but he left them before the main courses were brought out and took a seat at the bar. I thought that was rude, but it's none of my business. He was drinking a lot. Scotch, and not the cheap stuff either."

Watson was facing away from me, so I couldn't hear what he said, but her reply was clear.

"Hour ago, maybe? I'd say he left about fifteen to thirty minutes before I heard the yelling from outside. He wanted to meet me when I get off, but I told him I'm in a relationship. He said he'd be at the bar in the Ocean Side anyway, if I felt like dropping by."

Watson asked her something.

"As if. I get that all the time here. Rich guys on vacation, too much to drink. Wives and girlfriends at home. More trouble than they're worth. No thanks."

Watson thanked her and returned to our table of curious faces. "Jake, did anyone go out the kitchen door this evening before Ruth did?"

Jake scrunched up his face and thought. "We're in and out all the time. That's where my staff go for breaks. They don't stand outside the front door smoking. You can ask them if they saw anything, but I went out for some air about fifteen minutes before Ruth did, and he wasn't there then."

"Are you sure of the time?"

"I wouldn't set my watch by it, but round about then." He glanced over to the group of his helpers, sitting silently together. "Robyn, she's new, burned a steak. In my earlier days I would have torn a blue streak off her. But, under the influence of my loving bride"—he smiled at Josie—"I've learned to take myself away for a few minutes. Robyn didn't mean to do it, and she won't do it again. Me yelling at her wouldn't help the situation any. So, I stepped outside. Took a couple of paces, breathed a few times, and when I'd calmed down, I came back in and got on with it. I didn't see a body, and I would have if one had been lying at my feet."

"It's dark out there," Watson said.

"It's my place," Jake said. "I know what's happening around me."

Watson nodded.

"I didn't hear anything out of the ordinary either," Jake said. "No one arguing or fighting for sure. But then again, the kitchen's a noisy place."

"Thanks," Watson said. "I'll talk to your staff in turn. But first," he asked the people at my table, "did any of you see Richard Lewiston Junior this evening?"

"Never met him," Connor, Amos, and Ellen said as Mom, Dad, and I shook our heads firmly.

"I didn't know he was in town," Dad said.

"I suppose it's possible Evangeline called and told him where we were," Mom said. "Although that wouldn't explain why he was in Nags Head in the first place or why she didn't tell us she'd invited him."

"She left," Dad pointed out.

"That's right. But Ricky was still here. For a while, anyway."

"And then he left," I said.

"Butch," Watson said, "you're too close to these people to take statements. Go outside and supervise the scene and ask Officer Rankin to come in."

Butch nodded and left.

"You know what my schedule's like, Sam," Josie said. "I need to get home. Can I give my statement first? It'll be short. I saw nothing, heard nothing. Never saw the dead man before in all my life."

"Sure," Watson said.

When Officer Holly Rankin came in, almost bouncing on her toes at the chance to be of help to the detective, Watson told her to take statements—Josie's first—from my family and the restaurant staff. "I have to go round to the Ocean Side and speak to Mrs. Lewiston, and I hope to get there before she and her son hear the news."

Mom stood up. "I will accompany you."

"That won't be necessary. I'd prefer—"

"Not a problem." She gathered up her handbag. "Evangeline and I have been the closest of friends for forty years. She'll need all the comfort I can offer at this time. Lucille and young Ricky are also extremely close. She'll accompany me."

"I will?" I said. "I mean, yeah. Glad to be of help."

"Who's Lucille?" Watson asked.

"Me," I said. "I have the name of a ninety-year-old woman."

"You were named for—" Mom began.

"Yes, I know." I was honored, really I was, to have been given the name of Dad's maternal grandmother. I wasn't honored when people met me for the first time and said I was much younger than they'd expected.

Watson shrugged. "Might as well. Lucy will find some way to get involved, whether I want her help or not."

I didn't bother to protest. Somehow, that was the way things worked out.

Connor got to his feet. He put his hand lightly on my arm and led me a few steps away from the table while Watson instructed Holly Rankin. "Are you okay going with your mom? Want me to follow?"

I laid my hand on his chest, just for a moment to feel the beating of his heart. "Not necessary, but thanks. You go home, and I'll call you when I'm back at the lighthouse. Mom never liked Richard the Second, but this will still be upsetting for her, and I need to be with her. Particularly when Sam breaks the news to Evangeline and Ricky."

"Interesting that they've both disappeared."

"Isn't it just?"

Chapter Six

Mom and I followed Detective Watson outside. He'd been at home when he got the call, so he'd come in his own car, but he waved for a uniformed officer to join us, and Butch broke away from the line of police tape that had been strung between the corner of the building and a fence post. An unadorned white van I knew to be the forensics vehicle was parked near the tape, as was the coroner's van. A few people had gathered in the parking lot to watch the goings-on, and another officer kept them back. Beyond them, traffic continued to move steadily on the Croatan Highway.

"Detective!" a forensics officer called. "Something here you'll want to see."

"Give me a minute," Watson said to us. He ducked under the crime scene tape and accepted a small, clear bag. From what I could see, it contained a single sheet of paper. Watson took his reading glasses out of his jacket pocket, studied the paper, nodded once, handed it back, and put his glasses away. He said a few words to the watching officers and then rejoined us.

"What was that?" I asked casually.

He didn't answer but indicated that we could get into the car.

"Not the first time I've ridden in a police car," Mom said as she settled her skirts under her in the back seat. "I do hope it's the last."

"At least you're not being taken in for questioning this time," I said.

"You didn't ask me for my alibi, Detective," Mom said. "Unlike the unfortunate events of the last time we met, tonight I was with my daughter, my husband, my sister, her husband, my daughter's fiancé, my—"

"We get the point, Mom," I said.

"Simply ensuring everything is clear, dear," she said. "Nice to see you again, Butch. We didn't get a chance to chat at Lucy's party. I hope all is well with you."

"It is. Thank you, ma'am."

"Tell me about Richard Lewiston, father and son," Watson said.

It wasn't far to the Ocean Side Hotel, but that didn't matter, as we didn't have all that much to tell. Both men lived in Boston and were lawyers at Richardson Lewiston. Richard the Third was the only child of Richard the Second and Evangeline née Walker, and he was not married. Richardson Lewiston was a corporate firm and, as far as Mom and I knew (which wasn't much), they didn't do work for the mob or other underground figures. Mom saw Evangeline and Rich regularly at social events and company gatherings, but if he'd had a secret life, she didn't know about it. I thought about the encounter earlier with the company client, Gordon Frankland, and how he'd implied there was trouble in the firm, and I recalled Ricky and Evangeline's whispered conversation in the hallway, but I didn't say anything. That was hearsay. It would be up to my dad to fill the police in on the situation at the firm. If he didn't want to,

I'd give him a nudge. Keeping secrets from Detective Watson never worked out well.

Butch parked the cruiser at the bottom of the steps leading to the front doors of the Ocean Side Hotel. The valet trotted toward us, but Butch waved him away.

"Do you have Mrs. Lewiston's phone number and that of her son?" Watson asked my mom.

"I have hers, but not his."

"Give her a call. Tell her you need to speak to her and are coming up to her room, if she's there. If she's not, ask her where she is. Don't tell her what this is about, and tell her to invite her son to join us."

Mom made the call. "Evangeline! Dear! It's Suzanne." Her voice was so unnaturally high-pitched that Evangeline would immediately know something was wrong. I laid my hand on Mom's arm and gave her a slight shake of the head. She took a breath before continuing. "I'd like to talk to you for a few minutes, dear. Are you in your room?"

Evangeline said something, and Mom replied, "I know it's late, but it is important. Thank you. We'll be right there. Oh, can you ask Ricky to join us?" She hung up. "Room two twenty-two. She's calling Ricky."

We got out of the car and climbed the steps into the hotel. It was ten thirty and the restaurant was almost empty, but the lobby bar was busy. I glanced in as we passed, but I didn't see Ricky.

Mom knocked, and from inside the room we heard a dog start to bark. "Shush," Evangeline said. She opened the door a crack, using her right foot to keep Fluffy inside. She was still wearing the dress she'd had on at dinner but had taken the jacket, the jewelry, and her shoes off. She didn't bother to smile at Mom and me, and she blinked when she saw the two men standing behind us. Sam Watson might have been casually dressed in chinos and a beige shirt, but he always looked as though he had COP tattooed across his forehead. Butch, six foot five, two hundred or so pounds, was a formidable presence in his dark uniform, even if he wasn't trying to be.

"What on earth? Suzanne, what's the meaning of this?"

"I'm Detective Sam Watson of the Nags Head Police. Are you Mrs. Evangeline Lewiston?"

"I am, but I don't understand."

"May we come in?"

Good manners took over, and Evangeline stepped back. She leaned over and grabbed Fluffy by the collar before the little dog could attack the invaders. "Be quiet!"

Fluffy ignored her and kept barking. Evangeline scooped her up.

Watson gave Mom a nod, and she got the message. "Why don't you sit down, Evangeline, dear. But first, maybe you could put the dog in the other room."

Room 222 was a suite. I glanced around me, trying not to be too obvious about it. Evangeline's gold jacket had been tossed onto the neatly made king-sized bed in the other room. The bed was draped in a blue-and-gold duvet and piled high with matching pillows. The drapes, made of similar fabric, were closed. In the main room, an iPad lay open on the desk, the screen black. The big-screen TV hanging on the wall played a costume drama— women in big skirts and men in wigs and white stockings. A bottle of white wine sat in a silver bucket on a side table next to the sofa, and a single glass graced the coffee table, next to an iPhone in a sparkly pink case. I glanced at Evangeline. Her eyes were wide and frightened. She knew this was no friendly social call. She clung to Fluffy for a moment, then nodded and carried the dog into the bedroom, put her on the floor, and shut the door before the little animal could escape. Evangeline crossed the room and dropped onto the sofa, lifted a hand to her mouth, and started to cry. "Ricky! What's happened to Ricky?"

"Nothing. Nothing." Mom sat next to her. "He's perfectly fine. As far as I know. Did you not get him on the phone?"

"No answer. I . . . I left a message. Why are you here, then? What's happened?"

"Would you turn the television off, please, Mrs. Lewiston?" Watson asked.

Evangeline didn't move. I crossed the room, my shoes sinking into the deep carpet, grabbed the remote off the coffee table, and pressed buttons. The voices died and the screen went dark.

"It's Rich," Mom said. "I'm sorry, dear."

"Rich? Good heavens, Suzanne, have you lost your senses at long last? Rich is home in Boston." Evangeline stood up and smoothed her skirt. "You've frightened the life out of me for nothing."

My mom didn't stand.

"I'm sorry, Mrs. Lewiston," Watson said. "Your husband was found dead earlier tonight."

"He was? Where? How did that happen?"

"That's to be determined," Watson said. "But it doesn't appear to have been an accident."

Evangeline didn't sit back down. The fear had faded from her eyes, and it didn't reappear. She didn't resume crying. The dog stopped barking and settled into a long, continuous whine. "That is cryptic. Not an accident. I can guess what you mean.

I've told him repeatedly he wasn't to drink so heavily before driving, but I'm afraid he rarely listened to me these days. Thank you for coming to tell me, Detective, Officer. My son and I have already made bookings to fly home tomorrow, and I'll contact my husband's PA first thing in the morning to make the necessary arrangements. Suzanne, do you know where they've taken him?"

"Uh . . ." Mom said.

"Your husband isn't in Boston," Watson said. "He's in Nags Head. He was found outside the kitchen door at Jake's Seafood Bar a short time ago."

Evangeline dropped onto the couch. "What? That can't be right. Isn't that where we had dinner, Suzanne? What would Rich be doing there?"

My mom shook her head.

"I was hoping you could tell me," Watson said. "Did you know your husband was in Nags Head?"

"No. There must be some mistake. He didn't come with us."

"No mistake," Watson said. "I understand you left the restaurant early, before dinner was finished. Why?"

"My son and I had an argument. I no longer felt like making polite conversation."

"What was this argument about?"

"I'm sorry, but that's none of your business."

"Everything that happened in Jake's Seafood Bar and the vicinity tonight is my business," Watson said.

Evangeline glanced at me. She had the grace to look embarrassed. Mom noticed and gave me a curious look.

Evangeline patted her hair. "Nothing at all important. I think . . . I thought . . . my son was . . . uh . . . ignoring romantic opportunities he should have been taking better advantage of."

"What on earth does that mean?" Watson said. "How old is your son?"

"Thirty-five."

"Thirty-five? And you're advising him on his love life?"

"I am his mother," Evangeline snapped. "I know what's best for us—I mean, for him."

"What Mrs. Lewiston isn't telling you, Detective," I said, "is that Ricky and I were in a relationship at one time. That ended before I moved to the Outer Banks and met Connor. Mrs. Lewiston wants her son to marry me rather than Connor because she mistakenly thinks I have money to bring to the marriage."

Evangeline caught one word in my statement. "Mistakenly?"

"Okay," Watson said. "Is it possible your husband decided to surprise you by joining you here?"

"We do not have that sort of marriage." Evangeline picked up her phone and punched buttons. "Richard! Call me immediately! No matter the time." She hung up and clutched the phone in both hands. She looked at my mother with wide, frightened eyes. "He's not answering."

"He's probably gone to a bar or maybe a movie or . . . something . . . and he can't hear the phone ringing," I said.

"What time did you leave Jake's?" Watson asked.

Evangeline shook her head. "I can't possibly say. I didn't check my watch."

"Before the main courses were served," I said. "We arrived around seven, had a round of drinks and appetizers. So you probably left not long after eight."

"Possibly," Evangeline said.

"You drove yourself?" Watson asked her.

Butch said nothing. He stood by the door, his feet apart, his arms crossed over his chest, as though it might be necessary to block our escape, and watched and listened.

"I didn't want to inconvenience anyone," Evangeline said. "My son had driven us to dinner in our rental car. I assumed he would get a ride back to the hotel with Lucy, who'd come in her own car."

"Yeah," I muttered to myself. "Like that was going to happen."

"Did you come straight back to the hotel after leaving Jake's?" Watson asked.

Evangeline stared into space, thinking. That is, she pretended to be thinking. She knew exactly what she'd done. "I might have gone for a little drive," she finally admitted. "I was naturally upset. My son and I have a close, loving relationship—isn't that right, Suzanne?"

I thought Mom showed great restraint in not saying, *Are you kidding?*

"Any rare disagreement we occasionally have is highly upsetting to me. The beach is so lovely at night, isn't it?"

"What time did you get back to the hotel?"

"I . . . uh . . ." Evangeline looked directly at Watson. "I don't remember exactly. I came straight to my room. I spoke to no one. I took Fluffy for a short walk, settled myself down for the evening, and called room service."

"Did the valet take your car?"

Evangeline's eyes flicked around the room. "Yes," she admitted.

"They'll have a record of the time you turned it over to them," Watson said. "As will you." His eyes wandered to the little piece of paper on the desk half tucked under the iPad alongside the room key.

"How clever you are," Evangeline said cheerfully. "Why yes, so I will."

Watson crossed the room and picked up the valet stub. "Nine twenty-five."

Mom and I exchanged glances. By 9:25, Richard Eric Lewiston Junior was dead.

"Quite a long drive," Watson said. "If you left the restaurant around eight. Jake's is less than a five-minute drive from here."

"I like to drive," said Evangeline. "It helps to clear my head."

Once again, Mom refrained from saying, *Are you kidding?*

The phone in Evangeline's hand trilled. She almost leapt out of her skin and dropped the phone onto the sofa next to her. She scrambled for it and fumbled to push the button and hold it to her ear. "Ricky! What? No, I do not want an all-expenses-paid vacation to the Bahamas. You call this number again, and I'll sue you for every penny you have. I am quite sure that is not much." She threw the phone across the room. It landed on the carpet and bounced once. She burst into tears, and my mom gathered her into her arms. Fluffy resumed barking.

"Is that the dress you were wearing to dinner this evening?" Watson asked her.

Evangeline mumbled, "Yes."

Following Watson's train of thought, I studied the front of Evangeline's black dress and her bare arms for signs of . . . gulp . . . blood. I saw nothing out of the ordinary.

"She had a jacket over it," I said. "The jacket's on the bed."

Watson gave me a nod, then turned to Butch. "The bartender at Jake's said Ricky told her he'd be in the bar here. Go and see if he's there. Have you met this guy?"

"No," Butch said.

"Lucy?"

"I'll go with Butch."

"Why would Ricky have told a bartender his plans for the evening?" Evangeline sobbed to my mom. "And what did Lucy mean, she doesn't have any money?" Mom didn't answer as Butch and I left the room.

"She wants her son to marry you? And he doesn't want to?" Butch said. "Guy sounds like a fool to me."

I smiled at my friend. "Thanks for the vote of support. Ricky and I dated all through college and for years after, but it was more what our mothers wanted than what we wanted. That's why I came to OBX in the first place, to get away from all those family expectations. Mom's come around to understanding. Evangeline, apparently not so much."

We arrived at the lobby bar, and I looked quickly around. No sign of Richard Eric Lewiston III. "He's not here," I said.

"Let's ask if he's been in." Butch crossed the floor, and I trotted along in his wake. Everyone stopped what they were doing to stare, even if they were pretending not to.

The bartender, a grizzly older guy, finished pouring a pint of beer, shoved it at his customer, and sauntered over to us. " 'Evening, Officer. Something up?"

"Just a quick question," Butch said. "I'm looking for a man who might have been in earlier. Age thirty-five, uh . . . Lucy?"

"About five nine, slightly chubby around the middle. Short brown hair thinning in the center. Fashionably rough stubble, some sunburn on his face. He was wearing dark jeans and a white golf shirt under a white blazer, loafers with no socks. He would have been on his own, or maybe with a young woman."

"Yeah, I think I saw him."

"When was this?" Butch asked.

"I started shift at six. He was here then." The bartender jerked his chin to the end of the bar. "Nursing a Scotch and fiddling with his phone. I didn't see him talking to anyone, and he left not long after."

"He hasn't been back?"

"Not that I saw, and I've been here all night."

"Thanks," Butch said.

"What's he done?"

Butch didn't answer. When we were taking the stairs to the second floor, he said, "Sounds like your friend Ricky blew off the bartender from Jake's."

"Fair enough, as she told him she wasn't coming."

Butch knocked lightly on the door to the suite, and Watson opened it. Evangeline was on her feet. The tears had stopped, but she clutched a tattered tissue in one hand. She stared at the door. When she saw that Butch and I were alone, she resumed pacing up and down, twisting her tissue in her hands.

"I'm going to stay here tonight," Mom said. "Evangeline shouldn't be alone. I've called down to the desk and asked them to send someone to make up the pullout couch and bring me a bag of toiletries."

"You're going to sleep on a pullout couch?" I said.

"I'm sure Ricky will return his mother's call shortly and I can go back to my sister's place."

"Do you suppose he's lost his phone, Suzanne?" Evangeline asked. "That's possible, isn't it? Or perhaps the battery died."

Or he met a woman and isn't taking calls from his mother, I thought but didn't say. I glanced at Detective Watson. What *he* was thinking and not saying was that Ricky might be on the run after killing his father.

"I have to get back to Jake's," Watson said. "If you hear from your son, Mrs. Lewiston, notify me immediately."

"I'll see that she does," Mom said.

"I'd appreciate it." Watson held a plastic bag in one hand. Evangeline's shoes were no longer on the floor, and the size and shape of the bag indicated that the gold lamé jacket was inside. Watson had taken her things for analysis, I realized.

"You going to be okay, Mom?" I asked.

"You go home, dear. I'll be fine. I'm sure we can find something enjoyable to watch on television. Evangeline and I will have a nice evening." She was facing me, her back to Evangeline. Mom rolled her eyes to the heavens as she spoke.

"Before I go, Mrs. Richardson," Watson said, "a word?"

Mom and I followed the detective into the corridor. I shut the door behind me.

"She doesn't seem all that upset at the death of her husband," Watson said. "Would you say that's delayed shock or that she genuinely isn't all that upset?"

Mom thought. "The latter. Rich and Evangeline are not close. They haven't had a good marriage for many years. If ever. Right now she's worried more about her son. I have to tell you, Detective, Rich was having problems lately. Drinking, gambling, making bad legal decisions. My husband can tell you more, but that's what I observed and what I overheard."

"His wife—"

"No," Mom said firmly. "Evangeline would not have done something so crass as to kill her husband to get out of a failing marriage. Even in our circles, divorce is a common, acceptable practice these days."

I wasn't so sure. Yes, plenty of people got divorced and no one clutched their pearls over it. But Evangeline had known Rich was blowing through the family money at a rapid rate. An expensive divorce would not have helped the situation any.

His death, however, would put a stop to the financial bleeding. There might even be a handsome insurance policy involved.

I said nothing. Watson knew how to run an investigation. He'd find out about Rich's financial and legal situation soon enough.

* * *

Butch drove the detective and me back to Jake's. The parking lot was still full of cruisers, the forensics van was in place, and yellow police tape fluttered in the light wind, keeping the curious at bay.

Otherwise, the only cars in the lot were mine, Connor's, Jake's, and a Mercedes with Massachusetts plates, which I didn't recognize.

Holly Rankin trotted toward the cruiser as we drove up. Unlike Butch, who looked every inch a cop, Holly was short and stocky with a sprinkling of freckles across her nose and red hair pulled back into a tight ponytail. She was young, and her uniform didn't fit her too well, giving her an air of play-cop. But she was intelligent and eager to learn, and I was confident she'd soon grow into the job. "I took statements from Jake's staff and Lucy's friends and family," she said, "and then I said they could go. That was okay? Right?"

"Fine," Watson said. "I'll read the statements when I get back to the office. In the meantime, did anything stand out I should know about?"

"No one claims to have seen the deceased at any time today, spoken to him on the phone, or otherwise communicated with him. He didn't come inside the restaurant. Only Lucy's dad knew him, and he said he didn't even know the guy was in North Carolina. None of the staff heard anything, and none of them went outside between the time Jake did and then Ruth."

"Thanks," Watson said. "Good job."

She trotted away, visibly pleased with the bit of praise.

We found Connor, Jake, and my dad sitting at the big round table having a beer. Connor leapt to his feet when we came in and gave me a hug. "I decided to wait until you got back. Everything okay? Where's your mom?"

I hugged him back and then let go—reluctantly—to talk to Dad. "Mom's staying with Evangeline tonight."

"What about Ricky?" Dad asked.

"Evangeline can't get hold of him, and she's worried. He didn't go to the bar at the Ocean Side like he said he would."

"Ricky does his own thing," Dad said. "He's not one to report to his mother on his whereabouts."

"That's what we all said, but she's leaving messages he's not answering, and she's getting increasingly frantic." I pulled out a chair and dropped into it with a sigh.

"Get you a drink, Lucy?" Jake asked.

"No thanks."

"You have no idea what brought your law partner to Nags Head tonight?" Watson asked my father.

"Absolutely none," Dad said. "Although something odd did happen earlier tonight."

"What was that?"

"A client of Rich's recognized Ricky and Evangeline. He knew of me, although we've never met."

"Is that common? You not to know your partner's clients?"

"We're a big firm," Dad said. "A very big firm. We have offices in several cities, twenty-seven partners, and more than a hundred associates."

"Oh," Watson said.

"So, yes, I can't possibly know all our clients on sight. Although I did recognize the man's name."

"What happened tonight that you call odd?"

Dad let out a long breath. "He approached our table. Said hello. He implied that he had problems with the way Rich and Ricky were representing him. Amos cut him off, reminding him this wasn't the time or the place."

"You don't know what he was talking about?"

"I do not, but I can assure you I'll be calling my office first thing in the morning. After we make arrangements for Rich, of course."

"It was Gordon Frankland," Connor said.

"Gordon Frankland?" Watson said. "Of Nags Head?"

"The Nags Head pest. Yes."

"Who's Gordon Frankland?" I asked.

No one answered me. "That is interesting," Watson said. "Did you notice what time Mr. Frankland left the restaurant?"

"No," Dad said. Connor shook his head.

"He was gone by the time we got up to leave," I said. "I noticed that section of the deck was empty, but I can't say what time he left. He was on his own."

"I know who you're talking about," Jake said. "Gordon Frankland's a regular here. He comes in for dinner at least once a week, sometimes more. Always on his own, far as I know. My staff has been warned—advised—to treat him with kid gloves."

"I'll have a word with him. I'll also need to talk to your customers who might have been outside when Mr. Lewiston arrived," Watson said to Jake. "Most people pay by credit card, I assume."

Jake stood up. "Yeah. We ask for telephone numbers when we take reservations, so I can get you those as well."

"If you don't need me anymore," I said. "I'd like to go home, and I'm okay to drive myself. I'm bushed. If you don't mind, Dad, I'm going to withdraw the offer of a nightcap."

My father stood up. "I don't mind. I'm glad we had a chance to spend some time together, Lucy. Despite how it turned out." He approached my chair, and I got to my feet. He gave me an awkward hug. My dad isn't one for displays of affection, but he was making the effort, and I was pleased. He turned to Connor. "You take care of my daughter, young man."

"I intend to do precisely that."

"Why don't you take my car, Dad," I said, "rather than call for a cab. Connor, can you drive me? I don't feel like driving home alone tonight. I can pick my car up tomorrow."

"Good idea," Dad said.

The three of us headed out into the night as the lights inside Jake's Seafood Bar were turned down behind us. Mom did not call to say Ricky had turned up.

Chapter Seven

A fog moved in as we drove out of town, getting increasingly thicker as the lights of Nags Head dropped behind us. Swirls of mist wound themselves around the car, and Connor's headlights struggled to illuminate the road ahead.

"Spooky," I said.

He took a quick glance at me. "You going to be okay tonight?"

"Fog's common enough around here, as you well know, so it's not anything to worry about. I rather like the moodiness of it. I'm reading *The Hound of the Baskervilles* for book club, and this puts me in mind of the 'great Grimpen Mire.' "

"Is that a real place, do you know?"

I'd done my prereading research to get ready for leading the book discussion. "No, it's not. It's believed to be based on a real place called Fox Tor. I like that name better—Fox Tor. It's in Dartmoor. I'd love to visit it someday, it sounds so fascinating."

"How about England for our honeymoon, Lucy?"

"I'd like that. We could go to Fox Tor and to Yorkshire to see where the Brontë sisters walked, to the Jane Austen House Museum in Hampshire, to Baker Street in London, to Bath where—"

"A literary honeymoon," Connor said dryly. "How nice."

"Then again," I said, "maybe the Caribbean like we've discussed."

He chuckled. "As long as you're with me, I'll go anywhere you like."

"I wasn't planning on going on my honeymoon by myself."

He reached out and took my hand, and we turned into the fog-shrouded laneway to the lighthouse, passing beneath the row of tall red pines, their thick trunks indistinct in the mist.

* * *

Charles ran to greet me when I let myself into the library. I bent over and gave him a rub on the top of his head as he wound his body around my legs. I live alone, and I like it, but it's always nice to come home, particularly when it's late after an emotionally troubling day, to be greeted by someone happy to see me. Although, I suspect, Charles is more excited about having his food bowl refreshed than seeing me.

Most of the lights in the main room were off, only the lamp in the alcove and one at the bottom of the twisting iron stairs lit. I glanced around the library. I love being alone in the library after closing. I believe that when it's very quiet, I can hear the rustle of conversation as the characters chat to each other, the wind moving through the sails of ships of old, the chug of a steam-powered train passing through the countryside, or the roar of jet engines bearing a heroine off to adventure and romance.

Louise Jane maintains that the lighthouse is haunted, and she has plenty of stories about people who came to their unexpected and sudden end within these round walls. But I've never sensed anything—other than my literary characters, that is. And that's more than enough for me.

I didn't bother switching on any more lights as I made my way up to the fourth floor. I knew this building so well by now. Around and around I went while Charles ran ahead, neatly balanced on the railing. I unlocked my door and hit the light switch. Charles ran for the food bowl. He gave it a sniff and turned to stare at me, shocked—*shocked!*—to find it empty.

I threw my purse onto the kitchen counter, kicked off my shoes, and took the kibble out of the cupboard. I know in what order my priorities lie.

Once Charles was happily tucking in, I grabbed the phone and curled up with it on the window seat. Something had come to mind that I'd not thought to ask Connor earlier. This apartment is so small there's not room for much more than a bed, a small bathroom, and a kitchen alcove with a table and two chairs. The walls are round and white, with just one tall window set in the four-foot-thick stone walls above a small window seat covered with bright cushions, perfect for reading and gazing dreamily outside. The walls are so thick cell phone coverage is unreliable, so I still have a landline.

I love my Lighthouse Aerie, and I've been very happy here. But it'll soon be time to leave, and I'm not regretting it. Time to move on to the next phase of my life.

With a smile on my face, I called Connor.

"Hi," he said. "You're safely inside?"

"I am. Charles is dining, and all is right with the world."

"The world according to Charles must be a nice place to live."

"I feel so bad for Evangeline and Ricky. Mom, who should know, says she and Rich didn't have a particularly good marriage, but they had been married for a long time. And Ricky . . ."

"I get the feeling Ricky will be fine. I suspect Ricky always is."

"Hum."

"How about you? Are you okay?"

"I'm okay, as in I didn't know Richard the Second very well, but the whole thing is still upsetting. On the bright side, this time it didn't happen here at the library."

"For once," Connor said.

Charles finished his meal, checked the entire kitchen floor and under the chairs to make sure he hadn't overlooked anything, and then leapt onto the bed to wash his whiskers.

"I have a question for you. Who was that guy who came up to our table and knew Ricky and Evangeline?" I asked. "He knew you too, and I got the feeling you don't like him. You later called him a pest."

"To put it mildly. I shouldn't have said that in public, but Gordon Frankland is a pest. Worst of all, he's a pest with deep pockets. He's always complaining about something or other, sticking his nose where it isn't wanted, threatening to sue all and sundry for nothing more than the fun of doing it. He's mainly based in Boston—"

"Thus he uses my dad's firm."

"Right. He has a vacation home in Nags Head as well as a lot of business interests here. His current bugbear is opposition to plans to tear down a bunch of homes that are too close to the waterline. He claims they're of historical value, which is true, but that's largely irrelevant, as another big wave is going to wash them all out to sea."

"Historical value? Not some of the unpainted aristocracy, I hope." I was referring to several big old cottages, beloved of Bankers for their history and admired by tourists for their charm, so called because their natural wood has been allowed to age gracefully over the decades until they match their ocean-side surroundings.

"Thank heavens, no. Not them. It would be nothing short of a tragedy if any of the unpainted aristocracy have to come down."

I smiled to myself at his tone of voice. Every time we drove past one of those marvelous old houses, Connor sighed wistfully. Connor's family has lived in the Outer Banks for many generations, and its history is important to him. He'd love nothing more than to live in a historic house or cottage, but the unpainted aristocracy in particular are family heirlooms and almost never come up for sale.

"What do the homeowners have to say about Frankland getting himself involved?"

"They're furious. They want to rebuild on firmer ground, and they're in danger of being tied up in court for years. As for me personally, I used the word *pest* advisedly. He's always on his high horse about something or other and demanding I drop everything on my plate to meet with him. He was out of state through most of the last election, thank goodness, but now he's threatening to back a challenger to me next time around, on the grounds that I am, and I quote, 'uninterested in the concerns of the average Nags Head citizen.' "

"How do you feel about that? You said you aren't going to run again."

"And I'm not. I've done my bit, Lucy, and as I've told you, seeking higher office isn't for me. I intend to return to my practice and to enjoy married life."

"I like the sound of that."

He chuckled. "I can say that until I'm blue in the face, but no one believes me. They all think I'm biding my time until it's right for a state or even federal run. I was interested to hear Frankland's not happy with his legal representation. That might be significant. The death of his lawyer—if 'Richard the Second,' as you call him, was the head of his legal team—has the potential to set his plans back."

"Don't say that! Not even to me. We don't need anyone implying that Rich's death has benefited you."

"I can't ask for a better alibi than I had."

"There is that."

"One thing before I go. I got a message earlier from our realtor saying she has a house for us to view tomorrow night. Are you free?"

"Yes." Connor and I were trying to find a house to buy together. It was not proving to be easy. We wanted to stay within the town of Nags Head, both because he was the mayor and so I wouldn't be too far from my own work, but as in most hugely popular tourist destinations, prices are exorbitantly high for residents.

"I'll pick you up at seven, and we can meet her there. Good night, Lucy."

"Good night, Connor."

As I went through the usual going-to-bed routine, I thought about Rich Lewiston. I hadn't known him well; the man had been nothing but a vague background shape in my childhood—partner of my father, husband of Evangeline, father of Ricky. Ricky and I had gone on a couple of cruises with our moms over the years (yes, even when we were a couple, we holidayed with our mothers), but I don't recall either Rich or my dad coming along. The Lewistons had a lake home in New Hampshire, and my parents and I went there a few times when I was young. About all I remember about those visits was the time when I was twelve and my brother tried to drown me in the lake—ha-ha, such a great joke!—with Ricky helping him. Dad and Rich spent most of the vacation in Rich's study talking business, their heads enveloped in a cloud of cigar smoke and glasses of whiskey at their elbows. I vaguely recalled Mom telling me recently that they'd sold the New Hampshire property.

Maybe Rich had been coming to realize that things couldn't go on as they were: a listless marriage, an uninterested son, a failing career. Had he decided to pop down to Nags Head as a surprise for Evangeline? Maybe suggest they stay on for a few days and have a romantic little vacation together?

That didn't sound like something Rich would do, but then again, I didn't really know what he would do. I'd probably never know. But whatever had happened to him, Rich Lewiston hadn't deserved to end up knifed in the back and left to die alone in a back alley.

My copy of *The Hound of the Baskervilles* was resting on the blue-and-yellow cushions in the window alcove where I'd left it. I crossed the room and reached for it, intending to read for a few minutes in bed.

As I did so, something outside caught my eye, and I peered out into the night. My window looks over the marshes to the national seashore and the open ocean beyond. I'll miss this incredible view when I move, but there wasn't much of a view tonight: the thousand-watt light at the top of the lighthouse tower could do little to break through the dense fog.

A wooden boardwalk winds through the marsh, leading to a small pier bordering a pond with an outlet to Roanoke Sound. It's a popular spot for birders and hikers and anyone interested in the wildlife of a saltwater marsh.

No one goes there at night. Certainly not on a night as dark and misty as this one. A flash of light at about the midpoint of the boardwalk had caught my attention. The light was extinguished, and I blinked, thinking I must have imagined it. Then I saw it again. Vague and insubstantial in the drifting mist. On. Off. On again. And then off. I leaned toward the window, as though I could see better if I got an inch or two closer. High above me, the great first-order Fresnel lens flashed to life after its 22.5-second dormancy, lighting the way, as it would all through the night, to sailors at sea. Then it went out, darkness settled once again, and no more flashing lights appeared. I gave my head a shake; it *must* have been my imagination. I picked up the book and snuggled into bed with it. The perfect read for a spooky night.

* * *

Another thing I'll miss when I move is this commute. The next morning, I walked down the one hundred steps to the library. As usual, I was the first to arrive. The second if you count Charles, who ran on ahead of me, eager to start another day.

I wasn't quite so eager. I'd read long into the night, enjoying Sir Arthur Conan Doyle's story of the legendary hound, the race across the dangerous, gloomy moor, Sherlock Holmes's usual keen observations, and Dr. Watson's usual befuddlement. When I finally turned out the light and laid the book to one side, I hadn't thought about Sir Henry Baskerville and Sherlock Holmes but of Rich Lewiston, what might have brought him so unexpectedly to the Outer Banks, and who might have wanted to ensure he never left.

Over my usual breakfast of muesli and yogurt, I surveyed the local news, but I learned nothing new. The police had issued a statement saying they were investigating a suspicious death, providing few details. I gave Mom a call, and she told me she was still at the Ocean Side, where she and Evangeline were enjoying a room-service breakfast. Ricky hadn't called, and no one had answered Evangeline's frantic knocking at the door of his room. Evangeline had finally gone to bed, but Mom heard her all through the night, tossing and turning and pacing and periodically getting up to check her phone. "Her anxiety's transferring itself to Fluffy, who's more wired than ever. I wouldn't have thought that possible."

"Are you going to go home today as planned?" I asked.

"I don't know, dear. Let's see what the morning brings. Your father's been in touch with the office, and someone there will liaise with the police and take care of the arrangements."

"Nice to have an office," I said.

"It is, isn't it? I'll call you when I know more. Ellen is due here shortly, bringing fresh clothes for me."

Charles froze at the bottom of the stairs, staring at the front door. Suspecting a mouse had crossed the threshold in the night, I left him and went into the staff break room to put the coffee on. When I came back out, the big cat was standing at the door, the fur along his back erect, his ears at attention, still staring.

"What are you up to? Is someone out there already?" Obviously a staff member would just come in, but perhaps we had an early patron. It was five minutes until nine, so I unlocked the door and threw it open.

A body fell in.

Chapter Eight

I screamed. Charles hissed and swatted at the man lying in the doorway in front of us.

Richard Eric Lewiston III groaned and rolled onto his back. There he lay, spread out on the black-and-white tiles blinking rapidly up at me through red-rimmed eyes. He grunted.

"What are you doing?" I said in a louder voice than perhaps I'd intended.

"Good," he said. "You're finally open." Charles peered into his face. "Hello," Ricky said. Charles meowed. Ricky struggled to get up. I leaned over and held out one arm. Ricky grabbed it, and I hauled him upright.

"What are you doing here?"

"Is that coffee I smell?"

"Yes."

"I'd kill for a cup."

Bad choice of words, considering the events of last night. I didn't say so. Instead I said, "Sit down, and I'll get you one."

When I returned to the main room, an enormous mug of strong black unsweetened coffee in hand, Ricky had settled himself into the wingback chair next to the magazine rack. His head was thrown back and his eyes were closed. Charles perched on a high shelf, watching him.

Ricky looked, quite simply, dreadful, and he didn't smell all that good either. He hadn't shaved or combed his hair this morning, and deep purple circles lay under his eyes. He wasn't wearing his blazer, but he still had on the white shirt and jeans he'd been wearing last night. The shirt was white no longer but dotted with what looked like beer and grease stains as well as dirt off our front steps. The hems of his pants and his hand-made Italian loafers were covered in sand and mud.

"Ricky," I said. "Wake up."

He started and his eyes flew open. I handed him the coffee, and he took a long, grateful drink. "Thanks, Lucy. I needed that."

"It would appear that you do. What's going on? Where have you been and why are you here?"

" 'Morning!" Ronald called as he came in. "Oh, sorry." He looked at Ricky and then at me. "Everything okay?"

"Yes. This is a . . . friend of my family. Ricky Lewiston, Ronald Burkowski."

"Okay." Ronald studied my face. I gave him a slight nod to say everything was good here.

Ricky struggled to stand up. I grabbed the mug out of his hands as Ronald leapt forward and took his arm.

"I'm going to take him upstairs and throw him under the shower," I said.

"Are you sure, Lucy?" Ronald asked.

"Not really." I peered into Ricky's bloodshot eyes. He blinked at me and breathed out noxious fumes. "Ricky, have you spoken to the Nags Head Police today?"

"Why would I want to do that? I only had a couple drinks."

"More than a couple," Ronald muttered.

I reconsidered taking Ricky up to my apartment. Not that I was worried he'd attack me or anything, but I didn't think he could manage the stairs, and I wasn't about to get myself involved in trying to undress him. "We'll go into the break room. I'll hold his head under the tap in the sink. But first, I need to call Detective Watson."

"Why?" Ronald asked. "I heard about a suspicious death in town on the news, and I was thanking our lucky stars it didn't have anything to do with us this time. Does it?"

"Sorta," I admitted.

"I'll find out what *sorta* means later. First I'll take care of your friend here. You call Watson. Come on, buddy. We'll have you as fit as a fiddle in no time."

Ricky made no protest as Ronald led him away. I decided to step outside to make the call so I could have a look and see if Ricky'd left anyone else on our step. I've had reason to phone the good detective so often I have his personal number in my contacts list.

Last night's fog had cleared. The sun was rising in a cloudless sky, the heat of the day was already settling in, and a light salty breeze caressed my cheeks and ruffled my curls as a flock of Canada geese flew overhead, calling to stragglers to keep up. The barking of a dog came from the marsh, and I could see heads bobbing over the long grasses near the pond. Ronald's car was the only one in front of the library, although two cars were parked near the boardwalk, and I remembered that my dad had taken my car last night.

A square of thick white plastic lay on the steps, and I bent down to pick it up. A room key from the Ocean Side Hotel. It must have fallen out of Ricky's pocket.

What, I wondered, had he been up to last night after leaving the restaurant?

Was it possible that he—Ricky, whom I'd known since we were kids—had killed his father and run into the night to try to forget what he'd done? I told myself there was no point in speculating. It would be up to Detective Watson to figure out what had happened.

I placed the call, and he answered almost immediately. "Good morning, Lucy. Have you located Ricky Lewiston?"

"Uh, yes, actually. How did you know that's why I'm calling?"

"A guess. I didn't think this was a social call. Although CeeCee tells me your club's reading *The Hound of the Baskervilles*, one of my favorites. If I get this case cleared up, I might come to the meeting. Where are you now?"

"I'm at the library. Ricky was asleep on the step when I opened up."

"Did he have anything to say about last night?"

"I didn't ask. He seems to be hungover. Very, very hungover."

"I'm on my way. Would you say this is a normal pattern of behavior for him? Is he a serious drinker?"

"No, not really. He enjoys a night out, but I've never known him to drink to excess. He was drinking a lot last night at the restaurant even before—I mean, even before he left."

"Ten minutes. Don't let him leave." Watson hung up. I stared at my phone. Don't let him leave? What was I supposed to do if Ricky wanted to be on his way? Suggest he settle down with a good book? Tie him to a bookshelf? Tell Charles to stand guard over him?

All of that turned out not to be necessary. When I went back inside, I found Ricky and Ronald in the break room.

Ricky was sitting at the table, clinging to his mug of coffee as though it were a life preserver, his hair and shirt soaking wet. Ronald's sleeves were drenched up to the elbows, his Star Wars tie askew, and he was mopping the floor while Charles scowled at our visitor in disapproval.

"Thanks, Ronald," I said.

He handed me the mop. "It's Charlene's day off. I can watch the desk for a while, but toddlers' story time is at eleven."

"I'll be done by then."

"Sorry," Ricky said once Ronald had left, straightening his tie and muttering under his breath in disapproval. "Do you have any aspirin or anything? My head's killing me."

I got the little bottle off a high shelf and shook out two pills. I handed them to him with a glass of water, and he accepted them gratefully.

I poured myself a cup of coffee and sat down opposite Ricky. "What are you doing here?"

"I don't know, Lucy. I went on quite the bender last night, and . . . I guess I decided I needed to see you one more time before I leave."

"Before you leave? You mean you're going home?"

He nodded, winced as the motion reminded him that he had a headache, and sipped his coffee.

"To Boston?"

"That's where home is. For me, anyway. Obviously no longer for you."

"Today?"

"Yes, today. With Mom. Is there a problem with that?" He lifted his head and looked at me. His eyes were still bloodshot and his head hurt, but some degree of comprehension had returned.

85

"Ricky, are you aware the police want to talk to you?"

"What about? Okay, I went on a heck of a bender, and I don't exactly remember everything that happened last night, but I would remember if I'd been in an accident or something. I think." He lifted his unmarked hands and studied them.

"Have you spoken to your mother this morning?"

"I guess I should, eh? She can be overprotective sometimes, but she knows not to worry about it when I . . . don't show up for breakfast."

"I'll let her know you're here," I said.

He shrugged, not much interested, and finished his coffee. He extended the mug to me. "Any more? I should probably get some breakfast into me. Want to join me?"

I took the mug. "Ricky, I don't know what to say, but—"

I was saved from saying anything by the sound of firm footsteps in the hallway and the arrival of Detective Watson and Butch Greenblatt.

"Detective, Officer," I said in the way my mother had taught me was proper when greeting guests. "Please do come in."

Ricky started to stand. "Oh. I guess you're busy. I'll be going, then. Uh . . . can you call a cab for me, Lucy?"

"Not so fast," Butch said.

"What?" Ricky said.

"Sit down, please," Watson said.

Ricky dropped into his chair. I got to my feet and edged toward the door. I wasn't planning on leaving, but I thought that if I made myself unobtrusive, Watson would forget I was here.

"Are you Richard Lewiston the Third?" Watson asked.

Ricky blinked. "I might be. I might not be. Who the heck are you?"

"Detective Sam Watson, Nags Head Police."

"Is there a problem?" Ricky asked.

"Answer the detective's question." Butch didn't look happy. It was likely the police had been searching for Ricky all night, and Butch had been on duty since yesterday evening.

Ricky threw me a look, and then he shrugged. He didn't seem to know what was going on. He didn't seem to know that his father had died and that his mother, as well as the police, was frantically trying to locate him.

Then again, Ricky was a lawyer. A corporate lawyer, yes, but he had courtroom experience. Court was a stage and a lawyer an actor. He let the silence drag on for a few more seconds, then shrugged and said, "Yeah, that's my name."

"Where were you last night?" Watson asked.

"That's absolutely none of your business."

"I'll decide what's my business."

"Perhaps, *Detective*, you're not aware that I'm an attorney with—"

"Ricky!" I said. "Please. Don't be difficult. Just tell us—I mean, them—what you were doing last night after you left the restaurant."

"Why?"

Watson turned to Butch. "I haven't got time to play games. Let's go. Bring him along. We'll continue this conversation down at the station."

"Hey!" Ricky half rose as Butch took a step toward him. "I'm not going anywhere without—"

"Ricky," I yelled. "You do not want to do this. Please. Stop it. Your father's dead, and you need to tell the police what you know." Horrified, I snapped my mouth shut. Here I was, trying to be unobtrusive and silent, and I'd just blurted out what the police were not telling the suspect. I ducked my head. "Sorry."

Ricky's face was a picture of shock. He dropped into his chair. His mouth opened; it snapped shut. Surely he couldn't be that good an actor? "What? Lucy, what do you mean?"

"Ms. Richardson's right," Watson said. "Your father died last night."

"I still don't understand what concern that is of yours," Ricky said. "I have to go to my mother. We need to get back to Boston. Lucy, does Mom know?"

"Yes. My mother's with her."

"That's good, then."

"It is very much my concern," Watson said, "as your father was found dead in an alley in Nags Head under suspicious circumstances. Now, can you please tell me where you went last night after you left Lucy and her party at Jake's Seafood Bar?"

That was blunt, but clearly Watson had decided it was time to stop beating about the bush. Ricky wasn't making it easy for the police to ask the necessary questions.

"You think he was murdered?" Ricky said.

"We are presently acting on that assumption," Watson said.

"Can I have a glass of water? Please?"

Watson didn't tell me not to move, so I slipped over to the sink and got Ricky what he needed. I handed it to him with what I hoped was an encouraging smile and returned to my place against the wall.

Ricky drank the entire glass in one long gulp and then took a deep breath. "Okay. My mom and I had dinner at that seafood place overlooking the Sound with my dad's law partner and his family, including Lucy here. It wasn't a pleasant evening. My mother was making . . . shall we say, demands of me that I wasn't happy about." He threw me a quick look. "I went to the bar to get myself another drink, and I decided to leave. Mom and I'd come together in our rental car and she had the keys, so she could get herself back to the hotel without me. I paid my bar bill and walked out without saying good-bye to anyone. I went to that strip of restaurants and bars across from the oceanfront and settled in for the duration. The result of which is, I don't feel too good today."

"What bar?" Watson asked.

Ricky gave him a sickly grin. "I don't remember the name. Sorry."

"Will you remember it if you see it again?" Butch asked.

"I might. They all look much the same."

"Did you see your father at any time yesterday?" Watson asked.

Ricky shook his head. He winced and touched his forehead. "I did not. I didn't even know he was in town. He said nothing about any plans to come here."

"When you left Jake's, was there any police activity outside?"

"Not that I noticed."

"Were Lucy and her party still at their table?"

"Yeah. I figured no one would miss me if I just left."

"What about your mother?"

"Come to think of it, I didn't see her. I figured she'd gone to the ladies' room. Like I said, I wasn't worried about her. She could drive herself to the hotel. My mother's more than capable of looking after herself."

I kept my face impassive. Unwittingly, Ricky had established his mother as a suspect.

"What time did you return to your hotel?"

"Uh . . ."

"He didn't," I said. "His mother was knocking on his door all night. She's been worried sick."

"I didn't know that, did I?" Ricky snapped at me.

"Where did you spend the night, then?" Watson asked.

Another glance at me. "I'd like to be able to say I met a nice young lady, but I didn't. When the bar closed, I gave the bartender a hundred bucks to roll me into the back of his truck. When he came out this morning to get to his other job, I asked him to drop me off here. I gave him another hundred for the lift."

"Why come here?"

"I wanted to talk to Lucy. To say good-bye and wish her well. We were close, once."

"You maintain you didn't see your father yesterday?"

"I did not."

"Did you recognize anyone at all, other than Lucy, your mother, and other members of the dinner party, at Jake's last night? Inside or out?"

"No. I—wait, there was one guy. A client of my dad's and mine. Guy by the name of Gordon Frankland. He was having dinner in the same place and came over to say hello."

I nodded in agreement.

"Did you see Mr. Frankland after you left the restaurant?"

"No."

"Anyone else you're acquainted with?"

"No."

"Did your father have any enemies?"

Ricky snorted. "Outside the boardrooms of Boston, none that I know of. Inside, yeah, probably a lot. My dad's been an attorney for a long time. I can't say his ethics have always been entirely aboveboard. Not that I know anything about that, of course."

"Of course," Watson said. "I will point out that in my experience, even people intimately acquainted with the insides of corporate boardrooms can commit shocking acts of violence."

Ricky said nothing.

"Was your father a regular visitor to the Outer Banks?"

"He came about once a year or so on fishing trips with clients. He worked out of Boston, but our firm has clients all over the country. Like Gordon Frankland, who, as I told you, came over to our table to say hello. It wasn't a pleasant encounter. Guy's a difficult client, to say the least."

"What happened?"

"Nothing happened. He threw around a few insults and insinuations about our firm's capabilities and then went back to his table."

"I'm acquainted with Mr. Frankland," Watson said. "I'll be speaking with him. Leave your contact information with Officer Greenblatt."

Ricky stood up. "Great. Can I have a lift back to town?"

"I don't run a taxi service."

The police left, leaving the door open behind them. Ricky let out a long breath. "Wow. That's pretty hard stuff to take in."

"It is."

I heard voices in the hallway, and Bertie's head popped in. "Lucy, what's going on? Ronald said Sam's been here to speak to a friend of yours about a death in town?"

"Hi," Ricky said.

"Hello. I heard something on the radio this morning about that. I dared hope we wouldn't be involved. Are we?"

"No," I said firmly. "We are not. Unfortunately, my parents are. It was my dad's law partner who died."

"Goodness."

"You'll be wanting to check up on your mom, Lucy," Ricky said. "She's bound to be devastated about Dad's death. You can give me a lift to the hotel."

"I—"

"Take some time if you need it, Lucy," Bertie said. "You put in a lot of extra hours last week when Ronald was off sick."

Time I'd been hoping to spend with Connor in our search for a house. Before I could point that out, Ricky said, "Great! Let's go. I have got to get out of these clothes."

Chapter Nine

Connor had driven me home after dinner last night, and Dad had my car. I had to go into town to get it anyway, so I called a taxi to come for Ricky and me. We drove to the Ocean Side in silence. I had nothing more to say to Ricky, and he was wrapped in his own thoughts.

As we walked up the front steps together, Ricky began patting his jeans pockets.

"Looking for something?" I passed him the room key.

"Thanks," he mumbled. "Must have dropped it."

Ricky's room was next to his mother's. He knocked, the door flew open, and Evangeline threw herself at him while Fluffy danced around their legs, barking frantically.

"It's okay, Mom." Ricky patted her back. "I'm here now. Sorry if you were worried." He led her into the room, and I followed. I nudged Fluffy with my foot to get her inside and shut the door. The little dog kept barking. I was surprised the hotel hadn't thrown her out by now. I bent over and gave her what I hoped was a comforting pat. "It's okay. We're all okay."

She stopped barking as abruptly as though a switch had been thrown. Evangeline dropped onto the couch, and Fluffy leapt up beside her.

Watson and Butch stood silently, watching everything.

"Fancy meeting you here," I said.

"Don't push it, Lucy," Watson replied.

"Hi, Mom," I said.

My mother was sitting in the desk chair. Despite having spent the night on a pullout couch and being continually disturbed, she looked fresh and dewy and ready for another fun-filled day. She'd found the time to apply her makeup and fix her hair and was dressed in a different outfit of white capris, a blue-and-white-striped T-shirt, and blue espadrilles. Perhaps only I noticed that she was still wearing the earrings she'd had on last night, and the dangling diamonds didn't suit today's jaunty casual nautical attire.

"Ellen dropped off a few things for me a short while ago. She came in your car, and Amos drove her home." Mom passed me my keys, and I slipped them into my bag. "Your father's been up for hours, she tells me, making phone calls. He's going home as planned later today, but we think it best if I stay a while longer."

"I've been calling you all night," Evangeline said to Ricky. "Why didn't you reply? Where have you been? I've been so dreadfully worried."

"Sorry, Mom. I didn't hear the phone. I uh . . . ran into a friend." Ricky ducked his head and looked very boyish and chastised as he lied comfortably. I hoped he'd have more sense than to try to lie to the police.

"I'll forgive you. This time," she said. "Detective Watson was explaining to me that they can't release your father's body yet. Pending, as he put it, the results of his investigation."

"That's normal procedure, Mom." Ricky dropped onto the couch next to her, displacing Fluffy, who glared at him before hopping down. "Have you had breakfast?"

"I was up early. I scarcely got a wink of sleep all night. I was so worried. Didn't you at least see my messages?"

"Messages?" Ricky patted his jeans pockets once again. "I, uh, seem to have lost my phone. Lucy, did you see my jacket?"

"Nope."

Watson's eyes opened slightly. "You've misplaced your jacket?"

Ricky shrugged. "It'll turn up. I hope."

"Never mind, my darling boy." Evangeline patted his knee. "You're here now. You can worry about your phone later. Suzanne and I ordered from room service earlier. Would you like me to call down for them to bring you something?"

"Coffee, lots of it. Bacon and eggs and hash browns. Lots of toast. Tomato juice. I don't feel too good."

Evangeline rubbed the back of his hand.

"I might be coming down with a cold," Ricky lied.

Evangeline started to get to her feet, but Watson said, "Perhaps we can finish here first?"

"Nonsense," Evangeline said. "It won't take a minute. You can see my son is very hungry."

Ricky tried to look hungry. It wasn't difficult. He looked like a rabid dog that hadn't eaten recently.

"I'll take care of it." Mom reached for the desk phone.

"As I was saying," Watson said, "I'll need a list of Mr. Lewiston's clients and friends who live in the Outer Banks. People he might have been here to visit."

"And, as I was about to tell you, Detective, I do not know. I paid no mind to my husband's business dealings, and his fishing-trip companions were not acquaintances of mine."

Yet Gordon Frankland had known who she was and she had not appreciated seeing him. I didn't mention that.

"I'll see what I can do," Ricky said. "They'll have records of that sort of thing back at the office."

"I've checked with the front desk, and Mr. Lewiston wasn't registered here," Watson said, "nor did he have a reservation. We didn't find a hotel key on him."

"His PA would have made any reservations he needed," Ricky said. "I'll ask her."

"Thank you," Watson said.

Ricky didn't move. Finally Watson said, "Sooner rather than later would be good."

"Oh, sorry. Uh . . . a phone?"

His mother handed hers over, and Ricky placed the call. "Hey, Jackie, it's me. Ricky? Yeah. Yeah, thanks. Yeah, we're all upset. I don't know. I'll let you know. Right now I need to be with Mom. Did you make hotel reservations here for Dad? You didn't? You did? Wasn't that odd?"

Watson plucked the phone out of Ricky's hand. "This is Detective Sam Watson of the Nags Head Police. To whom am I speaking? Thank you, Mrs. McKenzie. Did you know Mr. Lewiston Senior was planning a trip to North Carolina? Was that normal behavior? Thank you. I'll be in touch if I need anything else."

He passed the phone to Evangeline, who said, "I'll call to let you know what I need when the police have left," and hung up.

"Your husband's personal assistant says he left the office Friday afternoon at the usual time, telling her to have a good weekend," Watson said. "She didn't hear from him over the weekend, and she would have if travel plans arose suddenly.

He didn't come into the office yesterday morning, missing several appointments. She attempted to call him and got no reply, but he called her at one o'clock when she was on the phone with someone else, and he left a message saying he'd be out of town for a few days and she was to reschedule all his appointments. According to Mrs. McKenzie, this was not a normal pattern of behavior for your husband. Would you agree, Mrs. Lewiston?"

"The very idea of Rich doing anything not scheduled a month in advance is preposterous. Jackie McKenzie makes appointments for him to buy shoes, never mind flight and hotel reservations." Evangeline snorted. "Saves me having to do it. Jackie has been with him for years, decades. She's paid very well for her troubles."

"That's true," Ricky said.

I threw my mom a look, and she raised one eyebrow. More than one lawyer has confused his wife and his secretary, and in more ways than one. I made a mental note to ask my dad about Mrs. McKenzie. Was she the sort to finally understand that her position as "office wife" wasn't leading to the real thing and decide to get her revenge for decades of "troubles," no matter how well paid she might be?

"Is that your understanding of your father's behavior?" Watson asked Ricky.

"Totally. I'd be surprised if my dad even knows—knew— how to make a flight or hotel booking."

"Yet in this case he seems to have come to Nags Head without anyone making his arrangements for him. A car registered in your father's name was found in the parking lot of Jake's. You told me you and Mrs. Lewiston flew and then rented a car?"

"That's right."

"If your father's car wasn't stolen, and it hasn't been reported as such, then it would indicate he drove down from Boston."

I remembered the Mercedes with Massachusetts plates I'd seen outside Jake's.

"Rich drove all the way down here?" Evangeline's shock was obvious. "I can scarcely believe it."

"Perhaps he decided to join you for dinner to celebrate Lucy and Connor's engagement?" Watson said. "As an old family friend?"

"If so," my mother said, "it would have been the first time anything like that happened. Ever."

"My husband was not," Evangeline said, "of a spontaneous nature."

"So you have no idea why he was here?" Watson asked.

She simply shook her head.

"None," Ricky said.

A knock at the door and a call of "Room service!" had Ricky leaping to his feet and Fluffy setting up another round of barking. Ricky opened the door, and a waiter pushed in a trolley covered in a white linen cloth and bearing nice china and cutlery, chafing dishes, and a giant carafe of coffee.

Ricky patted his pockets one more time and came up empty once again. He gave his mother a rueful shrug, and she dug in her bag for a ten-dollar bill, which she passed to him.

"Thank you for your time, Mrs. Lewiston," Watson said. "If I need anything further, I'll be in touch."

"I'll be here," she said. "Until I can take my husband home."

Ricky lifted the lid off a chafing dish, and the delicious scent of perfectly done bacon and hot buttered toast drifted through the room. "Once I've had breakfast, Mom," he said, "I need to take the car and try to find where I left my jacket last night."

"I'd like to see this jacket," Watson said. "When you find it."

"Surely you can buy another one?" Evangeline said.

"Yeah, but it had my things in it. I seem to have misplaced my phone and my wallet."

My mother and I followed the police into the hallway, and Butch shut the door behind us.

"Looks like you have two mysteries to solve, Detective," I said. "Not only who killed Rich, but why he was here in the first place."

"Once I find the answer to one question, I'll have the answer to the other. You know these people well, Mrs. Richardson. Is what they said about Rich Lewiston's habits correct?"

"Oh, yes," Mom said. "A more regimented man I never have met, and I gather from my husband that Rich is getting more so as the years pass. I've often thought the reason they only have one child is Evangeline couldn't find the opportunity to arrange a second appointment with her husband."

I choked. Butch's eyebrows rose.

Watson cleared his throat. "I need to talk to your husband about his law partner. Is he still at the O'Malleys'?"

"Yes," Mom said. "He's expecting you. He'll be going home later this afternoon." She looked at me. "I'll be staying for a while, dear. Evangeline's not always as stoic as she appears, and she has no one else to call upon. She has a younger sister, but they are not close. She told me yesterday her parents are traveling in Europe at the moment."

The elevator pinged, and a woman stepped out and headed our way. She was dressed in a neat but cheap baggy gray suit with the hotel's logo discreetly embroidered over the breast pocket. She smiled politely to us as she passed and knocked firmly on Evangeline's door.

Watson made no move to walk away, and so neither did I.

The door opened, and Evangeline peered out. "Yes?"

"I'm very sorry, ma'am, but we've had complaints about your dog barking."

"My dog does not bark. The sound must have been coming from another room."

"I'm sorry, ma'am, but I heard him myself a few minutes ago. The noise is very intrusive."

"Her."

"What?"

"Fluffy is a her. A girl dog."

"I don't know that the animal's gender matters."

At that moment Fluffy lunged for the hotel employee and broke into a chorus of high-pitched barking. She bared a row of small teeth, and the woman took a quick step backward. "Please, ma'am. You'll have to make other arrangements for your dog."

"That's preposterous. I'm paying good money to stay in this hotel."

Chuckling, Watson walked away, followed by Butch. I bent over and scooped Fluffy up.

"Thank you, Lucy," Evangeline said. "See, she's under control."

"Madam, please. The dog cannot stay."

"How tedious is this?" Evangeline turned her head and spoke into the room. "Ricky, take care of this, will you, my darling?"

"I don't have any money on me at the moment, Mom, as I seem to have lost my wallet, and I don't think a bribe will work in this case anyway."

Evangeline bit back a bad word and turned to face the woman. Tears welled up in her eyes. "I'm sorry. So sorry. I'm dreadfully upset, you see, and my dear little Fluffy is only reacting to my emotions. She's so very sensitive that way. I've been given the most horrid news imaginable. I'm sure you saw the police officers who just left. They were here to break the news to me of my husband's sudden death." A tear drifted ever so slowly down her cheek.

"My condolences. But the dog cannot stay. Unless you have a muzzle to put on it."

Evangeline recoiled. "That's positively barbaric. In any other circumstances, I'd check out immediately, but . . ." Her eyes settled on me. Fluffy had stopped struggling and was clearly enjoying the nice back rub I was giving her.

"Very well," Evangeline said with a martyred sigh. "If you insist. Suzanne, dearest, you'll look after Fluffy for me."

My mother started. "Me? Oh no, you're not unloading your dog on me."

"Aunt Ellen's allergic to dogs," I said. "She can't have one in the house."

"That's true," Mom said. "I always wanted a dog when we were children, but Ellen suffered too much."

Evangeline turned her smile on me. "Will you look at that? How sweet. She seems to like you, Lucy. I know she'll be comfortable with you."

"I can't take her," I protested. "I live in an apartment that's smaller than this hotel room."

"Won't be for long. Thank you so much, dear. I'll send you a text with feeding instructions."

The door shut in our faces.

The hotel employee grinned at me. "Have a nice day." She walked away.

I stroked Fluffy. "What does this mean?" I asked my mom.

"It means you have temporary guardianship of a small and excessively annoying dog." She rapped on the door. "Evangeline, I need my purse."

"Just a minute," came the voice from behind the door. I put my ear against it and heard Ricky and his mother talking, trying to keep their voices low. Eventually the door opened and Ricky slipped through. He carried Mom's purse over one shoulder, a pink leash over the other, a plastic bag containing cans and a bag of what was probably dog food in his left hand, and a hastily made bacon-and-egg sandwich and a cup of coffee in his right.

The door slammed shut behind Ricky.

"Mom needs the car," he said. "She has to go shopping."

"Shopping?" I said. "Now?"

"Unlike the queen," Mom said, "Evangeline doesn't travel with a full set of mourning attire in case it's unexpectedly needed."

"Right," Ricky said. "I need a lift. I need to find my phone and wallet."

"Have you tried calling your phone?" Mom asked.

"Yes, but voice mail picks up right away. It might be out of juice."

"I don't want this dog," I said.

"Not a problem," Ricky said. "Mom will collect her when she's ready to leave the hotel."

"It is a problem. I—" But I was speaking to their backs as Mom and Ricky walked down the hallway. I sighed, resigning myself to my fate, and Fluffy and I followed. Fluffy strained against me, wanting to be put down so she could run back to Evangeline. I held her tighter. "Looks like you're stuck with me, and me with you, for the duration," I said.

She bit my finger, and I yelped in surprise and pain. Her teeth might be small, but they were very sharp.

Chapter Ten

I dropped Mom at Aunt Ellen's and then took Ricky (and Fluffy) to search the bars of Nags Head.

"It wasn't too far from the restaurant," Ricky said. "I walked there. I had to cross a busy road."

"Big place? Small? Nice or a dive?"

"I'm not entirely sure. Not the sort of establishment you'd find my mother frequenting, in any event."

I drove slowly down Grouse Street and turned right on Highway 12 while Ricky peered out the window and munched on his bacon sandwich and Fluffy bounced around the back seat. "You should get the dog's harness out of the rental car," I said.

"Yeah, I guess. You and this guy, Connor. Are you going to be okay?"

"Whatever that means, yes, we're going to be okay."

"Mom said he's the mayor."

"That's right."

"Mom says you can never trust a politician."

"Your mother is not a neutral observer."

"Got that one right. There! That's it. I think."

"You think?"

"It's the right one for sure. I think."

I did a U-turn and pulled onto the cracked and broken pavement next to an establishment that you would definitely never find Ricky's mother in. Only one car was in the lot, parked next to the back door. Blue and red lights flickered in the windows, advertising brands of beer, along with an open sign. Ricky studied the door and finally said, "Yeah, this is it. I hope they put my stuff away someplace safe. Wait here."

"Happy to," I said.

Ricky got out of the car, and I twisted around and held out my hand to Fluffy, bracing myself for another bite. "How are you enjoying your vacation in the Outer Banks so far?" She studied me warily, then gave my fingers a quick lick in response.

"Do you like to go for long walks on the beach?" I eyed her carefully groomed pure-white fur and the pink collar studded with rhinestones. "Probably not."

The passenger door opened, and Ricky hopped into the car. He was not, I noticed, carrying his blazer. "Right place, but the guy I spoke to last night isn't in, and they wouldn't give me his number. I have to come back at five if I want to talk to him. I can only hope he hasn't sold my phone and used my credit card for a flight to Brazil. It's almost noon. How about lunch?"

"You just finished a sandwich five minutes ago."

"Still hungry. Still hungover, truth be told. I need some hair of the dog."

"Well, I don't. I'm going back to work. I'll drop you at the hotel." I switched on the car's engine and pulled into traffic. "You can get me the dog harness. I don't like the way she's bouncing around back there."

As long as the little creature had been forced on me, I might as well try to look after her properly.

"What are you going to do now, Ricky?" I asked. "Are you going back to Boston today as planned?"

He said nothing for a long time, and then he let out a sigh. "I'm not sure. I should probably stay with my mom, give her moral support and all that, but your mom's doing that. I should go back to the office, assure everyone the firm is in good hands, a steady hand on the tiller, that sort of rubbish. But it doesn't really matter. I don't do much there, and everyone knows it. Your dad'll do a better job of reassuring them than I ever could. Not that they need reassuring. They'll be glad Dad's gone. He can't do any more damage."

"Surely you don't mean that, Ricky."

"I do. Unfortunately. He'd been making a lot of bad decisions lately, taking on bad clients. People on the lower floors are always whispering in corners about overheard shouting matches coming from the partners' meetings. They stop whispering when I walk in, but I've heard enough to know they're whispering about me too."

I arrived at the Ocean Side. I drove past. Ricky needed to talk.

"Thing is, Lucy, Dad was a drain on the firm, and I'm in way over my head. I should have articled in another firm, got my feet wet somewhere I wasn't the boss's son. I should be doing smaller cases, less important ones, but Dad's been shoving the biggest and most high-profile cases onto my desk, and then he never follows up to see how things are going, and some of the partners are ensuring I don't get what support I need."

"Some of the partners? You mean my dad?"

"No. Never him. Your dad's not my biggest fan, but he'd never do anything to damage the reputation of the firm."

"But others would?"

"Your dad's never forgotten that Richardson Lewiston was started by his father and my grandfather. That history's important to him. Important enough that he's not on the side of those who want to push my father—and thus me—out. Guess that's all a moot point now."

I took a left turn onto a side street. "I had no idea. Ricky, the police think your dad was murdered. Is it at all possible that one of the partners or someone else at the firm decided to speed his departure along?"

"You mean by bumping him off? No, Lucy. This isn't the movies. Members of respectable law firms don't do that sort of thing. I'm not being sarcastic. The knives were out for Dad, and it was only a matter of time before he was pushed overboard, if I may mix my metaphors. Dad wasn't helping matters any, and he scarcely seemed to realize what was going on. Even your father couldn't do anything about it. Your dad was always loyal to my dad. I'm sorry to say it, but my dad didn't return the favor; all he cared about was saving his own bacon."

I took another left. "Someone killed him, according to the police. If it wasn't a random attack, then he had at least one enemy prepared to go to extremes."

"I don't know anything about Dad's private life, if he had one. We didn't spend much time together outside of the office—or even in it, lately. There were disgruntled clients, like that guy who showed up at the restaurant last night."

"Gordon Frankland. He recognized your mom, but your mom says she never had anything to do with the firm."

"They would have met at some charity do or another. My mom's big on charity dos. Gives her a chance to buy a new dress, wear her diamonds, and show off. Dad and I know we're expected to invite clients to her things. They're expected to put in an appearance, if they know what's good for them. Mom wasn't at all happy to see Frankland yesterday."

"To put it mildly," I said.

"Dad might have told her the man was causing trouble. My dad talked about business with Mom more than she let on. On the other hand, Dad had debts, gambling debts, and he made one bad investment decision after another. Probably a lot Mom and I didn't know about."

"What do you want now, Ricky? Are you going to stay on at Richardson Lewiston?"

"I don't know, Lucy. I really don't know. I do know, however, that you're driving in circles. I've seen that house before."

"Get my phone out of my purse and call your mom. Ask her where she is and where the dog's car harness is."

I told Ricky the password to my phone as I made another left turn and headed for the Ocean Side. He made the call, and his mother answered. They spoke briefly and he hung up. "She's still at the hotel. Says she decided to go shopping after lunch. She coulda told me that before I dragged you all over town, Lucy. Sorry."

"Not a problem."

Fluffy jumped up and down in the back seat, eager to be let out of the car. The sun was high in the sky and the temperatures in the eighties. I couldn't leave the dog locked in the car when we went in search of Evangeline.

Ricky seemed to read my mind. "I'll take the demon beast for a stroll around the property while you go in. I'd just as soon avoid Mom for a while longer. She's in the restaurant, and she has the valet slip with her. They'll get the harness for you."

"Thanks," I said.

I left Ricky and Fluffy glaring at each other and went inside in search of Evangeline. I found her in the restaurant, comfortably seated at a table for two with views over the garden, a glass of wine in front of her, but to my surprise she was not alone. A man leapt to his feet as I approached.

"I was telling Leon that I'm in town to congratulate you on your engagement, Lucy, and here you are in person." Evangeline laughed lightly. She'd reapplied her makeup, and all trace of tears and sorrow had been covered up.

Her companion thrust out his hand. "Leon Lions. Pleasure to meet you."

"Dear Lucy is the daughter of my oldest and dearest friend in all the world," Evangeline cooed. For a moment I thought she'd mistaken me for someone else. "Leon and I go a long way back, don't we, Leon?"

"So far back," he said, chuckling, "I don't dare try to remember how many years." He was a pleasant-looking man around the age of Evangeline and my parents, with a deep— probably permanent—tan, a round, completely bald head, cheerful gray eyes, and a big belly and equally big smile. He was casually dressed in pressed slacks and a golf shirt. A heavy gold signet ring marked with an ornate letter *L* graced the index finger of his right hand. "Won't you join us?" he said politely. "We haven't ordered our lunches yet."

Evangeline's narrow eyes and tight smile said, *Don't you dare.*

I almost accepted, just to see her reaction, but I shook my head. "Thank you, but no. I have to get back to work."

"Did Ricky find his blazer?" she asked me.

"The night staff wasn't there, so he has to go back later." I was pretty sure the police wouldn't be quite so patient. They'd be wanting to have a look at this missing white jacket. I didn't tell Evangeline so. "Uh, the valet ticket?"

Evangeline turned to Leon. "I love my son dearly, but he is such a scatterbrain sometimes. He certainly doesn't get that from me."

Leon smiled fondly at her. "I'm looking forward to getting to know him."

Okay.

"Do you live locally, Mr. Lions?" I asked.

"Please, call me Leon. Yes, yes I do. In Kill Devil Hills. Lived there all my life except for a few years spent in Boston in my youth, which is where I met this charming lady."

Evangeline actually tittered.

Okay.

"And you've kept in touch all these years," I said. "Isn't that nice?"

"Not as much in touch as I would have liked," Leon said. "Life gets ahead of us, doesn't it, as the years pass before we realize. We still have mutual acquaintances, and I was informed this morning about Rich's death. Naturally, I immediately contacted my old friend to offer any assistance she might require." He smiled at Evangeline.

"What do you want, Lucy?" Evangeline snapped.

"Fluffy's harness."

"Oh, right. The reason you're here." She dug in her Kate Spade bag. "Here you go, dear; mustn't keep you."

"Nice meeting you," Leon said.

"And you," I replied.

Back outside, I handed the ticket to the valet and told him what I wanted. When I had it in hand, I found Ricky watching Fluffy sniff around under a perfectly manicured bush. He handed me the leash. Fluffy sniffed my shoes.

"What are you going to do for the rest of the day?" I asked.

"I have to start making phone calls. I have *some* clients I need to reassure. Firm hand on the tiller and all that. I'll find out what I have scheduled for the rest of the week and then decide if I'm going to stay with Mom until . . . until we can take Dad home."

"If you need anything . . ."

He reached out and touched my cheek, ever so lightly. His eyes were very wet. "Lucy. My Lucy. What a fool I've been."

I turned and fled, dragging Fluffy behind me.

Chapter Eleven

Charles and Fluffy did not attempt to make friends. The moment I stepped into the library, the little dog trotting happily ahead of me, Charles flew across the room, hissing and spitting. Fluffy screeched, darted for the safety of the back of my legs, and began barking so loudly she probably had the ducks lifting off the pond in fright. The leash wrapped around my ankles and was jerked tight. Startled, laden with a bag of dog supplies, and yanked off my feet, I began to topple. I would have fallen flat on my face had not James Dalrymple been passing and grabbed my arm.

"What on earth!" Mrs. Peterson, library patron, said. "Lucy, do you think it's a good idea to bring that dog in here?"

"No," I said through gritted teeth. "I do not."

"Then why have you?"

Good question.

Charles feinted as though to go around to my right. Fluffy edged closer to me. Charles changed course and came by the left. Fluffy showed him all of her impressive teeth. "Stop that!" I yelled at Charles.

He paid me his usual amount of attention when I try to be firm, which is none. He arched his back and all the fur stood on end, appearing to add about twenty pounds to his already hefty frame. His whiskers bristled, his amber eyes narrowed, and he displayed his equally impressive teeth.

Fluffy turned and fled. James had let go of me, and before either of us could react, I was jerked completely off my feet. Fluffy dodged the returns cart, but I wasn't so lucky and crashed into it. The cart fell. The bag fell, split open, and cans of dog food rolled across the floor. Desperately flailing about, trying to keep myself upright, I stepped on a can, and my foot shot out from beneath me as the leash was pulled out of my hand. Books tumbled around me as I hit the floor and cans rolled under the shelves. A substantial hardcover volume of the history of Eastern North Carolina landed on the back of my head. I feared I heard bones crack.

People screamed, the dog barked, the cat screeched, cans clattered, books tumbled, hands reached for me, and other hands chased after the animals. Footsteps pounded down the stairs.

"Lucy, are you all right?"

"I've got him."

"Don't let him go!"

"Someone call an ambulance."

"Careful, he might bite."

"Geez, Mom. Don't be such a wimp. It's just a little dog," Dallas Peterson said.

"What on earth is happening out here?" Bertie cried.

"I . . . I . . ." I rolled over. James and Charlene peered into my face. "Are you hurt?" Charlene asked.

I performed a quick mental inventory on myself. Everything seemed to be in place, and nothing felt broken. "Only my pride." I held out a hand, and James grabbed it. He pulled me to my feet.

I glanced around the library. A circle of faces watched me. Dallas had picked Fluffy up and was murmuring soft words and stroking her. The dog's small body trembled. Charles, content with having established his place in the hierarchy of the library, perched on top of the shelf marked MORRISON–PROULX, washing his paws.

"You need to introduce them properly, Lucy," Dallas said. "Dogs and cats don't have to be natural enemies." She carried Fluffy over to the bookshelf and said, "See? What's your dog's name?"

"She's not my dog, and she's called Fluffy."

"Charles," Dallas said. "This is Fluffy, and she's Lucy's friend. Be nice."

Charles yawned. Dallas put Fluffy on the floor, gave her a reassuring pat, and handed me the end of the leash.

"You have a good way with animals," James said to the girl.

"Thank you. I'm going to be a vet when I grow up. I'd love to have a dog, but Mom says they're too much work." She threw a poisonous look at her mother.

"Well, they are," Mrs. Peterson said to no one.

James and Charlene began gathering up the fallen books, and Ronald went in pursuit of the bag of dry dog food, which fortunately hadn't broken open, and the escaped cans. Patrons dropped to their knees to reach under the shelves.

"Sorry," I said to Bertie. "I was hoping to slip in unnoticed and take Fluffy upstairs."

"Didn't work." Ronald handed me the bag of kibble.

"Apparently not."

"No harm done," Bertie said. "As long as you're okay, Lucy?"

"I'm fine. Thanks." I didn't dare touch the back of my head with all these people watching. Drama over, they began to disperse.

"Cute dog," Charlene said. "Where'd you get her?"

"She belongs to a friend of my mother's, and she can't keep her in the hotel any longer."

"I wonder why?" Ronald muttered.

"Let me take her upstairs and get her settled, and then I'll come back down and take over the desk. I thought you were off today?" I said to Charlene.

"I am. James and I are going to lunch. I came in to get him." She peeked at the Englishman from under her lashes.

"I'm still feeling a bit uh . . . wobbly," I said to James. "Would you mind carrying the dog upstairs for me?"

"Maybe you should go to the hospital," Mrs. Peterson said. "You had a nasty crack on the head."

"Perfectly fine," I said.

"I wouldn't mind at all." James scooped Fluffy into his arms as I accepted a bag containing the gathered-up food. "I like dogs. Come on, girl."

I glared at Charles as we passed his shelf, and he smirked.

"Charlene told me you live over the library," James said as we climbed the stairs. "Nice."

"It is. I like it a lot, but it'll soon be time to move on." We reached the fourth level, and I put the bag on the floor and dug out my key. I unlocked the door and went into the Lighthouse Aerie. James followed me and put Fluffy down. "Here you go, little lady. No trying to escape." Fluffy immediately began exploring her surroundings, the pink leash trailing behind her.

"Is this your first visit to America?" I asked.

"I was born here," James said.

"You were? Really?"

"Yup. In Nags Head, as it happens."

"Your accent's completely English."

"I didn't live here for long. My father was American, and he died when I was a baby. My mum was a PhD student studying American constitutional history; after my father died, she moved back to the UK to be close to her own parents."

"Do you visit often?"

"Not for many years. Mum brought me here a few times to visit with my grandparents when I was a kid, but I haven't been back since they died. My father was almost fifty when I was born, and he was an only child. Mum remarried not long after she moved back to the UK, so once my natural father's parents were gone, she had no reason to come here again. She enjoyed her time when she lived here, and she still talks a lot about it. Natural enough, I guess, that I wanted to learn more. Thus my interest in the history and legends of the Outer Banks. In a way, it's my history and my legends."

"That's interesting. It makes a field of research so much more special, doesn't it, when you have a personal connection?"

"It does."

I wasn't just being polite. I was, to be completely honest, being nosy. I'd seen Evangeline's powerful reaction on meeting this man, and I was wondering what had caused that. James said that before this research trip, he hadn't been to America since he was a child. Was that true? "Did you hear about what happened in town last night?"

"You mean that guy being killed? I did. I heard it was the husband of the woman who was in here yesterday morning. Your friend?"

"Friend of my family."

"Tough. Do the police know who did it?"

"Not as far as I know."

"Charlene said you've worked with the police before?"

"I wouldn't say 'worked with.' I've been of help to them in the past. I—" I looked directly at him. "I have a way of finding things out. Things about people."

He shifted his feet, clearly losing interest in this conversation. "If you're okay, I'll be off."

"Yeah, I'm fine. Is Daisy going to lunch with you?" I tried to keep my voice casual, as if I didn't really care.

"No. She's in Manteo today, having a look at some family's letters they found in a forgotten old box when they wrapped up Granny's estate." He chuckled. "All I can say is, thank heavens for pack rats. A researcher's dream. Cheers." James shut the door on his way out.

I let out a breath. I was worried for my friend Charlene. She'd recently told me about a bad relationship she'd had a few years ago with a married man. I didn't want to see her making the same mistake again. She'd told me, that other time, that her heart was fully capable of overriding the *Beware!* warnings coming from her brain. It can be awfully hard not to follow your heart where it leads.

Fluffy sniffed around the kitchen. "Try to stay out of trouble," I told her before going downstairs and back to work.

* * *

Louise Jane came in as I was shutting down the computer. "Closing time!" I called.

"I know when it's closing time, Lucy. I'm meeting James and Daisy. We're going out for a drink. They're coming across some interesting things, and Daisy's anxious to tell me about it."

"I'm sure she is."

"Sarcasm does not become you, Lucy. Unlike some people, James and Daisy are experienced enough academics to know the value of local stories. As a professor of American history, Daisy has a deep interest in—hi, Teddy."

"Oh, good. I'm not late," the new arrival said. "We're going for a drink, Lucy. Would you like to join us? Charlene's meeting us in town, so we're going to be a jolly old group."

"No thanks. Connor and I have an appointment to look at a house."

Louise Jane's eyes flashed. "Is that so?" she said, ever so casually. "I wonder what Bertie's going to do with your apartment."

"It's been empty before," Theodore said. "Not many people want to live this far out of town, and the space is very small. Never mind the lack of an elevator."

"I'm well aware of that, thank you, Teddy. Before Lucy arrived, I suggested to Bertie she rent it out. For the extra income."

"She can't do that," I said. "The place doesn't have its own entrance; only a library employee can be in here after hours."

The desk phone rang, and I reached for it as Louise Jane explained to Theodore that *some* people could be trusted around library property.

"I'm sorry, Lucy," Connor said. "I got a call from the realtor. A firm and final offer's been made on that house, so there's no point in us seeing it."

"Oh no. I liked the look of that one so much."

"And the price was right. She said she'll keep looking."

"I've been invited to go out for drinks with Charlene's researchers, Theodore, and Louise Jane," I said. "Do you want to do that?"

"If you do, sure. I've some stuff to finish up here, so I'll meet you in town. Send me a text when you know where you're going."

"Will do." I'd turned to face the wall to make the call, and I started when I turned. Louise Jane was standing very close behind me. "Can I help you with something, Louise Jane?"

"I couldn't help overhearing. Having trouble finding a house to buy, are you?"

I sighed. "Yeah. Finding what we like at a price we want to pay isn't easy."

"Aren't your parents helping you?"

"Louise Jane, that's none of your business."

"I'm simply making polite conversation."

"I need to take the dog for a short walk. Wait for me here. One of you can give me a ride into town, and I'll come back with Connor."

"What dog?" Louise Jane and Theodore chorused.

"Don't ask," I said.

The desk phone rang again. It was after closing, so I was about to let voice mail answer when I saw the number of the caller. "Hi, Mom."

"Lucy," my mother said. "I need a ride. Ellen isn't here, and I was in the shower when she called, so Amos has gone on ahead."

"When who called, and Amos has gone where ahead?"

"Evangeline called, and Amos has gone to the police station. They've arrested Ricky for the murder of his father."

Chapter Twelve

As it turned out, Evangeline had overreacted. Ricky had not been arrested but rather taken down to the station to answer more questions.

"Same thing," she said.

"It isn't the same thing," I said. "Not at all."

Mom and I'd found Evangeline pacing up and down in the stark, uncomfortable waiting area at the Nags Head police station, her sharp heels beating a furious rhythm on the tiled floor. "This brings back pleasant memories," Mom said as we went in. "Not."

"I'm going to sue," Evangeline said by way of greeting. "I'll take them for everything they're worth."

"I'm sure threats will help," I said.

"Why don't you sit down, dear?" Mom guided the other woman to a hard plastic chair. "No point in getting upset."

"You mean further upset," Evangeline snapped. "Why shouldn't I be upset? This is absolutely preposterous. My son is a lawyer, highly respected among his peers. His reputation is everything." She dropped into the chair, and Mom and I took seats on either side of her. Amos wasn't around, so I assumed he'd been allowed to be with Ricky in the role of attorney.

"Did they say why they were asking him to come with them?" I asked.

"Some silly little thing about needing to know his whereabouts last night after he left the restaurant. As if my son would creep about in the dark and bash his own father over the head."

Mom and I exchanged glances over Evangeline's well-coiffed head. Rich had been knifed, not hit on the head. Did Evangeline know that, and was she pretending not to? No reason for her to know, if the police hadn't told her. She hadn't been—*gulp*—at the scene, as we had been.

"We were in the bar," she continued, "having a lovely little catch-up, and the police barged in like a bunch of storm troopers. It was most embarrassing."

I doubted that. The storm-trooper bit. Not the Evangeline-being-embarrassed bit.

"Where's Fluffy?" she asked.

"What?"

"What have you done with Fluffy? You didn't leave her in your car, did you, Lucy? Not on a hot day like this."

"She's at my apartment. Comfortable and happy and well fed." I didn't add that Charles lurked malevolently outside the door, angry at not being allowed inside. I didn't dare leave the two of them alone together.

"Did you get my feeding instructions? It's important you follow them to the letter. She has a very delicate stomach."

"She's a dog, Evangeline!" Mom cried. "She'll be fine for a few hours."

Evangeline sniffed and decided—wisely—to change the subject. "Thank you, both of you, for coming down. I hope I haven't disrupted your evening plans."

"No plans," Mom said. "Millar's gone home. He caught an afternoon flight to Boston."

"I was planning to go out for a drink after work with some of my library friends and James, that Englishman you met at the library yesterday morning?" I tried not to look as though I was overly interested in Evangeline's reaction.

Something moved in her face. "There will be other times for drinks, I'm sure."

"I guess, but I'm not sure how much longer James and Daisy will be here. Their work's coming on well, so they tell me."

"Isn't that nice." Evangeline checked her watch. "It's nice that you associate with people from work. That young man who pretends to be an Englishman is rather odd, wouldn't you say?"

Nice diversion. So nicely done, I was now positive she had an interest in James, someone she supposedly didn't know. "Theodore Kowalski. He's a bit odd, yes, but he's a kind man and a good friend."

"Is he the one with the rare-book business?" Mom asked.

"Yup. He donated a handsome first edition to the library restoration fund earlier in the year. It helped to push us over the top so the work could go ahead."

"Did he?" Evangeline said. "I wouldn't have thought he had that sort of funds."

"He was very generous. Many of our patrons were." I gave Mom a grin. "And anonymous donors too."

"Good for them," Evangeline said. "It's important to support the arts, don't you agree, Suzanne?"

"Universities are important also," I said. "Do you have much contact with universities, Evangeline? Maybe some in England?"

My not-so-subtle attempt to interrogate Evangeline as to how she knew James came to naught when the door keeping us out of the main area of the police station opened. Ricky, still looking somewhat the worse for wear, walked between Detective Watson and Uncle Amos. Evangeline leapt to her feet with a cry and enveloped her son in a ferocious hug.

He pulled himself free. "Let's get the heck out of here."

"Keep me apprised of your whereabouts," Watson said.

Ricky threw the detective a filthy look, grabbed his mother's arm, and almost sprinted for the door.

Watson and Amos shook hands, and Watson went inside.

"What happened?" I asked. "Do they have anything on Ricky?"

"Later," Uncle Amos said.

Outside, we huddled on the steps of the police station.

"I've changed my mind," Evangeline said. "I'm going home. Tonight. You're coming with me."

"It's okay, Mom," Ricky said. "They can't pin this on me. Bringing me down here was nothing but an intimidation tactic."

"Don't get too cocky, young man," Amos said. "You're not in the clear. I was happy to help tonight, but I suggest you find yourself a lawyer."

"I am a lawyer."

"You know what I mean," Uncle Amos said. "If you like, I'll ask my partner, Stephanie Stanton, to represent you. She's done a lot of criminal defense work."

"My son is not a killer!" Evangeline shrieked.

A middle-aged woman heading for the police station gave us a frightened glance and a wide berth.

"Keep your voice down," Mom said. "No one is saying anything of the sort. Amos is being practical, that's all. I suggest we continue this discussion in a more private location."

"Good idea," Ricky said. "I, for one, could use a drink."

I glanced toward the town offices, which share the same property as the police station. Connor's window faced in this direction, and I wondered if he'd left yet. On the way into town, I'd given him a call to tell him why my plans had changed, and he'd said he'd wait to hear from me. In case he was watching, I started to lift my hand to give a little wave toward his window. My hand dropped.

A man stood at the side of the town hall, in the long shadows cast by the building. He was looking our way, and he made no move to turn away when he saw that I'd noticed him. He didn't react; he simply stood and stared at us.

"Check out the guy watching us," I whispered to Uncle Amos. "To the right of the steps of town hall."

"Gordon Frankland."

"He was at Jake's last night. He spoke to Ricky."

"I remember."

"He seems interested in us."

"So he does, but don't read anything into that, Lucy. The man makes a point of watching people, all the better for him to find some indiscretion he can use to sue them over."

"Dad was going to look into what he was talking to Ricky about. Do you know if he did?"

"What are you two whispering about?" Evangeline said. "Is my son's future not of interest to you?"

"Give it a rest, Mom," Ricky said.

"Don't you 'Mom' me!"

"Evangeline's upset," my mother said. "We're all upset— except for you, Amos, who I don't imagine have ever been upset in your life."

Uncle Amos raised one bushy eyebrow.

"I suggest we discontinue discussing our business in front of the Nags Head police station," Mom said. "Evangeline, I'm happy to stay in town with you as long as you need my support."

Evangeline glanced at her son, intently studying the ground beneath his feet. "Richard?"

"I called my office earlier, and they said there's nothing pressing I need to show up for this week. Imagine that, they can get along fine without me. We should stay, Mom. I've nothing to hide from the police. Hopefully we can take Dad home soon. Come on, let's go back to the hotel."

"I'll be at Amos and Ellen's," Mom said. "Call me if you need anything."

Ricky took his mother's arm and led her away.

"What do you mean, they can get along without you?" I could hear Evangeline asking him as their voices faded. "Don't they need your help sorting through your father's business affairs?"

"Family conference?" I said, once Ricky and Evangeline were out of earshot.

"Yes," Amos said.

"What does that mean?" Mom asked.

"It means we need to talk things over," I replied.

* * *

Aunt Ellen put a jug of tea on the table and pulled out a chair. "This is becoming a habit. One I don't care for."

She meant sitting around the table on the deck next to the kitchen at their beach house, talking over a murder case and trying to figure out "whodunit."

Ellen poured tea for herself and me. My mom and Stephanie had glasses of wine, and frosty mugs of beer sat in front of Connor and Amos. As we left the police station, Uncle Amos had called Steph and I'd called Connor to tell them what was going on.

"First things first," I said. "Why did the police want to question Ricky further?"

"Sam's been talking to employees at your father's firm," Amos said, "as well as your dad himself. It seems things with Rich were coming to a head. A substantial number of the junior partners wanted him gone, and your father was finding it harder and harder to argue against that. Rich would never have gone willingly."

"No," Mom said, "he wouldn't. The firm was his life. It was all he had. I feared for a while Millar was going down the same path, but he seems to have recovered his senses recently." She gave me a secret smile.

"Which is hardly a reason for Ricky to kill him," I said. "I suspect, from what I'm hearing, the only reason Ricky has a job is because he's Rich's son."

"Motive is a vastly overrated reason for killing. That's the stuff of mystery novels, not real cases." Stephanie looked up from the yellow legal pad in front of her on which she was jotting notes. She hadn't been hired by Ricky yet, but Amos had suggested she join us in case things went further.

"What does that mean?" Mom asked.

"People kill for lots of reasons and sometimes for no reason at all. Sometimes for what they think are good reasons and everyone else considers meaningless. An old grudge, a supposed insult in response to a threat that exists only in their mind. Determining a motive helps, of course, but it's often not a building block on which to build a prosecution."

"Steph means, if Ricky was mad enough at his father, that might have led to an argument, and an argument led to the death," Amos said.

"You're not saying—" Mom began.

"I'm not saying anything," Amos said. "Simply pointing it out. In this case, the timing doesn't look good for Ricky. He left the restaurant at roughly quarter to nine, according to the bartender at Jake's. He arrived at Skinny Jane's about nine thirty. No one can be located who saw him in the interim."

"He says he walked around looking for a bar," I said.

"He stayed at Skinny Jane's until closing time. He seems to have made himself unforgettable there. He bought expensive drinks for a couple of women, and when the boyfriend of one of them, who's a regular at that bar, arrived and took exception to that, things escalated. Ricky was lucky he didn't get a punch to the jaw; instead, he wisely withdrew from the field of battle. He took a table in the corner, and there he fell asleep. At closing time, when the bartender went to throw him out, he gave the guy a sob story about how he'd lost the only woman he ever loved . . ."

I assumed that was supposed to be a reference to me. I shifted uncomfortably in my seat, and my mother notably avoided my eyes. I had little doubt that if I did get back together with Ricky, he'd soon forget I was supposed to be "the only woman he ever loved." Ricky had inherited his mother's love of high drama.

"He went on and on about how no one appreciates him," Uncle Amos continued. "Said he didn't want to go back to his hotel because his mother would be on his case, and he offered the bartender a hundred dollars to let him sleep in his truck. Which he did. Ricky was asleep in the truck the next morning when the bartender got it to go to work. For another hundred bucks, the bartender dropped Ricky at the library."

"Why would he want to go there?" Mom asked.

"To tell me his sob story," I said. "I found him on the step when I opened up this morning. He was definitely in bad shape, and he looked like he'd spent the night in a stranger's truck. I poured coffee down him, Ronald held his head under cold water, and then I called Sam Watson, knowing he'd want to talk to Ricky. He claimed not to have known his father died. Did Ricky find his jacket?"

"When the police tracked the bartender down," Amos said, "he gave it to them. Ricky had left it in the truck. The wallet and phone were untouched."

"Okay, so Ricky doesn't have an alibi for the time of his father's death. That doesn't mean anything, does it?"

"No, but it would be nice if he had one."

"Evangeline doesn't have an alibi either," I pointed out.

"You can be sure that hasn't escaped Sam's notice," Steph said.

"Sam Watson plays his cards close to his chest," I said. "With someone like Evangeline, he's likely to give her plenty of rope in case she needs it to hang herself."

"What does that mean?" Mom said.

"It means she has trouble controlling her reactions. He'll be watching her."

"You're getting good at this, Lucy," Steph said.

"Too good," Connor said.

"Perish the thought," I said.

My mother shuddered.

"Does anyone know why Rich was in Nags Head in the first place?" Connor said. "I'd think that would be important."

"It is important. Vitally important," Amos said. "He doesn't appear to have told anyone he was coming, never mind why."

"The police found a piece of paper on Rich," I said. "When Watson saw it, he seemed to find it interesting. Do you know what it said?"

"No, I don't."

"What did Dad find out about Gordon Frankland and his relationship with Rich?"

"If I never hear that name again," Connor said, "it will be too soon. Frankland filed suit against the town this afternoon in opposition to our plans to expand the fishing pier. As though we haven't gone through extensive environmental consultations and worked hard to address community concerns and secure local approval. The guy doesn't live anywhere near the pier, but he's found some—"

"Maybe let Amos continue," Steph suggested.

"Sorry," Connor said. "I got carried away there. The guy gets under my skin."

"Frankland's been busy," Amos said. "He filed suit against Richardson Lewiston yesterday for conflict of interest."

"Yesterday?" I said. "Before or after Rich's death?"

"Good question, Lucy," my uncle said. "Before. Yesterday morning."

"Seems a heck of a coincidence," Mom said, "that he ran into us that very night."

"It does, doesn't it? Although that is entirely possible. I checked with Jake when I heard about the suit, and he tells me Gordon Frankland dines at his place regularly. Sometimes as often as two or three times a week. Always on his own. The man appears to have no friends."

"Wonder why?" Connor muttered.

Amos chuckled. "It seems he favors Jake's these days, as not many other places in town will serve him—he's threatened to sue them all. Jake lives in fear that Frankland's going to find something, anything, to take him to court over."

"Can't something be done about this constant stream of lawsuits?" my mom asked.

"Let's get back to the point," Connor said. "Why is he suing Richardson Lewiston?"

"He claims the firm was representing him while also advising the firm representing his opponents in a case he's brought against a homeowner who wants to do some much-needed renovations to a historic house in Boston. Unfortunately for representatives of Nags Head and Boston, he has homes in both those places; thus he can act as a concerned citizen. I believe he's not unknown in the courthouses of New York City either."

"Is he wealthy?" Mom asked.

"Oh yes," Amos said. "Exceedingly so. Rather than putting his money—all of which he inherited—to good use, or even to amusing himself, he uses it to mount court cases. Which, come to think of it, is how he amuses himself."

"In case you think he's being a good citizen, standing up for what he believes in," Steph said, "don't. He has no problem funding both sides of any situation. Before Connor's time, he sued the town to stop them extending a building permit to a bird sanctuary, and when he won that one, he turned around and sued them for interfering in a member of the public's right to use their land as they see fit. It's all a game to him."

A ping came from the kitchen, and Aunt Ellen stood up. "Dinner's ready. Keep talking, but do it loudly, and I'll bring the food out. We're having lasagna, and it's a good thing I made enough to freeze for a second meal so I can feed all you unexpected guests."

My mom leapt to her feet. "I'll give you a hand."

"The salad's made and in the fridge," Aunt Ellen said. "It only needs to be dressed."

"According to what Millar learned this morning," Amos said, "Richardson Lewiston has been attempting to fire Frankland as a client for some time, as his legal actions are getting increasingly erratic, to put it mildly, but he's not going willingly. He's suing them for failure to do their fiduciary duty in taking his cases seriously. If he can pay them and pay court costs if he loses, which he usually does, he doesn't see why they care if his cases are frivolous."

"Again, why would he kill Rich?" Connor asked.

"Again," Steph said, "we don't need to consider motive. Particularly not with someone like Gordon Frankland. No one's ever claimed he's not in possession of his faculties, but he's a mean one. Maybe he killed Mr. Lewiston because Mr. Lewiston laughed at him."

"That's possible," I said. "Did he run into Rich outside Jake's and they got into an argument?"

"Sounds to me as though if they did argue, this Frankland would have come up with some reason to sue Rich." Mom put a stack of plates, cutlery, and napkins on the table. "Not get into a brawl."

"There's a thought," I said. "Did he egg Rich into a fight that went beyond what he intended? Maybe Rich took a swing and missed, and . . . whatever happened happened?"

"Lucy," Amos said, "find out if Gordon Frankland's in the frame, as the police say."

"Me?"

"Lucy?" Mom said. "What's Lucy got to do with this?"

Aunt Ellen carried out an enormous casserole dish trailing the gorgeous scents of hot spicy meat and melting cheese. "Lucy has a way of getting Sam Watson to talk to her."

"I do not."

"For once, I'm going to put my two cents in," Connor said. "Leave Lucy out of this. You remember what happened last time." He rubbed at the side of his face. "Although, come to think of it, that happened to me."

"And then there was the time before that," Steph said. "Who knows what would have happened had Louise Jane not learned sword fighting skills from her mother."

"What!" my own mother screeched. "You're telling me this has happened to Lucy more than once?"

"Nothing ever happens to me, Mom," I said. "It happens to other people, but somehow I find myself in the middle of it. Against my will." I accepted a plate piled high from Aunt Ellen and smiled at Connor. "I'm soon to become a respectable southern married lady. My sleuthing days are over."

"Salad?" Steph asked.

"Thank you." I took the wooden bowl and added a hearty serving to my already-laden plate.

We were sitting outside on the big, comfortable deck overlooking the beach and the open ocean beyond. A huge round moon hung in the sky over the sea, throwing a line of white light across the water. The night was warm but not overly hot, and the rhythmic sound of the surf steadily pounding against the shore was accompanied by the laughter of people playing at the edge of the water or strolling on the sand.

"Lucy's right," Uncle Amos said. "I shouldn't have made that suggestion. If the police decide to pursue a case against

Ricky, and if Ricky hires O'Malley Stanton to represent him, then we, meaning O'Malley Stanton, will start asking questions. Not before."

"We can speculate," my mom said. "And I will continue to speculate as to what on earth brought Rich Lewiston, unexpected and unannounced, to Nags Head. How did he even know we'd be at Jake's restaurant? Evangeline says she hasn't spoken to him since Saturday evening. When she left the house for the airport on Sunday morning, he was still in bed. Ricky hasn't spoken to his dad in days. Or so he says."

"That's a good question, Mom," I said. "I bet the answer's in that letter the police found on Rich. Assuming it was a letter, anyway. Everyone says Rich had a lot of debts. You don't suppose this could have been a mob hit, do you?"

"No," Connor said. "If he was in debt to the mob—and we don't know that—they don't kill the goose that's laying the eggs."

I swallowed a forkful of lasagna. No one makes lasagna like my Aunt Ellen. It was hot and delicious, packed full of ground beef and spicy sausage in a rich tomato sauce layered with creamy white sauce and an abundance of cheese. "Maybe it was more than that. Maybe he was doing work for them off the firm's books and it wasn't going well and they decided it was time to end the relationship. Unlikely the mob would sue for failure to do his fiduciary duty, as would Mr. Frankland." I remembered overhearing Ricky and Evangeline whispering in the hallway at Jake's. What had they said? *When Millar hears about . . .*

Connor chuckled. "Unlikely is right."

"If Rich was doing work under the table, for organized crime or anyone else," Amos said, "Millar will find out. Rich's death means all his cases will be assessed and assigned to other lawyers in the firm. Millar intends to keep a close eye on that process."

"If underhanded stuff was going on," Steph said, "it's likely your friend Ricky was involved in it too, if he worked alongside his father. Did he have reason to want to put a stop to what his dad was up to? Had it gone too far?"

"And now," Mom said, "we're back to where we began. Ricky. I'm glad, dear, you took my advice and decided not to marry him."

I choked on a leaf of Bibb lettuce.

Chapter Thirteen

When I got home that evening, I found Charles waiting for me at the door to the Lighthouse Aerie rather than meeting me downstairs, and I took that for a bad sign. He did not look happy. "The dog won't be here for long," I said. "Try to play nicely."

Charles hissed.

I slowly opened the door. Charles shot in and headed straight for the kitchen, where he sniffed disapprovingly at the bowl of water I'd put down for Fluffy. Fluffy herself was nowhere to be seen. I decided to feed Charles before looking for the dog and did so.

While Charles dined, I searched. It didn't take long, and it wasn't hard to find her. I simply followed the sound of whining and peeked under the bed. "You can come out," I said. "It's safe. I hope."

Fluffy's little black nose appeared, followed by the rest of her. She kept her eyes fixed firmly on Charles. Charles appeared content to eat and pointedly ignored the dog. Hoping for the best, I opened a can of dog food, dropped a couple of spoonfuls into a bowl, added some dry food, and stirred it all together. I hadn't read Evangeline's feeding instructions, and I hoped the little creature wouldn't die before I got around to doing that. I put the bowl on the floor.

Fluffy edged closer, keeping one eye on Charles. Then, not sensing an imminent attack, she rushed for the bowl and dove in. Charles finished his own meal and, completely ignoring the newcomer, strolled across the apartment, leapt onto the window seat, settled himself comfortably, and began washing his whiskers.

I let out a sigh of relief. Peace in the home.

* * *

I woke with Charles curled against my back, snoring lightly. A snuffling sound came from the floor, and I leaned over to see Fluffy's intense black eyes staring up at me. The peace had continued, and as far as I was aware, no raging battles had broken out overnight.

Wednesday was my day off. I would like to have viewed houses, but Connor was in meetings all day. I lay in bed, contemplating what to do with my day. Maybe I'd call Mom and suggest lunch and shopping. For me, shopping isn't a recreational activity, but it is for my mom. Perhaps Aunt Ellen and Josie could join us and we'd have a true mother-daughter outing. That would be fun.

First things first. I got out of bed and threw on a pair of yoga pants, a T-shirt, and a light sweater. Dog duties needed to be done. I found Fluffy's leash and clipped it onto her collar, and we headed out. Charles, who usually ran ahead of me, eager to get to work, stayed where he was.

We were up early, and when I'd peered out the window to check the weather, the giant orange ball of the sun had been making its first appearance above the watery horizon.

The library was quiet, but I didn't have time to admire it, as Fluffy was in a rush to get outside. Who knew a creature so small could exert such a powerful pull? She galloped down the stairs in a flurry of white fur, and I scrambled to keep up, trying to keep from being yanked off my feet as we hurtled across the floor of the main room, out the door, and down the steps.

With an almost human sigh of relief, Fluffy settled herself on the grass.

The area surrounding the lighthouse was so beautiful in the soft orange light of the rising sun, and so quiet. I'd miss living here. I'd miss mornings like this one. I pushed aside a brief pang of regret. Yes, I'd miss my Lighthouse Aerie, but it was time to move on. I had no regrets or doubts about choosing to have a life with Connor.

"Come on, Fluffy," I called. "I need coffee, and when I've had breakfast and am suitably dressed, we'll come back for a nice long walk. You'll like it out here in the wild spaces." I wasn't so sure about that last comment; Fluffy looked like a city dog to me, more comfortable with her little feet on asphalt than on the spongy grass, used to running away from bigger dogs, not Canada geese.

I'd stuffed my phone into my sweater pocket, and it rang. I pulled it out and felt a jolt of panic when I recognized my mother's number. It was way too early for her to be calling to make plans for the day. " 'Morning, Mom. Is everything okay?"

"No, it is not. Evangeline called and asked me to come to the hotel. The police informed her they will be paying her a visit at eight o'clock this morning. They have further questions for her. She wants my support, and I want yours."

"Can't you ask Uncle Amos?"

"I did, but he's due in court first thing this morning. Most inconvenient. I'll meet you at the Ocean Side. I've borrowed Ellen's car, and I'm leaving now." She hung up, giving me no opportunity to protest.

What was it Sherlock Holmes said to Doctor Watson? "Come at once if convenient. Come at once if not convenient."

It was not convenient for me. Oh well, I had been thinking it would be nice to have a mother-daughter bonding day.

Some mothers and daughters do bonding differently than others.

I took Fluffy upstairs, fed her and Charles, and jumped into the shower. When I came out, I was surprised to see the cat and the dog both sitting on the window seat. They weren't exactly curled up together, but neither were they engaged in a fight to the death for possession of prime napping space.

I dressed quickly in capri-length jeans and a T-shirt, not much bothering about what I wore. This wasn't a social occasion. I told Fluffy I'd be home soon, I hoped, and we'd go for that walk. "Let's go, Charles," I said.

Charles eyed me from the comfort of the window seat.

I opened the door. "Time to go to work."

Charles stretched mightily and yawned.

"Charles, you're the library cat. Your contract allowing you to live in the Lighthouse Aerie and consume all the food you can eat says you have to put in six days a week in the library. You get no vacation time. Let's go. Oh, for heaven's sake. The dog's only visiting. She isn't usurping your position." I marched across the room, picked the big cat up, and put him on the floor outside. He sauntered toward the stairs without a backward glance, head high, hips swinging, tail erect. When I glanced behind me into the apartment, Fluffy was stretching luxuriously across the full length of the window seat.

I arrived at the Ocean Side Hotel at two minutes to eight. I was running up the steps when the cruiser with Watson and Holly Rankin pulled up. I waited in the lobby for them.

"I shouldn't be surprised to see you, Lucy," Watson said. "But I am."

"Evangeline called Mom, and Mom called me."

"This isn't a public event, Lucy. I could have had Officer Rankin escort Mrs. Lewiston to the police station, but I decided, in light of the early hour, I'd come here instead. Was that a mistake?"

"No. I'll tell Mom we can't stay."

He nodded and headed to the elevators. Holly and I scurried after him. It was early, but guests were stirring, ready for breakfast in the restaurant or going out for a day on the water or at the beach.

Quite a crowd had gathered in Evangeline's suite. Mom was there, once again fresh and dewy and perfectly turned out. Ricky looked rumpled, badly shaven, and not happy. A man I didn't know stood next to Evangeline. He was about my age, short and slight, with Coke-bottle-bottom glasses and brown hair artfully arranged to stand up above his forehead. He wore a dark suit with a perfectly knotted blue tie and a spotless starched white collar and cuffs.

Watson focused on him. "I'm Detective Sam Watson, NHPD. Who are you?"

"Stephen Livingstone. Attorney with Richardson Lewiston."

"You called a lawyer, Mrs. Lewiston? That is, of course, your prerogative, but you are not under arrest. I simply have some further questions about the death of your husband."

"I didn't call Stephen," Evangeline said, "but I'm glad he's here. We can't have you continuing to browbeat my son and I."

I decided this wasn't the time to correct Evangeline's grammar. The proper phrase would have been *my son and me*.

"Hardly browbeating," Watson said. "If the rest of you will excuse us . . ."

My mom stood up. Ricky crossed his legs and leaned back in his chair.

"All of you," Watson said. "Please leave. Except Mrs. Lewiston and her attorney."

Ricky huffed and slowly got to his feet.

"Hi." Stephen grabbed my hand and pumped it enthusiastically. "So pleased to meet you. You must be Lucy, Mr. Richardson's daughter. I've heard so much about you."

"You have?"

"Come along, Lucy," Mom said. "Don't dawdle."

Mom walked out of the room. I followed, and Ricky brought up the rear.

"Where'd he come from?" I asked when the door had closed behind us. "Did you ask the firm to send a lawyer, Ricky?"

"I didn't. If I need representation, I'm good with your uncle and his partner. I looked them up last night, and she's got a mighty powerful track record."

"Your father called me last night after you left," Mom said, "to say he was sending someone down. If the reputation of the firm is in anyway threatened by these events, he wants someone here, on the ground."

"Fair enough," I said.

"Have you had breakfast yet?" Ricky asked.

"I haven't had time for so much as a cup of coffee," I said. "It's supposed to be my day off."

"Good. I'm starving."

"Might as well," Mom said. "Evangeline will call when they're finished."

"Let's get a seat by the door," Ricky said. "So we can see the cops leave."

"Did Evangeline say why Watson wanted to talk to her again?" I asked Mom when we were seated at a spacious table for six in the hotel's bright, cheerful restaurant, with full coffee mugs and open menus.

The restaurant was less than half-full, and the low buzz of conversation swirled around us. The morning sun streamed through the east-facing windows, and the air was fragrant with the delicious scents of morning: coffee, toast, bacon.

"She doesn't know," Ricky answered. "At least they didn't haul her down to the police station as though she were a common criminal. Like they did to other people I could mention."

I added a healthy slug of cream to my coffee and stirred. "Mom?"

"She didn't say. Unlikely Watson told her."

"It might not be about anything new. They have people go over their statements more than once, looking for inconsistencies or forgotten details."

"Ready to order?" the waitress asked.

Mom chose the yogurt parfait, Ricky asked for a double stack of pancakes with sausages, and I threw caution to the wind and ordered the smoked-salmon eggs Benedict. My relaxing morning and my day off had been ruined, so I might as well get something out of it.

"I don't suppose," I said, once the waitress had left, "you thought of anything new last night."

"Nope," Ricky said.

"What did you do after leaving the police station?"

He avoided my eyes. "Nothing much."

"If you've stayed on to be a support to your mother," Mom said, "going out and leaving her alone isn't the best way to go about it."

He lifted his head and stared at her. "I don't believe that's any of your business, Suzanne."

She sipped at her coffee. Somehow, in all the turmoil of yesterday, she'd managed to find the time to get a fresh manicure. She put the cup carefully down in front of her. "It would appear, *Richard*, that you and your family have made it our business. Believe me, I'd rather be at home, and Lucy has better things to be doing. Instead we're here, because your mother has asked for my support. I'm happy to provide it out of respect for her loss and for the years we've known each other, although at times we could scarcely have been considered friends. If you believe I'm wasting my time, please tell me, and my daughter and I will be on our way." She plucked her napkin off her lap, folded it, and laid it neatly on the table beside her plate.

Ricky had the grace to flush. He fussed with his cutlery and napkin. He glanced at me, and then he looked directly at Mom. "That's not what I meant, Mrs. Richardson. I apologize."

"Thank you." Mom fluffed her napkin and returned it to her lap.

"In my defense," he said, "I suggested Mom and I go out for dinner, and she said she wanted to be alone and would order room service, watch TV, and go to bed early. I told her to call me if she changed her mind, and yes, I went into town and found a low-life bar. It was not only low-life but low action, and I was back at the hotel by ten." He glanced at me. "Alone."

"Have you given any more thought as to why your dad would have been in Nags Head?" I asked.

"I've thought of little else, Lucy. I've been talking to people at the office—those who will take my calls, at any rate. Everyone says Dad seemed perfectly normal on Friday when he left at his regular time. A couple of people were in over the weekend, and they didn't see him. Dad was still in bed when Mom left for the airport early on Sunday morning and she didn't wake him. He simply didn't show up at the office on Monday morning at his usual time. As for me, I haven't seen or spoken to Dad for days."

"What does your housekeeper say?" Mom asked.

"Mrs. Lopez? Mom and I both spoke to her. She wasn't at the house on Sunday, she doesn't work weekends, and she didn't see Dad on Monday, which is normal, as he goes into the office before she arrives for work. She didn't know anything was wrong until she got Mom's call on Tuesday morning to say we'd be home later than planned and why."

"Has she been with your parents for long?" I asked. "Meaning, is she likely to know their secrets?"

"Less than a year," Ricky said. "Mom has . . . uh . . . trouble keeping staff. When I spoke to Mrs. Lopez, she told me a suitcase seems to be missing from Dad's closet, as are some of his clothes and shoes and his traveling toiletry bag."

"How many clothes?"

"Does that matter?"

"It matters very much. Two days' worth? A week? What you'd take if you were skipping the country forever? What about his passport?"

"I didn't ask her."

"Ask," I said.

Ricky made the call and asked the housekeeper to check his dad's closets again. While he was waiting, our meals arrived, and we picked up knives and forks. Ricky tucked the phone between his chin and shoulder and sliced his sausage, and I applied a liberal helping of ketchup to my home fries and sprinkled hot sauce on top.

I saw my mom, who was picking at the blueberries on her parfait, eye the mountain of food in front of me. Once upon a time, she would have made a comment about keeping oneself slim or the perils of overeating.

Demonstrating how things had changed between us, she said nothing.

"We haven't decided when we'll be home yet, but I'll keep you posted. Thanks." Ricky put his phone away. "She can't tell for sure, but not much seems to be gone, and he took a carry-on suitcase, not one of the bigger ones. She's never seen his passport and doesn't know where he keeps it. It's probably in the safe—always was when I lived at home. The police, by the way, have been to the house asking the same sort of questions." Ricky speared a slice of sausage and put it in his mouth. "You think Dad might have been planning to leave?"

"The thought crossed my mind. If he had more debts to unsavory elements than he could possibly hope to repay, he might have thought fleeing was the best option. That would explain why he came to Nags Head. To either get your mother or to say good-bye to you both."

"I can't see it," Mom said. "Rich simply didn't have the imagination."

I wasn't so sure, but I said nothing. Who knows what lengths people will go to if they believe they're in danger.

If Rich had been fleeing organized crime, and if, realizing his intent, they'd killed him, then it really would be none of my business.

I could only hope. But, until we knew that for sure, I intended to keep asking questions. "This is going to be difficult for you to answer, Ricky," I said, "but the question has to be asked. Was your dad perhaps involved with another woman?"

Ricky's head jerked up. "What kind of a question is that?"

"I'm just thinking out loud. Maybe he was planning to run away with his secretary or someone and came to tell your mom so."

"He wasn't involved with Jackie McKenzie, who's happily married."

"That doesn't always—" Mom began.

"In this case it does. Jackie's married to a woman."

"Oh," I said.

"She was in the office all day Monday, remember, scrambling to rebook Dad's appointments. As for anyone else— honestly, Lucy, I've never heard so much as a whiff of any rumors like that, and I would have if they'd been going around the firm. I hadn't recently noticed any change in his behavior either."

That, I thought, meant nothing. It was unlikely Ricky had ever paid much attention to his dad at all.

I was scraping my plate clean when Mom said, "There they go."

I threw down my fork, grabbed my bag, leapt to my feet, said, "Catch you later, Mom," and ran out of the restaurant.

"Detective," I called. "A moment, please."

Watson stopped. He sighed and slowly turned around. "How can I help you, Lucy?"

"A quick question, if you don't mind."

"Only one?"

"One to start with. Did Rich Lewiston have his passport on him?"

"He did not."

"Oh."

"You sound disappointed."

"No one knows what he was doing in Nags Head. I thought maybe, if things were getting bad enough financially for him, he might have been thinking about leaving the country and came to get his wife."

"That doesn't appear to be the case," Watson said. "Let me ask you a question. Why do you think Rich Lewiston was in financial difficulties?"

"Because everyone from his son to my father to the junior partners in the law firm say so. He was about to be asked to take retirement. More like *told* to take retirement, whether he wanted to or not. And he did not. Did you know that?"

"I know how to run an investigation, Lucy."

"Without your interference," Officer Rankin added.

"Only trying to be of help," I said.

"Because you have been of help in the past," Watson said, "I answered your question."

I dared to ask one more. "Have you spoken to Gordon Frankland about Monday night? He was at the restaurant when we were—you know that, right? He had words with Ricky about his dad. He was suing Richardson Lewiston for—"

Watson raised his hand. "I've spoken to Mr. Frankland, and what we discussed is confidential."

"If you're afraid he's going to sue you, I won't tell." I smiled.

Watson might have been about to crack a smile in return. Or he might not. It's hard to tell sometimes.

"Have a nice day, Lucy." Watson turned and walked away. Rankin wiggled her eyebrows at me in a gesture I couldn't interpret, then followed him. I watched them leave.

Watson held the door for a man hurrying into the hotel. The man caught sight of me and headed my way. "Lucy, good morning. How nice to see you."

I struggled for his name. This was Evangeline's friend, the one she'd been having lunch with yesterday.

"Leon Lions," he said.

"Sorry. Yes. Good morning."

"I'm looking for Evangeline. She called and suggested we have breakfast this morning."

"She called you? She's been rather busy, I would have thought. When was that?"

"Oh, a few minutes ago." He glanced around the room. "Fortunately, I happened to be passing, so I could come right away. There she is now!"

He abandoned me and just about sprinted across the lobby, barely avoiding colliding with an elderly lady tapping her way carefully across the room, trailed by a cohort of family laden with beach bags, colorful balls, flotation devices, spades and shovels, and a bag clanging with cans of soft drinks.

Evangeline stepped out of the elevator with Stephen Livingstone. She broke into a smile—a real smile—when she saw Leon and hurried toward him. He wrapped her in an enthusiastic hug and kissed her on both cheeks. She pulled away eventually, laughing and blushing.

Interesting.

I joined them and asked, "Everything okay? Did the police have any updates for you?"

She sighed. "Nothing new. The same tedious questions. Why was Rich in Nags Head? Who might have wanted to kill him? What was the state of our marriage?" She turned to Stephen. "You should have stopped them asking that question. The state of our marriage has nothing to do with anything."

"I thought it was a fair question, Mrs. Lewiston."

"I didn't. Never mind badgering me about where I was at the time Rich died."

"They weren't badgering, Mrs. Lewiston. Just asking. I thought—"

"I don't know that I care what you thought. My husband was a senior partner in one of Boston's most respectable law firms, not to mention scion of one of Boston's oldest families. Why Millar sent me a wet-behind-the-ears, scarcely-out-of-law-school apprentice, I—" She walked away, heels tapping, still talking. Leon caught up to her, and they went into the restaurant together.

Stephen stared after her, his mouth flapping.

"Don't take it personally," I said. "She talks to everyone that way. My dad would have chosen you to come because he knows you can do the job. And that you can keep her out of trouble. That's not always easy."

"Thanks," he said. "I can handle her. I've had . . . encounters with Mrs. Lewiston before."

We walked into the restaurant together. Ricky was on his feet, shaking hands with Leon Lions, who was grinning from ear to ear. If he were a woman, I would have said he glowed with pleasure. He finally dropped Ricky's hand and allowed Evangeline to introduce him to my mom. He barely glanced at her, and that was unusual. Men in that age group usually fuss over Mom. She's slim and beautiful, she's obviously rich, she's gracious, and she has that *soooo delighted to meet you* air about her that men like. Come to think of it, men a lot younger than Leon Lions fuss over Mom.

He turned back to Evangeline. "Shall I find us a table?"

"First, I need to talk to my so-called lawyer," Evangeline replied.

Stephen's mouth tightened.

Mom stood up. "In that case, Lucy and I will be on our way."

Evangeline took my vacated chair and shoved the dirty plate to one side. "I can't spend any more time in this hotel. Suzanne, let's have lunch in town and do some shopping. I saw an outlet mall the other day. That'll be fun. Lucy and Ricky can join us for lunch. Shopping isn't exactly Ricky's thing, now, is it, dear?" She reached behind her and patted her son's hand. "You and Lucy can find something fun to do. I've heard the Wright Brothers Memorial is very interesting."

"You truly are persistent, I'll give you that," Mom said. "Lucy won't have time. She's . . ." Mom foundered to think of something for me to do. "She has people to interview about what happened to Rich."

"I do?" I said. "Oh, right. Yes, I do. People to interview. Not interview as in formally take statements, just ask questions. Sorta." I stopped talking. No one was paying any attention to me.

"You do remember what happened to Rich, don't you, Evangeline?" Mom said. "The reason we're all still here?"

"Of course I remember," Evangeline said. "Don't be ridiculous, Suzanne. If I was inclined to forget, the police are popping up constantly to remind me."

"I'd like to see the Wright Brothers," Ricky said. "If you're busy, Lucy, I can go by myself."

"I've had a great idea," Leon said. "Ricky and I can have lunch with the ladies and then go to the memorial while they do their shopping. I haven't been in years."

"Why would Lucy have people to interview?" Stephen asked.

"My daughter," Mom said, with what to my considerable surprise sounded like a note of pride, "has helped the police solve cases before. She's full of interesting talents, as I'm finding out on this visit."

"Excellent." Evangeline clapped her hands together. "We're all set. Leon, you can recommend a nice place where we can meet for lunch. Oh, Lucy darling, is Fluffy managing all right? She has such a delicate stomach, you know, and I'm worried it will get worse with all this stress. She must be missing me so very dreadfully."

"She's okay," I said. "She and my cat are making friends."

"Your cat? Do you mean that horrid library creature? Most unfortunate. Fluffy doesn't care for cats. Neither do I. Nasty animals. Try and keep them apart, will you. Oh, one other thing before you go. She has an exceptionally weak bladder."

"She has what?"

"She needs to be taken out regularly." Evangeline smiled at me. "I hope that's not too much of a problem, Lucy dear."

"Not at all." I gritted my teeth.

Ricky disguised his laugh by stuffing an abandoned slice of toast into his mouth.

Chapter Fourteen

I drove back to the lighthouse to take Fluffy for the promised walk. I'd seen no signs of a weak bladder last night. I didn't know if that was true or if Evangeline was trying to mess with my head. Which would be exactly like her.

Traffic was heavy going out of town as people headed for the beaches of the National Seashore or the towns of Rodanthe and Buxton. I tapped the steering wheel impatiently and thought about all the people swirling around this case. Leon Lions was a strange one. Around Evangeline he acted like the school nerd in the presence of the head cheerleader. He basked in her presence as if he were a sun worshiper at the beach.

Had they once had a relationship? If not, it wasn't because he didn't want to.

Was it possible Evangeline's visit to Nags Head had not been entirely to stop my engagement to Connor? Had she had another reason for coming? Such as to see an old lover?

Maybe even a current lover?

Probably not. If Leon was her lover, past or present, she had more common sense than to bring him out in public in the days immediately following the mysterious death of her husband.

I came to an impatient halt, watching a long line of rear lights glowing red ahead of me. I briefly considered telling Sam Watson about Leon but decided not to. What could I say— that Evangeline had run into an old friend and they'd had lunch together?

Which brought me to thinking about her and James Dalrymple. Again, what on earth could I say to Watson? That Evangeline had appeared to recognize a man, but he didn't react to her, and then she denied knowing him?

Hardly grounds for an arrest. If my report did lead to an arrest, it would be of me for wasting police time.

At last the traffic broke through whatever the holdup was, and I sped out of town on Highway 12.

A substantial number of cars were parked outside the library when I arrived, and more followed me down the long driveway between the tall red pines. Schools were on break, and Ronald had a full schedule of children's activities planned. I noticed that many of the kids, as well as their parents, were wearing high boots.

"What's on the program for today?" I asked Janelle Washington as we walked up the path to the library together. Her twins, Charlotte and Emily, had run on ahead, hair ribbons flying, rubber boots slapping the ground, squealing with excitement.

"Ronald's invited an expert in marsh wildlife to lead an expedition. The girls are so excited; they've been looking forward to it all week."

I eyed her long-sleeved shirt, the heavy khaki pants tucked into pink-and-purple rubber boots. "You're going too?"

"Oh yes. The marsh isn't usually a place you'd find a girl from Manhattan wandering around in, but Ronald needs parent volunteers to keep an eye on the kids. I can only hope we don't come across anything that doesn't have legs." She shuddered. "Or Ronald will have more to worry about than the kids."

Inside the library, we were greeted by a cacophony of voices of excited children and equally excited parents. I waved to my aunt Ellen, who as a member of the Friends of the Library was staffing the circulation desk, and headed for the stairs before anyone could stop me.

"Lucy! Lucy!"

I stopped. I swore only to myself, plastered on a smile, and turned. "Mrs. Peterson, good morning. What can I do for you?"

Mrs. Peterson, library supporter, literacy advocate, mother of five daughters, and all-around nuisance, was also helping with today's expedition. Although she might have mistaken the Bodie Island marsh for some unexplored jungle, dressed as she was in a multipocketed jacket, pith helmet, khaki pants, and hiking boots that showed no sign of ever having been worn. An orange whistle hung from a thick rope around her neck. "I'm so glad I caught you. Ellen said it's your day off." She dismissed that trifle with a wave of her hand. "But I know you never mind chatting to *me*."

I continued to smile. I minded very much. When I moved, I would not miss being waylaid by eager patrons as I was attempting to enjoy my personal time.

"About book club. Charity's enrolled in several summer sports camps, and she insists she hasn't had time to read *The Hound of the Baskervilles*. Although, I have to point out, in the interest of honestly, she did get through that massive science fiction thing she took out last week. She says she's seen the episode of the *Sherlock* series called 'The Hounds of Baskerville.' Is that sufficient preparation for the meeting, do you think?"

I stifled a sigh. Mrs. Peterson meant well, and she only wanted the best for her daughters, but she was convinced that the best meant what she wanted the girls to be interested in, not what they were interested in. Charity was a bright girl, and she was more than welcome in our book club, but if a fifteen-year-old would rather read modern science fiction than the choice of her mother's book club, that was fine with me. "The meeting's tomorrow night, Mrs. Peterson. It's too late for Charity to read the original, in any event. I hope part of the discussion gets into modern adaptations of the original novel, and Charity's contribution will be welcome."

"If you say so, Lucy."

"What did you think of it?"

"Me? I uh . . . I thought it was . . . maybe a bit longer than it needed to be."

"It's not long compared to other novels of the era."

"If you say so. I don't see Ronald yet, but it must be time to go." She bustled away. Mrs. Peterson rarely read the club's selection. She came to our book club because she thought her daughters should be reading classic literature. I worried she'd turn them off reading for life.

And wouldn't that be a tragedy.

I climbed the stairs. Eager little wildlife adventurers rushed past me as not-so-eager parents yelled after them not to run on the stairs.

"Have fun!" I called to Ronald as he came out of the children's library.

The door to Charlene's third-floor office was cracked open, and I decided to stick my head in and say hi. She was bent over her computer, typing away. Her ever-present earbuds clung to her ears as she worked to the music she loved so much. I tapped lightly, and she didn't react. I knocked harder.

She just about leapt out of her chair. She spun around so quickly she knocked her elbow into her bookcase. Her office isn't very large. "Lucy," she snapped. "What are you doing sneaking up on me?" She hit the power button on her computer monitor, and the screen went black.

"Sorry. I wasn't sneaking up. I wanted to say hi and ask how things are going with your visiting professors."

"They're going fine. I'm busy; is there anything else I can do for you?"

"No, I guess not." I backed away. Charlene rolled across the few inches of floor and slammed the door in my face.

* * *

I closed my iPad with a sigh. I'd been looking at properties for sale that Connor and I might be interested in, and I was mightily discouraged. Not much was available that I liked and that fell within our price range.

I could always move into the house Connor was renting. That had been suggested, but, as nice as it was, it was *Connor's house*. We wanted a place that would be *our house* from the beginning.

I looked around the Lighthouse Aerie—the curving white-washed walls, the colorful cushions, the bright watercolors of Outer Banks scenes, the single tall window with the comfortable window seat and great view.

The bed taking up most of the available space, the two chairs around the tiny table in the kitchen that wasn't even a kitchen but more a nook in which one could throw together a quick meal.

Not exactly a great home for a newly engaged couple.

The phone rang, and to my surprise, it was Detective Watson, and he wanted to speak to me. "In person."

"What about?"

"Why don't we discuss that when we meet? I could use a walk in the marsh, get my head cleared. Ten minutes?"

"Sure." I hung up before I remembered that this morning the marsh wasn't going to be any sort of head-clearing place—not with Ronald, his pack of children, and all the helpers.

"Feel like a walk?" I asked Fluffy.

She seemed to recognize the word and jumped to her feet, ears up, tail swinging, entire rear end wagging. I'd tried a few simple commands on her—*sit, stay*. She'd responded, so she clearly had some training.

I got the pink leash off the coat hook, snapped it onto her pink collar, and picked her up. Charles was downstairs, hard at work in the library. I hoped Charles wouldn't realize that the dog didn't have to work but spent the day lazing around, snoozing, going for walks (outside!), and keeping me company.

Charles on strike would not be a pleasant cat to live with.

I hadn't made up my mind about whether to take Charles to live with Connor and me. Charles was the library cat. He'd been the library cat before I arrived, and he'd simply followed me upstairs one day after closing and made himself at home.

Would he miss me when I was gone?

Would he want to live in a house, even if I brought him to work every day?

I glanced at Charlene's closed door when I passed. That incident earlier bothered me, a lot. It had been totally out of character for her. Charlene was a warm, friendly person. She was passionate about her work and always delighted in sharing that passion with anyone who showed an interest. She loved her music and wanted everyone else to love it too. That people fled when she tried to press her musical selections on them made her only try all the harder.

No one ever minded. Not too much, anyway, because everyone loved her.

Something was up with Charlene, and I feared I knew what it was. If she was falling in love with James under the nose of his wife, that could not possibly end well.

What about James himself? Did he return Charlene's feelings? Was he having fun stringing her along, or did he simply not realize what was happening with her?

The latter was possible. He was quiet but generally friendly to everyone. Had Charlene mistaken that friendliness for something more personal?

What a mess.

Again, that led me to wonder what had caused Evangeline to react so strongly to James. He'd said he'd not previously been to America since he was a child. Was that true? If he was a cad, cheating on his wife, giving Charlene false hope, what else might he be capable of?

Fluffy was sniffing a patch of grass and I was reminding myself that I'd not be thanked for interfering in Charlene's love life when Watson drove up. He'd come in his own car, and he'd come on his own.

Fluffy and I met him at the top of the path.

"Is this Mrs. Lewiston's dog?" he said, bending over to let her sniff his hand. "Looks like it."

"Her name's Fluffy, and I'm looking after her while Evangeline's at the Ocean Side, from which Fluffy has been evicted for misbehaving."

Watson straightened up. "That's nice of you, Lucy."

"No, it's not. I was given absolutely no choice in the matter."

"You could have taken her to a kennel."

"Now that you mention it . . ." I grinned at him. "Maybe not. I'm growing rather fond of the little thing. Fortunately, she's small enough to fit in my apartment. Thank heavens Evangeline doesn't have a Saint Bernard."

Watson chuckled. "Let's walk." He pointed to the boardwalk. "There seems to be a lot of people over there. What's going on?"

"Ronald has a marsh wildlife expert visiting, and they've taken the kids out. We can go the other way."

"Let's," he said.

I fell into step beside him and we walked down the lane, which took us southwest toward the path to Blossie Creek, which opens onto Roanoke Sound. Fluffy trotted happily at my side. Watson walked with his hands thrust into his pockets, his gait slow and casual, appearing to be enjoying the feel of the warm sun on his head and the salty wind on his skin. He was, I thought, appreciating the chance to be outside in the fresh air, taking a moment to relax, even if the reason he was here had to do with murder most foul. Two yellow-and-black butterflies fluttered past his face, and he smiled as he watched them go. A flock of ducks took off from the calm waters of the creek, wings flapping, calling loudly to each other to keep up.

"Evangeline Lewiston," Watson said, when the ducks had passed and all was quiet once again. "Tell me about her."

I sucked in a breath. "Why do you want to know?"

"Just tell me, Lucy. You've known her a long time."

"Her husband—her late husband—and my dad are law partners. Their fathers founded the firm. I've known her for a long time, my entire life, but I know next to nothing, apart from what's obvious to everyone, about her. She was one of those people who was simply around when I was growing up. You should ask my mom about her, not me. I didn't pay a whole lot of attention to anyone in my parents' crowd. What kid does?"

"Fair enough. I have spoken to your mother, but she neatly brushed aside my questions about Evangeline's personality and other aspects of her life. She claims they were wives of partners, not friends."

"Mom's good at that. I bet you were out the door before you realized she hadn't actually answered your questions."

"And here I thought I was a good interrogator. In my years with the NYPD, I dealt with some of the toughest people in the world, but I fear I've met my match in your mother."

"My mother was an eighteen-year-old girl named Susan Wyatt from a North Carolina fishing family who'd barely finished high school when she married my dad. Which means she married his blueblood family, his father's law firm, his mother's social circle, and generations of expectations. She swam with sharks far sharper than any you've had to deal with, Detective. She not only survived but thrived. Evangeline would have been one of those circling sharks, just waiting for her to fail. *Friends* is a nebulous term. An outside observer would think Mom and Evangeline are friends, but they only spent time together as required by their husbands' positions. They never liked each other. Even now, Mom's stayed on in Nags Head out of a sense of duty, not any bonds of friendship."

"That's why I'm talking to you, Lucy. You observe things. You'd be surprised at how rare that can be. You know people."

Fluffy stopped to sniff at yet another patch of grass, and I gave the leash a tug. I considered letting her run free, but I didn't know if she'd stay close or come when I called, and I didn't want to risk it. If I lost Fluffy, Evangeline's wrath would be terrible to behold. "You're thinking Evangeline killed her husband."

"Not necessarily. She can't account for her time between roughly eight and nine thirty on Monday night, and that means I can't dismiss the possibility. You've told me before you and your mother came to the Outer Banks regularly over the years."

"Mom brought the kids here every summer to visit her sister. I remember those summers as some of the best times in my life." I thought of Connor and picnics at the beach and smiled to myself. "Until now."

"Did Evangeline ever come with you?"

"No. Definitely not. Mom wasn't trying to reconnect with her sister or even give her kids a great vacation. Coming here was her escape, a few weeks away from the pressures of that life—keeping up with the country club circuit, the constant disapproval of Dad's partners' wives, not to mention her own in-laws, always waiting for her to slip and display the slightest trace of working-class southern habits." I didn't mention that in the latter years of my childhood, Mom had been escaping from her own husband and a lonely, failing marriage.

Two people approached us, large binoculars and cameras with long lenses hanging around their necks and bulging backpacks slung over their shoulders. They nodded politely and paid no mind to Fluffy, who was dancing on her hind legs in greeting.

"Did you ever run into Evangeline on any of those visits?" Watson asked. "Have you seen her since you moved here?"

"No and no. Why are you asking me that? She told me she's never been to Nags Head. Isn't that true?"

"It would seem she's not been entirely truthful with either you or me. She originally told me the same—she'd never been here before—but a minor amount of digging proved that to be a lie."

"That's interesting."

"Isn't it? She got a speeding ticket in Duck three years ago. Five years ago her purse was stolen from a restaurant in Manteo, and the theft was reported to the police. When people lie to me, Lucy, I have to ask why they would do that."

"Have you asked her?"

"I did. She bluffed, badly, and said she thought I meant had she ever been to Nags Head specifically, not the general area. She then admitted she's come to the Outer Banks on occasion. For short, spontaneous getaways, in her words. Always on her own. Would you say she's the sort of woman to vacation alone?"

"No, I wouldn't. My mom needs what she calls her 'me time.' She'll check into a spa for a weekend or even go to New York City on her own for shopping and to see a play, but Evangeline's the sort of woman who's not comfortable in her own company. I could be wrong, Detective, but that's my impression."

"It's because I trust your impressions that I'm asking you, Lucy. I've got people going through records with a fine-toothed comb. I intend to find evidence she's been to Nags Head itself. And if I do, when I do, I want to know why she's lying."

"Do you know a man named Leon Lions?"

"Never heard of him, and that's not an easy name to forget. Why?"

"He lives in Kill Devil Hills, and he and Evangeline are old friends. Apparently they met years ago when he lived in Boston. He's been to the hotel to see her. They had lunch together yesterday and breakfast today and are meeting for lunch later."

"What are you saying, Lucy? How much of a friend of hers is this guy?" Watson's face rarely showed any emotion or reaction, and it didn't now. But his voice lifted slightly, and I knew I was telling him something he didn't know. I was strangely pleased. "On his part, he wants to be very friendly, and that's quite obvious. On hers, I can't say if she regards him as an old acquaintance or if there's something more. She called him this morning, immediately after you left her, to invite him to join her for breakfast, and he walked through the door so soon he had to have been circling the block. So soon that you passed him on your way out. You held the door for him."

"What's he look like?"

I tried to describe Leon Lions, but the words I used were mostly "average" and "normal." Not particularly helpful. I finished with "bald."

"I'll see if I can find anything out about him."

"Has Evangeline ever been to England?" I asked.

"Why do you ask?"

"She had a strange reaction when meeting one of Charlene's visiting researchers from Oxford University. Like she recognized him and was surprised to see him. He, on the other hand, didn't seem to know her. I thought it was odd, that's all. I wasn't going to mention it to you, except . . ."

"Except that 'it has long been an axiom of mine that the little things are infinitely the most important'?"

"Sherlock Holmes?" I asked.

"A suitable quote for every occasion. What's this researcher's name?"

"James Dalrymple. He's in his midthirties, so highly unlikely to be a former lover of hers."

"Never assume, Lucy."

"Stranger things have happened. He told me he was born in Nags Head but his mother took him to the UK, where she's from, when his father died, and he hasn't been back since his American grandparents died when he was a child. If that's true—and you should be able to find out easily enough—if Evangeline knows him, she has to have gone to the UK. Then again, a heck of a lot of Americans go to England, so I don't suppose that means much."

We hadn't reached the water's edge yet, but Watson said, "Shall we turn back?" and we did so. "You asked me earlier if we found Rich Lewiston's passport on him or in his car. That was a good question, Lucy, and as I said, we did not. Evangeline told me they keep their passports in a safe in the house, and I had Boston police look for it. They found both his and hers. The suitcase in his car contained clothes for a day, maybe two. He hadn't cleared out his bank accounts, made any transfers to overseas accounts, or even had an excess of cash on him."

"So he wasn't planning to skip the country, with or without his wife and son."

"Without going into details, I'll tell you we have forensic accountants going through his personal accounts as well as those of his firm's financial records which he had control over, and what you told me about his monetary situation seems to have been correct."

"Meaning he had debts."

"More than he could reasonably pay while still maintaining his lifestyle, not to mention his personal and professional reputation. Those debts, by the way, at least the ones I've been told about so far, are to banks, credit card companies, and reputable credit agencies. Not organized crime."

"Too bad."

"Why's that too bad?"

"Because if the mob offed him, then Ricky and Evangeline didn't, and I don't have reason to be involved and I can go back to planning my wedding, which I haven't even started doing yet, and finding a house to buy, which I have started and isn't going well."

"Things aren't easy for a young couple starting out today."

"No, and Connor and I are in a better position than many."

"I want to show you something we did find in Rich Lewiston's possession." Watson took a piece of paper out of his jacket pocket. "This is a good-quality photocopy. Tell me if it means anything to you."

He handed it to me. I studied it carefully, trying to think like Sherlock Holmes. The paper was white and plain, with a crease in the middle, indicating it had been folded in half. It contained nothing but a single line of text. The print appeared to be from a computer, the typeface Times New Roman 12.

We have to talk. Jakes Seafood Bar in Nags Head. 9 o'clck.

The letter writer had spelled *clock* wrong, which indicated the sender must have been in a hurry. Even if they couldn't spell the word, the spell checker would have put a red line under it, and anyone paying attention would have corrected it before printing the note. I pointed that out to Watson and added, "If they had spell checker turned on, that is."

"It's possible not to?"

"Yes."

Watson grinned at me. A rare occurrence. It made him look almost handsome. Human, even. "I knew there was a reason I wanted to show you this. No one else told me that. My desktop computer was set up for me, and I've never dared go into the settings. I'm afraid of breaking something. Same as the one at home. CeeCee fixes it if there are any problems. I assumed spell check was always on. Never assume, Sam," he added to himself. "First rule of policing."

"Other than that," I said, "this doesn't tell me much. We now know why Rich was at Jake's when he was, but we still don't know why he was in the Outer Banks in the first place. The note isn't signed, meaning Rich must have known who it came from. Or he thought he knew, but it was someone other than the person who sent it."

"Could his wife or son have sent it?"

"I wouldn't have thought they'd have such a formal relationship, but I can't say for sure. Why not phone or text? Did you find his phone?"

"It was on him. He'd received no calls or texts since Friday afternoon that hadn't come from clients of his or people he worked with. Nothing from Evangeline or Ricky. I haven't shown this note to anyone else, not yet. Please don't mention it."

"I won't."

Now that Watson was in what passed for him as a chatty mood, I asked, "When I saw him, it looked as though he'd been stabbed. Was that what he died of?"

"He was knifed in the back, yes. We're searching for the weapon, but I've little doubt it's at the bottom of the Sound or the ocean by now."

"Not many people carry knives around with them. Certainly not the sort of people Rich Lewiston was acquainted with."

"Which means the murder was an act of malice aforethought. The killer arranged to meet Rich at Jake's with the intention of killing him. By the way, Jake has done an inventory of his steak and cooking knives, and all are accounted for."

We arrived back at the parking lot and went to Watson's car. Fluffy sniffed the tires.

Detective Watson got in his car and drove away.

*   *   *

About the last thing in the world I felt like doing today was having lunch with Mom and Evangeline. Yes, I wanted to have some mother-daughter time, but not with Evangeline tagging along. Not to mention Ricky and Leon Lions and Stephen Livingstone and whoever else might be invited to participate in the cheerful outing.

Connor called as I was considering joining Ronald and the gang in the marsh. Since I've come to live in the library, I've spent a lot of time exploring the wetlands, but I hadn't gotten to know as much as I should about the flora and fauna and the other creatures who are my neighbors.

"I got a call from Lisa," Connor said, referring to our realtor. "She has word of a house that's coming onto the market today, and she can arrange a showing for us tomorrow evening, if you'd like."

"Book club's tomorrow."

"Oh, sorry, I forgot. I can ask her if we can see it around lunchtime instead. How's that sound?"

"That should work. Let me know the address and time and I can meet you there. What did she say about the house?"

"It's in an up-and-coming area and needs a tiny bit of work."

"Did she actually use that word? *Tiny?*"

"Yes."

"Let's hope." We'd agreed we didn't want a house that needed a lot of renovations or repairs, but if the price was low enough, we'd consider it. My home-maintenance skills stop at changing a lightbulb, but Connor's dad was a carpenter and Connor grew up helping him out, so he could do a lot of the work if needed, himself or with his dad's help.

A friend of mine in college maintained that the most important thing in choosing a life partner is that you love each other. The second most important is that he be handy. Although, as she pointed out one evening when we were celebrating the end of exams, love doesn't always last, but handyman skills never expire.

"While I've got you on the phone," Connor said, "I ran into Butch a few minutes ago in the parking lot, and he said he and Steph are going to the Dockside Lounge Bar to have a bite and listen to the band tonight and asked if we'd like to join them."

"Sounds like fun. I would."

"I'll swing by at seven."

The call had scarcely disconnected before my phone buzzed to announce a text.

Mom: *Lunch at Owens. 1:00*

Me: *I'd rather not*

Mom: *Lunch at Owens. 1:00*

Me:

Mom: *Please?*

Me: *Ok*

*   *   *

I let myself into the Lighthouse Aerie at three. Finally, at last, I could have some time to myself.

Lunch had been uneventful. Evangeline had been surprisingly quiet and Ricky on edge. Mom tried to make polite conversation about the delights of summer on the Outer Banks, and Leon Lions joined in with his praises. Evangeline said she'd never been here before and was finding it very nice, and Leon suggested that, in that case, she might want to come more in the future.

Did that mean she hadn't visited Leon the times she'd been here, or was he in on her attempt to lie about it?

I threw her a look, and she avoided my eyes.

Eventually Mom and Evangeline began talking about plans for the country club's Christmas ball. Leon turned to Ricky, seated on one side of him, to ask if Ricky wanted him to act as a tour guide and show him all the sights, while Stephen Livingstone, on the other side of Ricky, tried to get the lowdown on the gossip from Richardson Lewiston.

I enjoyed my chowder and plotted my escape.

"Book club." Evangeline's voice dragged me out of my thoughts. "I suppose that would be something to do, if we're still here tomorrow."

"What?" I said.

"Suzanne tells me your library book club meets tomorrow evening."

"Uh, yes."

"You're reading *The Hound of the Baskervilles*. I love that story, although it's been many years since I read it."

Something was up: earlier Evangeline had been highly dismissive of Sherlock Holmes.

"Ricky and I would like to attend, if we may," she said.

"We would?" Ricky said.

"Yes. We would."

"You'd be welcome," I said.

"You have nothing to do this evening," Evangeline said to Ricky. "You can download the book and read it tonight."

"Don't assume I have nothing to do, Mom."

"Do you?"

"I haven't decided."

"That's settled, then." She tapped her lips with her napkin.

"Maybe this'll all be over by tomorrow and you can take Rich home," Mom said.

"I hope so," Evangeline said. "But, if that is not the case, we'll attend the meeting of this book club."

The waiter brought the bill, and Leon snatched it directly out of his hand. He smiled at Evangeline and said, "Lunch is on me."

"Thank you. That's very kind of you. Suzanne, I feel a headache coming on. I hope you and Lucy don't mind if I bow out of our visit to the outlet shops."

I refrained from leaping to my feet and performing a victory dance.

"Not at all," Mom said. "I'd enjoy a quiet afternoon myself. It's been a stressful few days."

We all got to our feet.

"Ricky and I'll drop you off at the hotel," Leon said to Evangeline, "and then carry on to the Wright Brothers."

"What's the scoop on Melissa in human resources?" Stephen said to Ricky. "I heard her cousin got taken on, even though he was bottom of his class in law school."

Not interested in the scoop on Melissa in human resources or her relatives, I hurried Mom out of the restaurant and to my car.

"Thank you for coming," she said to me when we were on our way. "I'm grateful for your support, Lucy, while I'm supporting Evangeline."

"Is she doing okay?"

"No, she's not. I suggested she'd be more comfortable at home. She can wait for news there and come back when the police are ready to release Rich's body. She refused. She wants to be near him. She said they'd never been close in life but it's her duty to be with him in death."

"That's sad. Did you believe her?" I thought of Leon, so eager to please.

My mother gave me a smile. "I'm giving her the benefit of the doubt."

"Mom, I have to ask this. Do you think it's possible Evangeline killed Rich? She can't account for her time when he died."

My mother gave me the credit of taking my question seriously. She thought for several minutes. "No. I do not. If she wanted to, she would have had more than enough opportunities to do it in Boston, in a less dramatic fashion. She's intelligent enough to know she'd need an alibi. That she doesn't have so much as the shards of one indicates to me she did not arrange that unfortunate circumstance."

"She might have acted without thinking. Impulsively. Seen him at Jake's, been angry that he'd followed her, they got into an argument, and . . ."

"I doubt she's committed an impulsive act in her entire life. Evangeline thinks things through before acting. Besides, as far as I know, she's not in the habit of carrying a knife in her purse. The purse she carried Monday night wasn't much larger than necessary to hold her phone and credit card."

I didn't mention that even a small knife can do the job, if it's sharp enough. "Yes, I noticed that." I'd also noticed that there hadn't appeared to be any blood on her jacket. The police had taken it away for forensic analysis. If they'd found any-thing of significance, they'd have questioned Evangeline about it. And not in a polite interview in her hotel room.

"What's your impression of Leon Lions?" I asked.

"He's clearly in love with Evangeline, and I assume you noticed that also, thus the question."

"Hard not to."

"Quite. He's probably been in love with her for a long time. I don't know if the feelings are returned. Evangeline can be a closed book, when she wants to be. They met when he lived in Boston, many years ago. He might have continued to see Evangeline over the years, I don't know. A surprising number of Boston people seem to be in Nags Head these days. The death of Evangeline's husband has clearly given our Mr. Lions an opening to make his move. Is it possible, do you think, he's responsible for that?"

"You mean, might he have killed Rich? Anything's possible."
I remembered Watson telling me that Evangeline had visited

the Outer Banks, despite her saying she hadn't. Why would she lie? Surely, lying had to mean she'd been here to do something she didn't want anyone to know about. "He is, by the way, on the police radar for reasons you mention."

"You told Detective Watson."

"I did."

"You're full of surprises, Lucy," my mother said. "I'm beginning to realize that."

* * *

It was nice to get thoughts of Rich and Evangeline Lewiston out of my head. After dropping Mom off, I'd returned to the library and managed to sneak up the stairs unnoticed. I curled up in the window seat with Fluffy's chin resting on my lap and finished *The Hound of the Baskervilles*.

I wasn't entirely happy—okay, I wasn't at all happy—about Ricky and Evangeline coming to my book club tomorrow night, but I could hardly tell them to stay away.

I was ready for my date with Connor at the appointed time, and we met Butch and Steph in town. To my delight, they'd managed to get Jake and Josie to join us, and we had a fun evening. The band was popular and the place was crowded, but we managed to snag a table close to the wide windows, thrown open to the night. Beyond the line of lights cast by the houses and hotels lining the shore, lights twinkled from boats in the harbor. The moon hung high in the sky, and I could hear the low mummer of the sea rushing to shore. We drank beer, ate chicken wings and hush puppies, listed to some great music, and talked about our lives and our friends.

I laughed at something Butch said as I started to get to my feet to go to the ladies' room. At that moment, the crowd in front of the bar separated, and I caught a quick glimpse of a woman who looked very much like Charlene coming through the door. The same tall, thin frame, the same short brown hair. She was not dressed, however, in Charlene's usual library uniform of neat skirt suit or well-tailored trousers and blouse but a short, tight, colorful dress above strappy high-heeled sandals. The waiter stopped at our table to ask if we wanted anything more, and when he'd moved on, Charlene, or whoever the woman was, had gone. I scanned the crowd but saw no sign of her.

"You okay, Lucy?" Steph asked.

"What?"

"You look like you've seen something."

Connor's head popped up, and he glanced around. "Not that blasted Ricky again, I hope."

"No. Not Ricky. His mother has him sitting in his room at the hotel preparing for tomorrow's book club. I'm fine. I thought I saw someone I wouldn't have expected to see here, that's all. I guess I was wrong."

It might not have been Charlene, I said to myself, and she might not have left because she spotted my friends and me. Then again, the man standing next to her had looked very much like James Dalrymple.

* * *

"I have to take the dog out," I told Connor as we walked up the path to the lighthouse after our evening with our friends. The night was warm and clear and the big white moon was rising in the sky. High above us, the lighthouse flashed its pattern: steady, reliable, and comfortable in a changing world.

"How's he working out?" Connor asked.

"You mean having a dog? It's a she, and it's working out fine having her here, but that's only because I live where I work, so I can pop up and take her out a couple of times a day."

I unlocked the door, and we stepped inside. Charles was beside us immediately, winding himself around Connor's legs, purring happily.

"I don't usually get such an effusive greeting," Connor said. "Charles knows I don't ever feed him."

"Charles is attempting to remind you who's the number-one animal around here. He and Fluffy seem to have come to a tentative truce. I was worried I'd have to take sides. Do you want to come on the walk with us?"

"Sure. I'll wait for you down here."

I ran upstairs for Fluffy. When we got back, I found Connor sitting in the wingback chair with Charles on his lap and a book in his hand. He held up the book. *The Hound of the Baskervilles.*

"Found this on the returns cart, which reminds me, I won't make book club tomorrow. I had to reschedule the budget meeting so I can see that house with you, and somehow it turned into a dinner meeting."

He put Charles on the floor and stood up. He bent over and held his hand out to Fluffy to let the little dog sniff at it. Acquaintance made, Fluffy ran for the door, pulling me—at the other end of her leash—after her.

We stepped into the fresh night air. "One good thing about having a dog," I said, "is it forces you to get outside regularly and go for a walk."

Overhead, the thousand-watt bulb flashed, illuminating the ground in front of us. Connor took my free hand and we walked slowly toward the boardwalk, letting the moon and the occasional flash of light guide us.

We hadn't gone far before the light went into its dormancy and a bank of clouds slipped across the face of the moon.

At that moment, up ahead, a light flashed once in the distance before being extinguished.

I stopped walking abruptly. Fluffy tugged at her end of the leash. "Did you see that?"

"Yeah, I did. Someone's out there."

"There aren't any cars in the parking lot."

"They might have come by boat."

"Maybe." I was suddenly very cold. The darkness that moments ago had seemed so peaceful pressed on me. Last year, in the days leading up to Halloween, I'd seen mysterious lights moving in the marsh. Those lights had been faint, colored, drifting. Almost, I'd thought, beckoning me. Corpse candles, the ancients called them, luring the living to their doom. I'd fled and never experienced anything like that again, and I'd pushed the incident aside as a natural phenomenon I'd misinterpreted due to all the talk of the night when the veil between the worlds is at its thinnest.

This wasn't the same. This light was steady, white, powerful. Electric.

"Is something wrong, Lucy?" Connor said.

"I . . . I don't know. I don't like that light. There it is again." A series of flashes this time. A long, a short, a short, two longs. "Do you know Morse code?"

"I learned it as a Boy Scout but have almost completely forgotten." He peered into the darkness. "You don't think someone's signaling, do you?"

"I don't know."

"It's nothing but random flashes, Lucy. If it bothers you, do you want to go over and check out what's going on?"

"No!"

He dropped my hand. "I'll go. You can take the dog back inside."

I grabbed his hand and clung to it. "No!"

"The dog isn't reacting."

I glanced down. Fluffy sat at my feet, scratching behind her ear. "They might be too far away for her to smell anything. And the wind's blowing in the wrong direction for their scent to carry to us."

"It's nothing to worry about, Lucy. People are in the marsh. Lots of people visit the marsh."

"In the daytime or at twilight or sunrise. Not in the middle of the night. And they don't come at night without a car. Let's go back inside. I'm cold."

"Okay."

I tugged at the leash, and Fluffy stopped scratching her ear. She stood up, looked around her, and let out one loud bark. Connor hesitated and then came with us. I almost dragged both of them after me. When we reached the safety of the lighthouse, I glanced behind me. All was dark once again.

Chapter Fifteen

"How was the house you saw today?" Josie asked.

"A complete and total disaster. The thing's barely standing upright. We didn't stay more than a couple of minutes. Connor was furious at the realtor for wasting our time."

"You don't want a fixer-upper?" Louise Jane asked.

"We don't mind a fixer-upper," I said. "That is, Connor doesn't mind, and he'll be the one doing the work. If it's within reason. Not only was that place not within reason, but if we do get a house needing a lot of repairs and renovations, the price has to reflect that. They want top dollar for a bottom-dollar property." I stuffed an oatmeal cookie into my mouth.

"Help yourself," Josie said.

"Don't mind if I do." I took another.

Thursday evening we were in the third-floor meeting room of the library, getting ready for book club. As always, Josie had brought treats from her bakery to accompany the lemonade and iced tea provided by the library.

"I probably shouldn't be eating all these myself," I said. "I'm expecting a full house tonight. Not only is *The Hound* a popular book, but Mom and her friends are coming."

"I mentioned it to Daisy and James," Louise Jane said. "Daisy said she'd try to make it."

"Not James?"

"He's busy with something or other," Louise Jane said.

"Is that so?"

She gave me a look. "Why do you say it like that?"

"No reason," I said quickly. "Just making polite conversation."

"They're due to go back to England next week. Daisy said they've accomplished a lot in their time here and she can't wait to get to writing it up. I'll miss her."

"Maybe you can go and visit her in Oxford," Josie suggested.

"I went on that tour of the haunted castles of England last year, and it was great. I'd like to go back sometime."

I checked the time. "Almost seven. I'll go downstairs and greet people."

I stood on the front steps as cars began to arrive. At seven o'clock the sun was still up, although dipping in the west, casting long shadows between the trees lining the drive and across the lawn. I'd spent some time today think-ing about book club and coming up with questions I could ask to start the discussion off. I found my thoughts con-stantly returning to the convict Selden, hiding out in the great Grimpen Mire, signaling his sister at Baskerville Hall to make sure the coast was clear.

Was that what had happened last night? Not escaped pris-oners hiding out on the moors but me allowing the Conan Doyle story to take control of my imagination and run with it? Connor had been right: people had come by boat or had left their car in a copse of trees to observe the marsh at night. They hadn't been signaling to anyone in Morse code but waving their arms in front of the beam of light they needed to guide their way.

Cars began bouncing down the long driveway, pulling me out of my thoughts. Most of the regulars had come tonight: Mrs. Fitzgerald, head of the library board; Josie and our friend Grace Sullivan; Mrs. Peterson with Primrose and a sour-faced Charity; Steph and Butch, who as usual shouted a quick "Hi, Lucy," and galloped upstairs for the baked goods before they were all snatched up; Theodore Kowalski, complete with Harris Tweed jacket, paisley cravat, clear-glass spectacles, surrounded by the scent of tobacco even though he didn't smoke; CeeCee Watson, wife of the detective, who told me Sam had hoped to make the meeting but was held up at work; and Louise Jane. Plus several library patrons who weren't club regulars but came to meetings if the book was of interest to them. Daisy skipped down the path, her long golden hair swaying around her shoulders, and greeted us all warmly. Tonight she wore a light summer dress with spaghetti straps, and I could see that her tattoos covered not only her arms but most of her right shoulder as well. The light over the front door reflected off the silver ring in her nose.

"So glad you made it," Louise Jane said. "Come on, we have to hurry if we want to get a seat. Lucy's been in the cookies already." They bustled off before I could casually ask what James was up to tonight.

I greeted everyone as they arrived and directed them to the meeting room on the third floor. At quarter after seven, when I'd decided I couldn't wait any longer and was about to lock the door and head upstairs to start the meeting, two pairs of headlights broke through the trees.

"Sorry we're late, dear." Mom spoke to me, but she glowered at Evangeline.

"Yes, sorry," Evangeline said, sounding not sorry in the least. "I couldn't decide on suitable shoes." I glanced down, wondering what she considered suitable. I suppose the open-toed stilettos with four-inch heels were suitable to match her perfectly tailored pale-blue suit jacket, navy-blue blouse with a big bow at the neck, and tight knee-length skirt.

"I don't know what was the matter with the ones you had on," said Mom, who'd been known to arrive at a dinner party an hour late because every pair of shoes had to be tried and retried, discarded, and pulled out of the closet once more. And then, shoes decided upon, maybe the dress wasn't quite right.

Evangeline was obviously getting on Mom's nerves.

"We're here now." Evangeline gave me an air kiss heavy with perfume. "No harm done. The boys are right behind us."

A second car had pulled in behind them, and Ricky, Leon, and Stephen joined us on the steps.

"We're on the third floor," I said. "Go on up, help yourself to refreshments, and grab a seat. If you can find one—we've got a full house tonight."

Evangeline touched my arm as I turned to go inside. "How's Fluffy getting on?"

"She's good. I think she's enjoying it here. We're going on lots of lovely walks."

Evangeline glanced around us, taking in the boardwalk, the long grasses of the marsh, the ducks flying overhead, honking to each other. The not much of anything else. "I hope you're not taking her too far, Lucy. She's not used to all this . . . nature."

"She's fine. Shall we join the others?" I pulled the door shut behind us.

"I trust you're keeping that horrid cat away from Fluffy," Evangeline said as we climbed the stairs. "He looked like a bad-tempered beast to me, and Fluffy has a delicate disposition."

"Well away," I said. When I'd called Charles to come for book club, he and Fluffy had been curled up together on the window seat. They had almost—not quite, but almost—been touching. Charles, who loves book club, had to be encouraged to jump down and follow me.

"After your little meeting, I'll pop up and say hello," Evangeline said.

Instantly I mentally surveyed my apartment: laundry put away, bed made, dishes washed, trash taken out, floor swept. "Sure, we can do that."

It was standing room only in the meeting room. Butch, Ricky, and Stephen leaned against the walls. Butch munched on an oatmeal cookie and clutched a napkin containing a pecan square and a mini cupcake in one massive paw, and Ricky balanced a fully laden napkin and a glass of lemonade.

Beside me, Evangeline sucked in a breath when she caught sight of the crowded room.

I turned and looked at her. "Are you okay?"

"Perfectly fine." She patted her chest. "Those stairs are quite the climb, aren't they? Suzanne, you should have warned me to wear a pair of sneakers."

My mom's the only person I know who can roll her eyes without physically doing so. It is, I've always thought, a neat trick.

"The laws of succession are very strict, even now," Theodore was saying as Mom and Evangeline edged into the room. "Entailed property can only be inherited down the male line, regardless of the number of female offspring one might have." He leapt to his feet when he saw Evangeline and offered her a slight bow. "Madam, welcome. Please take my chair."

"I . . . thank you." She sat and patted her skirt neatly around her. She threw a sideways glance at Charles, curled up on Mrs. Fitzgerald's lap. Charles lifted his little chin and turned away. The snub was almost human.

"Can I get you a treat or a glass of something?" Leon asked Evangeline.

"What? Oh, sorry. Yes, thank you. A drink, please. Whatever they have."

"Like in *Downton Abbey*," Primrose Peterson said. "Lady Mary couldn't inherit, so she had to find someone to marry."

"That's not fair," her sister Charity said.

"The royal family recently changed their rules of succession," Mrs. Fitzgerald said. "Princess Charlotte, being the second child of Prince William, is now second in line after him and her older brother, rather than third after her younger brother, as she would have been before. Isn't that right, Daisy?"

The Englishwoman chuckled. "I hope you didn't invite me here tonight for my keen insider knowledge of the workings of the English aristocracy. My field is North American colonial history. The closest I've been to the monarchy is the time my mother met Prince Charles when he toured the university where she worked. As for any potential inheritance to sort out, my parents are determined to spend every last cent they have visiting the tourist traps of the world." She smiled fondly at the thought.

"I'm the oldest in our family," Charity said, "so I'll inherit all your money, Mom."

"Hey!" Primrose, the second daughter, protested.

"Fortunately for you girls, your family is not English and you are not landed aristocracy," Mrs. Fitzgerald said. "Your parents can leave their property to whomever they choose."

"Yeah, but if so, if not us, then who would inherit all your and Dad's money, Mom?" Charity said. "You have five daughters."

"I don't think we want to get into a discussion of our family's financial situation," Mrs. Peterson said. "Besides, your father and I plan to be around for a long time still."

"Drat!" Primrose fell back in her chair and crossed her arms.

Everyone, with the exception of Mrs. Peterson, burst out laughing.

"I assume you're talking about this because of the inheritance of the Baskerville title and estate," I said. "An excellent point at which to begin discussion of the book. Imagine being a young American man who suddenly finds out that a relative he never knew has died and left you everything."

"Including a family curse," Grace said.

Ricky chuckled. "Including that." He smiled at Grace. She smiled back.

"And then," my mom said, "spoiler alert for anyone who hasn't finished it—but I assume we're here to discuss all of the book—the next heir is someone no one even knows about."

"It did get rather ridiculous," Daisy said, "in real life as in the book: the hunt for someone, anyone, to inherit the estates and the title, particularly when there were perfectly acceptable female relatives around."

"Like in *Downton Abbey*," Primrose repeated.

"I'm an only child," Ricky said to Grace. "No inheritance worries for me."

His mother frowned at him.

"Previously unknown and illegitimate relatives still pop out of the woodwork at will-reading time," Butch said.

Evangeline shifted in her seat. She glanced at Theodore as he said, with great relish, "The very stuff of crime fiction."

"Mom's right," I said, "but let's not get ahead of ourselves. That happens at the end of the book. It begins with the death of Sir Charles, supposedly at the hands—or jaws, I should say—of the spectral hound. Did you for a moment think the legend might be true?"

It was a good meeting. *The Hound* is a great book, drenched in atmosphere as Holmes and Watson bound across the desolate, remote, deadly moors in pursuit of the mysterious and legendary hound. Ricky and Stephen didn't have much to say, and I guessed neither of them had read the book. Leon hadn't either, but he had seen some of the movie versions. Every time he made a point, he glanced at Evangeline out of the corner of his eye, hoping for her approval, but she scarcely seemed to notice. She sat quietly, ankles crossed, hands in her lap, almost pulled into herself, and I couldn't read her thoughts.

"If anyone would like to get a feel for the atmosphere of the Grimpen Mire," Louise Jane said, as the meeting began to break up, "the marsh outside these doors can be a mighty spooky place at night."

I was about to tell Louise Jane to stop spreading her ghost stories in the library when Daisy gave an exaggerated shiver. "Even if mists aren't swirling around your feet and dogs howling in the distance."

"Even if Sherlock Holmes isn't shouting, 'Come, Watson!' " Louise Jane laughed. "Although we did get a fright last night when we heard that silly little thing of yours barking, Lucy."

"What silly—" I said. "You mean that was you? You were on the marsh last night?"

"What silly little thing might that be?" Evangeline snapped.

"Some ridiculous dog poor Lucy's been stuck looking after," Louise Jane said.

Mom choked. Ricky stifled a laugh.

Louise Jane looked from one of them to the other. "Oh. Is that your dog? Sorry. Cute little thing. Feisty."

"Fluffy is not feisty! I'll have you know, her mother was a kennel club winner," Evangeline said.

I struggled to get a word in edgewise, having more important things on my mind than Fluffy's parentage. "You were in the marsh, Louise Jane? Last night? With flashlights?"

"Yup. We heard you and Connor and that . . . uh . . . nice little puppy. I wanted to sneak up and yell, 'Boo,' but Daisy said that wouldn't be nice."

"No, it wouldn't," Daisy said. "We've been out a couple of nights. Louise Jane says, and I agree with her, that the best way to get a feel for how things were in the past is to try to get away from all the noise and the bustle of modern civilization, as hard as that can be sometimes. Your marsh is so beautiful at night. And so quiet, I can almost believe I'm walking through it two hundred years ago. Until a plane flies overhead, anyway."

"Or someone brings a yappy dog," Louise Jane added. "Not that anyone did. Bring a yappy dog. Last night."

"Are you ready to go, Evangeline?" Mom asked.

Evangeline broke off glaring at Louise Jane. "I want to see Fluffy. I need to let her know we'll be together again soon."

"Were you in the marsh on Monday night?" I asked Louise Jane.

"Yes, we were," Daisy said. "It was brilliant with all that mist swirling around. Really spooky. It's still early. Anyone up for going round the pub?"

"Sounds good," Louise Jane said.

"Splendid idea," Theodore said.

"I'll give James a call," Daisy said. "See if he's ready to join us."

"Where is he tonight?" I asked, ever so casually. "Not interested in our little book club?"

"He went over to Charlene's house to have dinner with her and her mum," Daisy said.

"That's nice." I studied Daisy's pretty face while trying not to look too obvious about it. Did she and James have a truly open marriage, or did Daisy not realize that Charlene was in love with her husband? Or did Daisy trust James completely?

"Although," Daisy added, "it's starting to get a bit much, him always saying he has other things to do or going off without telling me. We only rented one car, and I hate having to keep begging Louise Jane for a lift if we want to do something in the evenings."

"I don't mind," Louise Jane said.

"Well, I do," Daisy said.

Theodore turned to Mom and Evangeline. "Nice seeing you again, Mrs. Richardson, Mrs. Lewiston."

"And you too," Mom said.

Evangeline said nothing.

The meeting began to break up and book club members clattered downstairs, chatting about the book, about venturing into the marsh at night, making plans for the weekend.

"Fluffy," Evangeline said to me.

"I'll take you up. Only one more flight to climb."

"A drink sounds like a nice idea," Stephen said. "I've been meaning to ask you, Ricky, if you've any idea what's going to happen to the Frankland cases now that Rich isn't around."

Leon jerked his head in the direction of Evangeline. "That's hardly a polite way of putting it."

"Sorry," Stephen said, sounding not at all sorry. "We'll wait for you downstairs."

"I don't know," Ricky said as the two men left the meeting room. "I was hoping you could tell me . . ."

Their voices faded away. I called to Charles, and Mom, Evangeline, Leon, and I left the meeting room. Evangeline glared at Charles, who returned her glare before nimbly leaping up the stairs.

The moment I opened the door to the Lighthouse Aerie, Evangeline dropped to a crouch and held out her arms, crying, "Come to Mommy!" Fluffy leapt off the window seat in a flurry of white fur and almost tripped over herself in her rush to do so. They greeted each other joyfully. Fluffy yipped. Evangeline cooed.

Charles headed for his food bowl to see if it had miraculously been filled while we were out. He was to be disappointed.

"Nice apartment," Leon said.

"Thanks," I replied.

Fluffy flipped over onto her belly and allowed Evangeline to rub and scratch at it. Finally, Evangeline started to stand. She wobbled on her heels and grunted softly. Leon grabbed her arm and hoisted her to her feet. She smoothed down her skirt. "My darling seems to be well cared for, Lucy. Thank you. And thank you for the . . . uh . . . pleasant evening."

"I'll walk you downstairs," I said.

"That drink sounds like a good idea to me," Leon said. "How about you ladies?"

"Not for me," Mom said. "I've had a long day."

"Perhaps a quick one," Evangeline said. She waved her fingers at Fluffy. "Good-bye, my darling. Don't worry, we'll be going home soon. I won't leave you in this place a moment longer than necessary."

"It's not dog jail," I muttered.

Charles hissed at Leon, who quickly made his escape.

Downstairs, Ricky and Stephen were waiting by the door, talking shop. That is, Stephen was talking shop. Ricky was fingering his phone and didn't seem at all interested in anything the other man was saying.

Mom hugged me good-night and said she'd call in the morning, and they left.

Chapter Sixteen

Friday at lunchtime I headed upstairs, once again thinking how much I'd miss this commute when I moved in with Connor. If we ever found a house to move into together, that is. Anything we liked was too expensive, and anything we could afford, we didn't like.

I could ask my parents for a loan, and they'd give it without question, but I didn't want to start our married life that way. Connor might not think of it as being indebted to my family, but I would.

Fluffy greeted me at the apartment door, dancing and yipping in excitement. Her excitement only increased when I got down the pink leash. I had to admit, the little thing was beginning to grow on me. She seemed to be starting to like me too.

I intended to hurry through the library, let the dog have a brief walk, and then go upstairs to eat my lunch and make a call to my mom.

I should have known better. The preschool story time was getting out, and every one of the kids wanted to stop and pet Fluffy. Fluffy wasn't used to children, so I kept a careful eye out, but she appeared to enjoy their attention.

Charles, not used to not being the center of attention, perched on a high shelf and scowled malevolently. I hoped Charles wouldn't be so offended he'd end their truce. Still holding the leash in one hand, I reached up and plucked Charles off the shelf with the other. I put him on the floor in front of a green-eyed, freckle-faced little girl with the wildest mop of red hair I'd ever seen. She squealed and dropped to her knees next to him. "Charles! Are you jealous? Don't be jealous. You know you're our favorite."

Fluffy and I left Charles basking in compliments, as was his due. We had a quick walk and then scurried back inside for lunch. I opened and heated a can of vegetable soup, which I ate with a piece of toast and cheese. Then, disappointed that there'd been no leftover baked treats last night, I called my mom. "Any developments?"

"If you mean have I heard from Evangeline about her returning to Boston, no."

"How long are you planning to stay?"

"As long as Evangeline does. She's having lunch with Leon—again—and we're going to the spa later. Would you like to join us?"

"I have this thing called a job. I'm on my lunch break now."

"Oh yes. A job. So tedious."

I briefly wondered what it must be like to have never had a real job. Then again, as "wife of," Mom had worked hard enough.

"I'm getting the feeling you're starting to get a bit impatient with Evangeline, Mom; that's why I'm asking."

"Impatient would be an understatement. I don't expect you to understand, dear. Your life is so . . . different than mine." A long silence came down the line. "I envy you, Lucy, but that's neither here nor there. Yes, I don't like Evangeline and I never have, but our lives are entwined in a way that's difficult to explain. We've always had to pretend to be close, and that has made us close."

"Even though you don't like each other."

"Even though."

I hadn't reacted when Mom said she envied my life. I've always known I never wanted hers. The pretense of a happy marriage, the country club circuit, the "frenemies," the social expectations. No thanks.

Mom and I were getting on so much better these days, but I couldn't forget that she'd tried to push me into following in her footsteps and marrying Ricky. Into marrying for social status and to keep the firm in the family rather than finding my own way and my own path to love.

"I'll stay," Mom said, "as long as Evangeline needs me to stay. And before you ask, Ellen and Amos are fine with that."

Maybe. Mom and Ellen had never been friends either. Despite growing up in the same house, with the same parents, their life paths had been too different. In that, I was more like my aunt Ellen than my mother. Mom had not been happy that it was Ellen who introduced me to Bertie James when Bertie was looking to hire an assistant library director for the Lighthouse Library.

All water under the bridge, I reminded myself.

"Ricky might be going home soon," Mom said.

"Before his mom? Why?"

"They dragged me into joining them for a quick drink after your book club last night, and Ricky said certain things are happening at the office that he needs to be, in his words, on top of. Evangeline was obviously surprised at that. He'd told her he'd stay here, in Nags Head, until they could take his father home. She started to have words with him about leaving early, but he cut her off. Too many people listening, I suspect."

"Meaning Leon and Stephen?"

"Yes."

"Speaking of Ricky—Mom, do you know anything about the state of Evangeline's finances?"

"Why do you ask?"

"We know Rich was carrying a lot of debt. I'm wondering if Evangeline has money of her own."

"It's possible but unlikely. Her parents are both alive and seem to be in reasonably good health. They're people of comfortable means but not excessively so, as far as I know. Evangeline has one younger sister, so I assume the family's money will go to Evangeline and her sister eventually. Why do you ask?"

"All that talk last night about the estate of Sir Charles Baskerville and the search for an heir got me thinking."

"Surely you're not thinking Ricky killed his father for the inheritance?"

"To protect the inheritance, if Rich was squandering what money he had. Watson's thinking it."

"Do you know that for sure?"

"No, I don't, but if I were him, I would be. If Rich was in danger of losing everything, and if Evangeline doesn't have immediate prospects in that area, then maybe . . . You have to admit it, Mom, both of them had a motive."

"I will not admit anything of the sort. The idea's preposterous."

"Ricky doesn't seem all that interested in his legal career. As feeble as it seems to be."

"What does that mean?"

I nibbled on a piece of toast and thought. "I honestly don't know, Mom. Then again, maybe his career will start to be important to him now that his father's dead and he's next in line to be the Lewiston name on the door. You did say he's thinking of heading in to work."

"I have no idea what's going through Ricky's mind, dear. Millar has never been what I'd call full of praise for Ricky's legal acumen or his work habits. But people can change, and the sudden death of a parent is a powerful incentive for reevaluating one's life. Enough of that. I enjoyed your book club last night. It was fun and an interesting discussion. You have some intelligent friends."

"That I do," I said. "Talk to you later, Mom."

We hung up. I finished my soup, washed up my few dishes, and headed downstairs to the library.

I was wearing a light pair of ballet flats today, so my feet made no sound on the iron stairs as I descended. Charlene's door was open just a crack. Remembering how she'd shut it in my face the other day, I was about to hurry past when I heard voices. Louise Jane and Charlene don't usually see eye to eye on the pursuit of historical knowledge, so I was surprised that Louise Jane was in Charlene's office. I pricked my ears up, and I might have leaned slightly to one side in order to catch snatches of their conversation.

Louise Jane: "So soon? . . . wait a moment longer than . . . have to."

Charlene: ". . . England. Mom will . . ."

"What does Bertie . . ." Louise Jane must have turned, so I didn't hear the rest of the sentence.

Charlene: ". . . good timing. You'll be . . ."

"Have you lost something, Lucy?"

I jumped and felt color rushing into my face. Louise Jane stood in the doorway, her hands on her hips.

"No. Nothing. I haven't lost anything. I was wondering what I'd been intending to do. Getting absent-minded in my old age. Nice seeing you, Louise Jane. Have a nice day." I took the steps two at a time.

Behind me, Charlene's office door slammed shut.

* * *

Friday afternoon the board of the Bodie Island Lighthouse Library met for their regular meeting. Recent departures from the board meant several new members would be joining them today for the first time.

"I'm not looking forward to this, Lucy," Bertie said as I laid pens and paper and water glasses on the long table in the staff break room.

"You never look forward to board meetings," I said.

"This one less than usual. I hate numbers, as you know, and the board will be going over the proposed budget for next year with a fine-toothed comb. I suppose I should be grateful Mrs. Fitzgerald managed to talk Cindy McMaster into coming on board. Goodness knows we've long needed a proper accountant, but Cindy's a stickler for accounting for every penny. I've lost count of the number of times she's called me over the last week for a full explanation of one line item or another."

"Does she love libraries and books?" I asked.

"Oh yes. With a passion."

"Then we're lucky to have her."

"That's true, although sometimes I almost miss Diane and Curtis. They might have hated the library and everything it stood for, but Curtis always insisted on having our meetings at a restaurant and enjoying a nice lunch—"

"With free-flowing wine."

"With free-flowing wine. All on the library's budget, of course. Cindy balked at getting in cookies from Josie's. I believe Mrs. Fitzgerald's baking today's treats herself in order to economize."

I smiled at my boss. The look on Bertie's face didn't match her words. The library had been preciously close to having to close recently when unforeseen expenses threatened to exceed our ability to pay for them. The library community had come through and we'd been saved. But money was always on our mind.

"Connor's been invited to come and say a few words to the new board," Bertie said. "How's the house hunting going?"

"Don't ask," I said. We went into the main room to greet the board members as they arrived.

Connor held the door for Mrs. Fitzgerald, and the rest of the board trailed in behind her. I was introduced to the new members, including Cindy McMaster. I recognized Cindy as a regular patron, but it was nice to formally meet her. She was in her early sixties and couldn't have looked less like an accountant in a calf-length, multicolored, multilayered dress, rows of earrings in her left ear, clanging bangles covering her wrists, and spiked gray hair dyed purple at the tips.

Then again, I'm often told I don't look like a librarian—whatever a librarian looks like.

I took Mrs. Fitzgerald's cookie tin from Connor, and he gave me his private smile.

"If you'll follow me." Bertie had begun to lead the way when the door flew open and Gordon Frankland stomped in.

He checked out the group and said, "Good. You haven't started yet."

"Mr. Frankland," Connor said. "Are you a member of the library board?"

"No, but I have a few things to say to them."

"This is a preliminary budget meeting, so it's closed to the general public. When the budget's ready for approval and discussion, the public will be invited to participate."

"You mean, when you've decided what you want to do, the so-called public will be allowed to parrot their approval."

"That's not the way it works."

"Of course it is. It's always the way it works. This library's a drain on the resources of the community. You need to be charging for access to the lighthouse and the marsh as well as your programs."

"We're a library," I said, shocked to my very core. "We exist to serve the citizenry, not to make a profit off them."

"My point exactly. It's time you expanded your mandate. I've brought a proposal for—"

Bertie glanced between Connor and Gordon. "I'm sorry, sir, but I don't believe we've met."

"Perhaps not, but I know who you are. Albertina James, library director. You own a business in town. I hope you don't take time away from what I'm paying you, as a taxpayer, to do while you run your yoga studio."

"I—" Bertie said.

"Mr. Frankland," Connor interrupted. "You've never before showed the slightest interest in the business of this library. I have to assume you're here today in an attempt to up the stakes on the suit you recently filed against the town. If you have issues with me and with the town council, please don't bring them here. Let these people go about their business."

Charles had been watching the exchange from the top of a shelf. His ears were pressed flat against his head, his eyes narrow, his tail moving slowly back and forth. When Gordon Frankland took a step toward Bertie and the board members, Charles, staunch defender of the library, made his move. He sailed through the air, a ball of furious white-and-tan fur and flashing claws, and landed directly in front of Gordon.

Frankland screeched, threw his hands in the air, checked his stride, lost his balance, and pitched forward.

He would have crashed into a shelf had Connor not grabbed his arm in the nick of time.

Rather than graciously extending his thanks to Connor, Frankland yanked his arm free and yelled at Bertie and the gathered board. "That cat's a menace!"

"I'm so sorry," I said. "He's usually very well behaved."

Frankland turned on me. "Doesn't look like it, does it? I could have been badly injured. You'll be hearing from my lawyers."

"Oh for heaven's sake," I said. "Nothing was injured but your pride. You should be thanking His Honor for helping you, not threatening us."

He stared at me. The spark in his eyes told me he was enjoying this. "I know you. You're Amos O'Malley's niece."

"I am." I should have known better, really I should. But this man's casual maliciousness pushed me over the edge of common sense. "I am also Millar Richardson's daughter, and I know you're acquainted with his firm. You were at Jake's on Monday night."

"So I was. What of it?"

"Lucy, I don't think—" Connor began.

"Monday night. The night my father's law partner Richard Lewiston Junior was murdered moments after you insulted the same Mr. Lewiston in front of his son and his wife and his law partner. You left the restaurant shortly, very shortly, before Mr. Lewiston was attacked. Did you kill him?'

Bertie sucked in a breath. The assembled board members watched, wide-eyed. Connor took a step toward me. Charles, who'd leapt onto the returns cart to watch the action, hissed at Gordon and displayed his always-impressive teeth.

"I hope you've prepared the tea, Bertie," Mrs. Fitzgerald said. "I've developed a powerful thirst."

No one took the hint.

"Are you accusing me of being a murderer?" Frankland said to me.

"No, she isn't," Connor said. "This isn't the time or the place, Gordon."

I stood my ground. "I'm not accusing anyone of anything. I simply asked the question uppermost in my mind. Did you kill Rich Lewiston, Mr. Frankland?"

The edges of Gordon's mouth turned up, and too late I realized that I'd gone too far. I'd given him exactly what he wanted.

He smirked. "Sounds like an accusation to me. A baseless, unfounded accusation designed to slander my reputation in front of all these people."

"I didn't hear anything," Mrs. Fitzgerald said. "Did you hear anything, Bertie?"

"Not me," Bertie said.

"I didn't know you had a reputation that could be slandered, Gordon," Cindy said.

He heard the jab, but he didn't turn away from me. "I'll see you in court, young lady. Better get yourself a lawyer, and you'll want a good one. Not Richardson Lewiston. They have enough troubles these days."

Then, with his back to everyone else in the room, he winked at me, before turning and marching purposefully out of the library.

That is, he would have marched purposefully had Charles not jumped off the cart, charged across the room, and planted himself between Frankland's feet. Gordon swore and danced and stumbled into the door. He raised his right foot, aiming it at Charles. I yelled, "Don't you dare!"

He lowered his foot, wrenched open the door, and disappeared. The door slammed behind him.

I scooped Charles up. "That," I said, "didn't help."

Charles's eyes sparkled. Trying to trip Gordon Frankland a second time hadn't helped the situation any, but it made Charles feel better.

"I declare," one of the new board members said, "is this library always this exciting?"

"You haven't seen anything yet," Mrs. Fitzgerald said. "Shall we begin our meeting?"

"Do I need a lawyer?" I asked Connor.

"No. You didn't accuse him of murder, and you didn't even imply he'd done it. You simply asked."

"We all heard what you said," Bertie said. "The man's a pest." She looked at the cat, now washing his whiskers. "I hope Charles hasn't gone too far this time."

"Nothing will come of that threat either," Connor said. "Any suit would be frivolous, and although that wouldn't stop Frankland from pursuing it, his reputation is getting out of hand. He'll have trouble finding a lawyer to take it on."

"We can only hope," I said.

Bertie led the way to the meeting room, and Connor followed, after giving me an encouraging smile.

Fortunately, Gordon Frankland couldn't sue me for what I'd been thinking. Because I had been thinking he was an excellent suspect for the murder of Rich. He'd been in the area at the time, he'd had poisonous relations with the dead man, and only minutes before he'd had a confrontation with Rich's son. Had Gordon left the restaurant and run into Rich Lewiston coming in?

Had they exchanged words? Had one thing led to another and things gotten out of hand?

Had it been an accidental encounter, or had Gordon sent the note telling Rich to meet him? I needed to ask Watson what he knew about Frankland's movements after leaving Jake's. The detective had earlier told me that information was confidential, but now I had a good reason to insist—I had to defend myself against a threatened lawsuit.

It wasn't long before Connor left the board meeting. He greeted some of the patrons he knew and then came to the desk. We exchanged our private smiles.

"Plans tonight?" he asked.

"I'm meeting Josie, Grace, and Steph after work. Sorry, girls' night. You're not invited."

"I suppose I can live with that. If I must. Is your mom still in town?"

"Yes. She's staying until Evangeline can take Rich home." I lowered my voice. "Connor, would you say Gordon Frankland is mentally unstable?"

"I'm a dentist, not a psychiatrist, but I wouldn't say unstable, no. He gets a kick out of making trouble, and he's spoiled enough to have the money to indulge himself. Are you seriously thinking he might have killed Rich?"

"The thought has crossed my mind. Mrs. Johannsen, let me take those from you."

The patron dumped an enormous stack of cozy mysteries on the desk.

"You've got a lot of reading ahead of you," Connor said.

"I do wish Ellen Byron and Essie Lang would write faster," Mrs. Johannsen said. "I'm reduced to reading my favorites a second time while waiting for new books."

I checked her books out, dropped them into her canvas book bag, and she left. Another happy patron.

"It's nice," I said to Connor, "having a job where you help people and make them smile."

"Rather than listening to complaints all day," he said. "Speaking of complaints, I'd better get to the office and see what I need to clear up before the weekend. Sunday still on?"

"Yes, and the weather looks perfect." We'd planned a picnic at the beach for Sunday. "I don't suppose you've heard from the realtor lately."

His mouth twisted, and he shook his head. "Nothing new. You might have to reconsider moving into my house."

"Or you into the Lighthouse Aerie."

"That would hardly suit," Louise Jane said.

"Where'd you come from?" I asked. Louise Jane did seem to pop out of the woodwork at the most inopportune moments.

"I was upstairs doing some work with Daisy."

"Where's Charlene?"

"She and James went to the Elizabethan Gardens in Manteo."

"Is Daisy okay with that?"

"Why wouldn't she be? Historical gardens are one of James's specialties, and maps are hers. Back to the subject at hand. You wouldn't want to live in the library apartment, Connor. You couldn't get in and out of the building without people wanting to stop you and tell you about a pothole in their street or that time garbage collection was late."

He rubbed at the stubble on his jaw. "You're probably right about that."

"Of course I'm right. I always am. I'll be upstairs if you need me, Lucy," she said.

"Why would I—?" But Louise Jane was gone.

Once she'd left, Connor shook his head. Then he blew me a kiss and left.

*　*　*

The library board meeting ended and the members took their leave, clutching the budget papers and chatting excitedly among themselves. A few minutes later Louise Jane and Charlene came down the stairs together and slipped into the hallway heading to Bertie's office. Both of them so pointedly didn't look in my direction that my suspicions were instantly raised. What could Louise Jane and Charlene have to talk to Bertie about? And why was I not included in this talk? My suspicions only grew when they stayed in the office for a long time. Eventually the two of them emerged. Charlene went upstairs, and Louise Jane left the library at a rapid pace, head down, again avoiding glancing in my direction.

A couple of minutes later, Bertie came out of her office, purse over her shoulder, keys in her hand. "Have a nice weekend," she called to me.

"Bertie, is something—?" But I was talking to a closing door.

Oh well. Something was up, and I'd find out what it was sooner or later. I announced closing time and checked out the last of the books. Ronald and Charlene left together, and I locked up after them.

Aside from wondering what Charlene and Louise Jane were up to, I'd spent a good part of the afternoon thinking about Gordon Frankland. I wasn't as confident as Connor that the blasted man wouldn't try to sue me for slander; all he wanted was to cause trouble and distress, and he wouldn't care if the case was thrown out. If he'd killed Rich Lewiston, I wouldn't think he'd want to draw attention to himself by engaging in a spree of legal activity, but maybe he thought he was clever enough to pull off a double play. Be so obviously in the face of the law the police would look straight through him when searching for the killer.

Before going upstairs to dress for my evening out with my girlfriends, I called Sam Watson. It was after six o'clock on a Friday in summer, but he answered. I guess, when he's in the middle of a murder investigation, Detective Watson doesn't worry about getting a start on his weekend. I told him briefly what happened earlier.

"Frankland's a pest," Watson said. "But it doesn't sound like you have anything to worry about, Lucy. You didn't openly accuse him."

"I'm not worried," I said. "Much. But I did have a thought. The word everyone uses for Gordon Frankland is *pest*. You just did. Is it possible he's more than a pest?"

"Anything's possible, Lucy. I understand what you're saying, but I have no reason to think he was responsible for

Lewiston's death. He doesn't have an alibi for the time, but that means little. The hostess at Jake's saw him leave. She remembers because he complained about his steak. Said it was overdone."

"Yeah, that sounds like him."

"Right. The hostess didn't see where he went once he was outside. He says he went straight home, but as he lives alone and regularly parks his car inside his garage with the door shut, no one can verify that. You'll be interested to know he's threatening to sue the NHPD for harassment because an officer parked outside his house, in full view of the neighbors, and questioned him aggressively, according to Mr. Frankland."

"Pest," I said.

Watson chuckled. "While you're on the phone, Lucy. Significant parts of this investigation are being taken over by the Boston police. I'm telling you this because your father's aware of it."

"Boston police? Why?"

"Further digging has discovered that Mr. Lewiston had some associates that are, shall we say, known to the Boston authorities. He owed money to the sort of people you don't want to owe money to."

"You said earlier he was in debt only to banks and credit agencies and the like."

"It would appear Rich Lewiston's financial problems went deeper than first appeared. Your father's ordered a full internal investigation into his partner's clients to see if he undermined the reputation of the firm in any way. It's possible Rich angered people he shouldn't have."

"You mean it might have been a mob hit?"

"Boston thinks the origins of the man's murder are more likely to be found in that city than in Nags Head. This is not, Lucy, an entirely new case on their files."

Meaning they'd been watching Rich. Probably waiting for him to lead them to higher-ups in organized crime or do something to incriminate himself.

"I plan to release Mr. Lewiston's body on Monday and allow his wife and son to take him home, provided nothing new comes up on the weekend."

"Thanks for talking to me," I said.

He chuckled. "Take care of yourself, Lucy."

In a way, I was relieved. If this case belonged to Boston, then it had nothing to do with me or people I cared about. I was glad to be able to take off my sleuthing hat. Not that anyone ever asked me to put it on, or even that I wanted to. But that's what seems to happen all too often.

If it turned out that the roots of the case lay back in Boston, well and good. But I couldn't forget that Rich Lewiston's presence in Nags Head was still unexplained. He had to have had a reason for coming all this way, unexpectedly and unannounced. If that reason was directly related to his murder, then I couldn't turn my back and say it was none of my business. Not if it involved people I was close to. I'd keep trying to do what I could do to help sort all this out.

If the case did lead back to Richardson Lewiston and Rich's law practice, what effect might that have on Ricky? I had no idea how intertwined Rich and Ricky were in the firm's cases and client base. Maybe Ricky had turned a blind eye to whatever his father had been up to. And what of my father? Even if Rich had been acting on his own initiative and keeping any illegal or unethical activities from the rest of the partners, surely that had the potential to destroy the reputation of Richardson Lewiston.

I don't know anything about the law or the running of a law firm. My dad had never tried to interest me in following in his footsteps and potentially joining the firm, but I do know that for a major corporate law office, reputation is everything.

Regardless of what had happened to Rich or was happening to the case, Mom would be glad to be able to go home on Monday. I gave her a quick call to check in. "Hi, Mom. Just calling to see if there are any developments at your end." I could tell by the buzz of noise in the background she was in a restaurant or bar.

"Nothing I know of, dear," she said.

"Where are you?"

"At the Ocean Side for"—she lowered her voice—"yet another round of drinks with Evangeline and her entourage. This is all getting terribly tedious, Lucy. Evangeline's bored and restless and wanting people to entertain her."

A bark of female laughter echoed in the background.

"It's Lucy," Mom said. "I'll be right back. No, nothing more for me. Thank you." The voices and laughter faded as Mom walked away. "There, now I can talk easier."

"Is Evangeline okay?"

"No, she's not okay. Brittle is the word I'd use. Laughing too loud, drinking too much. She needs to go home with her son so they can grieve together, not be pretending to be the life of the party." She sighed. "Maybe I'm being too harsh. Easy for me to say."

"We all deal with grief in our own way."

"That we do. I suspect there's a substantial amount of guilt mixed in with Evangeline's grief. Probably on Ricky's part too."

"Meaning?"

"Meaning, one part of her is glad her husband is dead and she can get on with her life. The other part of her feels guilty about that. They were married for many years. As for Ricky, he and his father were never close."

"By get on with her life, you mean with Leon Lions."

"Not necessarily him. He's doting on her, but she's not responding in any way I'd consider to be beyond the normal bounds of a rekindled, casual friendship. Although she is enjoying making a fuss about leaning on his manly support." Mom snorted. "The police came by earlier with another round of questions for her and Ricky."

"What sort of questions?"

"I don't know. I wasn't here. Things to do with the law practice. Evangeline claims not to know anything about that. I don't necessarily believe her. She always seemed to know a great deal about the goings-on at Richardson Lewiston."

I had a flashback to that night at Jake's. Gordon Frankland approaching our table. Ricky getting to his feet, recognizing the man immediately. Evangeline recognizing him also, judging by the expression on her face. If he'd been nothing but a regular client of the firm, there was no reason she would have known him.

"Your friend the detective spent quite a lot of time with her," Mom went on. "Leon was upset about it. He says he should have been allowed to sit in on the interview to give the 'grieving widow,' in his words, moral support. The police didn't see it that way. She had Stephen, acting as her lawyer, with her to safeguard her rights. Ricky's talking about booking a flight home tomorrow. He says if the police are interested in the business of the firm, he needs to be there."

"About that. Don't tell the others yet—things might change, but if they don't, Watson's going to release Rich's body on Monday."

"Why do you know that and the man's family does not?"

"I called him to talk a few things over and he told me. You might want to go home too, Mom. The police are turning their attention to Richardson Lewiston, and whatever happens, it's unlikely to be pretty."

"That I am not happy to hear. I've been trying to convince your father that it's time for him to let go of some of the workload, to edge himself into retirement the way Amos is doing. This brief holiday was supposed to be the start of that. Instead, he's now working harder than ever, worried the firm's about to crumble around him. Thanks for calling, dear. Are you and Connor doing something fun tonight?"

"Not tonight. I'm meeting Josie and her friends for a girls' night."

"Sounds lovely. I'm going to make my excuses now. You've given me an idea. I'll tell Evangeline and her entourage that I need to spend some quality time with my sister. Good night, dear."

" 'Night, Mom." I hung up and then went upstairs to get ready for a night out with my friends.

Chapter Seventeen

And a fun night it was. We had dinner at a casual place in town, where I complained at great length about our house-hunting experience. My friends told me about all the people they knew who also couldn't find a suitable place at a reasonable price.

After dinner, Grace suggested a drink at the Ocean Side Hotel, and I might have shouted, "No!" a bit too forcefully.

When the laughter died down, we decided to head for the bar at Jake's. On the way to our cars, Grace said, "You might be interested to know, Lucy, that your friend Ricky asked me out."

"Ooh, do tell." Josie wiggled her eyebrows. "When was this?"

"Last night, as book club was breaking up. He suggested dinner tonight. Fortunately, I had a standing date with you guys as my convenient excuse."

"You don't need an excuse on my account," I said. "If you want to go out with him, that's okay with me."

"I do not want to," Grace said. "And not just because the picture you've painted of him in the past is so unappealing—"

Josie and Steph laughed.

"He's here because his dad died," Grace continued. "He should be dealing with that and supporting his mother, not trying to pick up women."

"Ricky can walk and chew gum at the same time," I said.

"Not with me," Grace said firmly.

We didn't stay at Jake's for long, as both Josie and I had to work in the morning. Josie had picked me up at the lighthouse earlier, and we exchanged hugs in the parking lot with the others before everyone headed off on their separate ways.

"That was fun," Josie said as we drove out of town.

"Always is," I said. "Even the closest of friends often drift apart and start to lose touch when they get married, but I'm glad that hasn't happened with you, and I hope it doesn't happen to me."

"It won't if we don't let it," she said.

It was reasonably early, but night had fallen and traffic was light heading out of town. A single car pulled out of Jake's parking lot after us and followed us through Whalebone Junction and down Highway 12. Darkness settled around us as the bright lights of Nags Head fell behind. In the distance, the lighthouse lamp flashed its rhythm, as it would throughout the night.

I leaned back in my seat and closed my eyes. "I'm going to miss living at the lighthouse. I love it there, but it's time for me to move on."

"Have you and Connor done much planning for your wedding?"

"I've scarcely had time to give it a thought. It's been so hectic with Mom here and all that stuff around the death of Rich. At least that's over and they'll be going home on Monday. I hope."

"Over? You mean they've arrested someone?"

I filled Josie in on what Watson had told me, that the police were investigating Rich's business affairs. I didn't add that I was still concerned about the Nags Head connection. "Once Connor and I find a place to live, we can concentrate on planning the wedding."

"The perfect house will appear, Lucy. Don't give up hope."

"I'm not," I said, speaking as much to myself as to my cousin.

Josie flicked on her turn indicator, slowed, and turned into the lighthouse drive. The car behind us sped past, its headlights illuminating the long, quiet road ahead.

I jumped out of the car, waved good-night to Josie, and trotted up the path. I turned to watch the red lights of her car fading in the distance, and then I let myself into the lighthouse to be greeted by Charles. It had been a long day, and I was bushed.

I let out a groan when I remembered that I had to walk the dog. I really, really didn't feel like it. Maybe tonight I'd forgo the walk and let Fluffy sniff around the bushes for a couple of minutes. That should last her until morning.

I unlocked the door to the Lighthouse Aerie, and Charles ran in ahead of me. Fluffy gave us a woof of greeting and leapt off the window seat. I threw my phone and my purse onto the bed and kicked off my shoes. "Let's make this a quick one," I said to Fluffy.

My phone buzzed with a text. It often didn't work inside the stone walls of the lighthouse, but whatever energy propels phone signals must have been strong tonight. I crossed the room and picked the phone up. I didn't recognize the number, but the words that flashed on the screen got my attention.

It's me. Josie. My phone's out of juice. Car broken down half way to town. Borrowed phone from a guy but he's heading other way. Help!

I replied immediately: *On my way.*

I thanked the god of phone signals that I did have reception here tonight. I didn't stop to wonder why Josie hadn't called the landline. She knows how erratic cell phones can be in here. In my panic and rush, I also didn't consider why she'd call me rather than her husband. If she was halfway to town, Jake's restaurant was not much further away than the lighthouse.

I swept up my purse, stuffed my feet into a pair of flip-flops, and ran into the hallway, heading for the stairs. Charles and Fluffy followed me. I hesitated. Charles couldn't come, and Fluffy would slow me down. I grabbed the cat, called to the dog, shoved them both into the apartment, slammed the door on them, and then I hurried down the stairs. I remembered to lock the door behind me and ran for my car. I jumped in, started it up, and sped down the laneway. I didn't like the idea of Josie stranded at night on the side of the highway outside of town. Some man had stopped and offered her his phone. It sounded as though she was being suitably careful, as she should be, and hadn't stepped out of the car. She'd probably rolled her window down an inch or two, just enough to accept his phone. I turned onto the highway. She'd said she was halfway back to town. That didn't necessarily mean she was at the five-mile point; she could be anywhere along the road. Traffic was light, and not more than one or two cars passed me heading in the other direction. No one was ahead of or behind me. Thick clouds covered the moon, and outside the beam cast by the lights of my car, all was pitch-dark. My headlights picked up flakes of sand scurrying across the pavement, and I kept my eyes peeled for deer; I'd once almost hit a deer at night on this stretch of road. I saw nothing but drifting sand and scruffy grasses moving in the wind.

I drove slowly, alert for the sight of a car ahead of me, pulled off to the side, its red rear lights facing my way, white headlights shining into the night. Maybe the car belonging to the phone owner would be parked protectively next to it.

Nothing. I reached Old Oregon Inlet Road and the traffic picked up slightly, people heading home after a Friday night out. Lights from the rows of houses lining the seafront appeared, but they were far from the highway. Soon I was well past what anyone would call "halfway to town." Could I possibly have missed her?

I hadn't spotted anyone stopped at the side of the road when the red and green traffic lights of Whalebone Junction appeared in the distance. I passed through the intersection and pulled off to the side of the road. I sent a text to the number she'd used: *Where are you?*

No reply.

Maybe the phone owner had left her. Left a young woman alone in a broken-down car on the side of an empty highway at night? Not a nice thing to do.

I made a right at the intersection, turned around in a restaurant parking lot, and headed back the way I'd come, going even slower than I had earlier. Apart from a couple of impatient cars who sped past me, I saw nothing and no one.

By the time I reached the lighthouse lane, I was seriously worried. I turned around once again and stopped the car. I had to call Jake.

If Josie was okay, she'd be angry at me for worrying Jake, but right now I didn't care. Something was not right.

"Hey, Lucy," he said. "It's late for you to be calling. What's up?"

His voice was so natural, so cheerful, I knew his wife hadn't called him for help, but I asked anyway. "Jake, I . . . Have you heard from Josie in the last twenty minutes or so?"

"Yeah. She called about ten minutes ago to say she was home and going to bed. Our schedules are so opposite, that's the way we usually exchange good-night kisses. Why do you ask?"

"She told you she was home?"

"Yeah. Lucy, what's wrong? Has something happened?" Panic began to creep into his voice.

"I don't know, Jake. You don't have a landline in the apartment, do you?"

"No. Almost no one I know has a landline anymore, except you."

"She called you on her cell?"

"Lucy. Tell me what's wrong."

"I don't know. I got a text about twenty minutes ago, supposedly from Josie but not her number. Saying she'd broken down on the side of the road and asking me to come and get her. I drove up and down the highway, but she's not there."

"She's not there because she's at home. Where are you now?"

"I'm parked on the lighthouse lane, just off the highway."

"I'm coming for you."

"No need; I'm sure everything's okay. It was a stupid prank."

"Not a funny one. Don't get out of your car, and don't stay where you are." He spoke quickly, issuing orders the way he did in his kitchen on a busy summer's night. "Get on the

214

highway and drive to Old Oregon Inlet Road; at least there's some traffic there. Wait for me, keep your headlights on, and do not get out of your car. I'll be there as soon as I can. I'm hanging up. I want to call Josie to check she really is at home and if she has any idea what's going on. I'll call you back when that's done."

He hung up, and I suddenly felt very alone. I sat in my car, in a small circle of light, surrounded by the dark night. When the lighthouse light flashed, the light I'd always found so reassuring and comforting, I realized how far away it was.

Until now, I hadn't thought to be afraid. I'd been worried for Josie, then annoyed at whoever was playing a joke on me. Now I was truly frightened.

I glanced around me, trying to see into the night. But all was dark. Dark and quiet. So quiet.

I threw the car into gear and sped down the laneway. I probably took the turn onto the highway on two wheels, and I made it to the intersection at South Old Oregon Inlet Road in record time. My phone rang, and I answered it using Bluetooth as I made the turn and pulled off to the side of the road to wait. "I'm here."

"Josie's home, safe and sound and wondering why I felt the need to check on her," Jake said.

"I tried texting her back, but no one replied. Should I call the number?"

"No. Don't do anything until we get there."

"We?"

"Of course *we*, Lucy. Don't hang up. Stay on the line."

An approaching vehicle slowed and turned onto the road. My heart stopped. The car sped up and continued on its way. My heart started again.

That happened a couple more times before Jake said, "I think I see you. Flash your lights."

I flashed them. Jake's car pulled up next to me, and he leapt out. I undid my seat belt and opened my door. My hands were shaking, and I wondered if my legs would hold me up. Jake grabbed my arm and helped me out of the car.

A police cruiser came tearing down the highway, siren screaming, red and blue lights breaking the deep night, and pulled in next to us.

"You shouldn't have called the police," I said. "I'm fine."

"I didn't call the police. I called my brother," Jake said as Butch got out of the cruiser.

"You okay, Lucy?" he asked me.

"I'm fine. I'm sure it was nothing." I tried to smile at the men who'd rushed to my aid. I feared it came out as more of a grimace.

Another car screeched to a halt beside us.

"You shouldn't have called Connor," I said to Jake.

"Of course I called Connor," Jake said.

Connor jumped out of his car without shutting off the engine. He reached me in three strides and wrapped me in his arms so tightly I was afraid I might suffocate. I made no move to pull myself free. It felt rather nice to be held. The dangers of the night silently receded.

"Thanks, guys," Connor said, over the top of my head.

"Anytime," Jake replied.

Connor finally let me go. He bent over and peered into my face. I reached up and touched his cheek. He grabbed my hand and pressed it to his lips.

Jake and Butch shifted their feet.

"Can you tell us what happened, Lucy?" Butch said at last. "Everything you can remember. Jake said someone lured you away from the lighthouse?"

"*Lured* is a strong word," I said.

"Strong is what's needed," Connor said.

I told them the story. It didn't take long. "Can you show me the text?" Butch asked.

I did so.

The three men leaned in and read the message. Butch pulled out his own phone and called the number. A tinny voice answered immediately.

"Either switched off or out of service," he said. "I'll get this checked out."

"If you don't need me any longer," Jake said, "I should get back. I left a twenty-dollar steak on the grill and a mess of crab legs in a pot."

I turned to him. "Thank you."

His warm hazel eyes smiled back at me, but lines of worry hadn't disappeared from the corners of his mouth. My cousin's husband is a good-looking man. He's slightly shorter and thinner than his brother, but otherwise the resemblance between them is strong.

"Let's go," Butch said. "I want to check out the lighthouse."

"I'm coming with you," Connor said.

"Why?" I asked.

"Maybe this was a practical joke and someone's hiding behind a sand dune giggling into his palm even as we speak," Butch said, "but I don't think so. Your Honor, you take the lead; Lucy, you drive in the middle, and I'll follow."

"Call me if you need anything," Jake said.

"Any sign of trouble," Butch said to Connor, "you and Lucy get the heck out of there and leave it to me."

"Will do." Connor held the door of my car for me and waved me in.

Jake went first, turning right toward town with a farewell blast of his horn; then Connor followed, turning left. I pulled in behind him, and Butch came after me. He drove close to my rear bumper, but he'd turned the cruiser's lights and sirens off.

I felt quite calm. Calm and safe and protected. And loved. I had no idea what had happened and whether or not someone wanted to only frighten me or if they intended to do me harm. Shock would settle in soon, but right now I was feeling surprisingly calm.

I didn't think this person—whoever it was—meant me physical harm. I'd been alone when I ran out of the lighthouse in answer to Josie's call, not paying attention to my surroundings. I'd driven up and down the dark highway, going slowly. It would have been easy to grab me before I got into my car or to force me off the road. I'd parked at the side of the lighthouse lane for a few minutes while I called Jake.

What, then, had been their intent?

We found out soon enough.

Butch told Connor and me to stay in our cars while he checked out the area around the lighthouse. Connor disobeyed that order immediately and got into the passenger seat of my car. We sat as close together as we could in my small Yaris, clutching hands as we watched Butch—powerful flashlight in one hand, the other on the butt of his gun—studying the grounds and the exterior of the building. I swallowed when he disappeared around the side of the lighthouse, and Connor gripped his phone in his free hand. I noticed he'd already punched in a nine and a one. Butch soon reappeared. He waved to us, and Connor and I got out of the car.

Butch met us at the bottom of the steps. "I've called for backup and asked them to notify Detective Watson. Someone left you a message, Lucy."

He turned his light to shine directly on the door. A piece of plain computer paper had been fastened there with a nail. The typing was neat, in Times New Roman 12, too small for me to read from where I stood.

Butch nodded, and Connor and I climbed the steps. We peered at the note but didn't touch it.

Stay out of what doesn't concern you. Or next time your cousin will be in trouble. Maybe even you.

Chapter Eighteen

Southerners love their sweet tea, but there's nothing like a hot, steaming cup of strong, fragrant tea for calming one's nerves. And my nerves needed calming.

I gripped my mug tightly. Charles stretched out on the couch next to me, and Fluffy snoozed on the carpet under the coffee table.

"Top you up?" Connor asked.

I held out my mug. "Yes, please."

He filled it and then sat at the other end of the couch. I stretched out my legs and put them into his lap, and he stroked my bare toes. "I don't like being threatened," I said.

"I don't like you being threatened. Sure you don't want me to call your mom?"

"Positive. Let me think this through and decide what to say. I'll talk to her in the morning."

Sam Watson had arrived at the lighthouse in record time in answer to Butch's call. The front door showed no signs of being tampered with, but I'd been guarded by a phalanx of police officers, not to mention the mayor of Nags Head, while I'd gone upstairs to collect Charles, Fluffy, and my toothbrush and pajamas. I'd had time, as I was hustled through the library, to notice that nothing seemed out of place.

Holly Rankin had been dispatched to follow Connor and me into town and make sure we reached Connor's house safely. In other words, the police were taking this evening's happenings very seriously indeed.

"Before we start speculating," Connor said, "you don't think it was Louise Jane trying to scare you out of your apartment?"

"Absolutely not. Louise Jane can be irritating at times and as annoying as all heck, but she's not mean."

"Agreed. Who, then?"

"Who indeed." I leaned against the arm cushions of the sofa, my feet resting in Connor's lap. "I know one thing."

"What?"

"The murder of Rich Lewiston isn't a Boston matter, and it had absolutely nothing to do with organized crime."

"Did you think it did?"

"The police were considering the idea. Sam told me the police in Boston are looking into an organized-crime angle. It would appear that Rich wasn't always operating on the right side of the law, and he might have been in debt to underworld forces. We can disregard that line of inquiry now. No one from the mob is going to make such a halfhearted attempt to frighten a Nags Head librarian."

"Don't discount yourself, Lucy. Maybe rumors of your detecting prowess have expanded beyond the confines of the Outer Banks."

I snorted and stroked Charles's ears. "You know as well as I do that I have no detecting prowess. I have a lot of dumb luck."

"I wouldn't put it that way, but never mind. I don't suppose you've been frightened off."

I lifted Charles off me and swung my legs to the floor. Fluffy awoke with a start and barked. I stood up and went for my purse. I rummaged around inside, finding a pen and a copy of the Lighthouse Aerie rental agreement I'd been consulting when I decided to think about moving. I resumed my seat. "Let's make a list of all the possible suspects. I've found that helps to clear the mind."

"Dumb luck, right," Connor muttered. "If we must. First things first. Whoever tried to scare you off—if we assume that was their attempt and not just a childish prank—doesn't know you very well."

I drew three columns on the back of the rental contract. "Why do you say that?"

"Anyone who knows you knows you can't be frightened off."

I smiled at him.

"And, as someone who knows you well and loves you beyond measure, I wish you could be frightened off. Leave it to the police, Lucy."

"I will. This is only a mental exercise. I'll tell Sam anything we come up with. Who do we have?" I started writing names in the left-hand column. "Evangeline. Ricky. Gordon Frankland. Leon Lions."

"Gordon Frankland," Connor said.

I looked up. "Why do you say that?"

"Because I want it to be him. Get him out of my hair."

"It doesn't work that way. Wouldn't it be nice if it did?" I hesitated, pen poised. "Not much of a list. One thing I do know is that it can't be someone who spends much time at the library. It was nothing but another instance of dumb luck that I even got the original text message tonight. Anyone who knows how

222

things work in the lighthouse knows not to text me or call me on my cell phone if they need me. They call the landline."

"Doesn't help much." Connor pointed to the list. "None of those people are regulars at the library."

"And thank heavens for that."

"Then we have person or persons unknown," Connor said.

"Evangeline," I said.

"You think she killed her husband?"

"I think something's up with her. I can't forget how strongly she reacted when she saw James Dalrymple at the library. I wonder if James should be on the list. Although he knows cell phone coverage isn't reliable in the building."

"You're clutching at straws, Lucy. Maybe James simply reminded Evangeline of someone."

"I suppose. I also suppose I am clutching at straws. We know why Rich was at Jake's that night: because someone sent him a note asking him to meet them there. But we have to wonder why he was in the Outer Banks at all. He left Boston and drove down without telling anyone."

"Anyone we know of. The person who sent him the note knew."

"Yes, our mysterious sender of notes. The person who lured Rich to Jake's with a computer-printed note has to be the same person who left that warning on the door for me. Who writes out notes anymore these days? He—or she—could have sent me a threatening text. He or she obviously has my number."

"Far more dramatic this way. A warning nailed to your front door. But that brings up a question." He gestured to the list. "Who among these people has your number?"

I thought about that. "Hard to say. Mom obviously does, and she could have given it to someone. Ricky does. I'm still on the same phone plan I had in Boston. If Ricky has it, then Evangeline might. And Evangeline might have given it to anyone at all. Anyone except Gordon Frankland. That probably destroys your hope that it's him."

"Not necessarily. I'm sure he has ways of finding things out." Connor rubbed the thumb and index finger of his right hand together in the universal signal for a payoff.

"The note asked Rich to meet the sender at Jake's, but as for why Rich was in Nags Head in the first place . . . Ricky said his dad came to OBX about once every year. Supposedly to go fishing with clients. I wonder . . ."

"If that's true?"

"If he was fishing with clients, he didn't bring any of his partners or associates with him. He didn't even bring his son. I suppose I could ask every charter fishing outfit in a hundred-mile radius if they've ever been hired by Rich Lewiston, but that would take a heck of a lot more resources than I have."

"Seeing as how you're a librarian simply engaged in a mental exercise."

"That reminds me. Evangeline's been to the Outer Banks several times over the years, although she denied it at first. I wonder if she followed Rich here. Was she checking up on him?"

"If you want to know the answer to that, Lucy, you're going to have to come straight out and ask her."

I pulled out my phone. Connor plucked it out of my hand. "It's two AM, Lucy. Not a good time to be calling anyone."

I squinted at the time on the display. "Oh. So it is. I suppose it can wait until tomorrow."

"I'd rather you didn't pursue this at all, but there's no stopping you sometimes."

"Don't you want to get at the truth?"

"Of course I do. But not if it puts you in danger." He stroked my feet.

I wiggled my toes in pleasure. "If someone meant to do me harm tonight, Connor, they would have." I wasn't feeling quite as brave as I was trying to make it sound, but the questions were in my head, and even if I wanted to, I couldn't get rid of them.

The questions were in Connor's head too. "Maybe Evangeline came to see this Leon Lions?"

"It's possible, but her attitude toward him doesn't suggest they've been conducting an illicit affair. Not currently, anyway. Clearly, he adores her, but equally clearly, the feelings are not returned. I mean, she seems to enjoy his company, but I don't sense any grand passion. Then again, Evangeline isn't the most demonstrative of women." I yawned.

Beside me, Charles yawned. Fluffy rolled over and yawned. Connor stood up. He held out his hand to me. "Let's go to bed. Maybe some of this will be clearer in the morning."

*   *   *

It wasn't.

As soon as I woke, I checked my phone for messages. Sam Watson had texted to tell me they'd found nothing out of the ordinary inside the library or upstairs; I could go home whenever I wanted, and the library could open for the day.

I smelled coffee and padded into the kitchen to find Connor dressed for the office and making breakfast. He turned with a smile when he heard my footsteps and crossed the room to give me a kiss on the top of my head. He smelled of good soap, and his hair was damp from the shower. "You slept well. I was worried you wouldn't."

"If you know that, then you didn't sleep well."

"No." He reached for the coffeemaker and poured me a cup. Charles and Fluffy watched us from the floor. "I've been up for a long time. I couldn't stop thinking about your list."

"Oh yes, the list."

Connor went to the fridge and got out eggs, butter, cheese, and a fresh loaf of wheat bread from Josie's bakery. Fluffy and Charles sat to attention when the fridge door opened. I leaned against the counter and sipped my coffee and watched him work. Nothing nicer than watching a man cook you breakfast.

"I should take the dog out," I said.

"I put her out for a quick moment, but she'll need a walk." Connor dropped a spoonful of butter into a frying pan, cracked eggs into a bowl, and added a splash of milk. While the butter heated, he grated cheese and sliced a green onion. "I haven't fed her, though. Her or Charles. I didn't know how much to give them."

I took care of that while Connor cooked the eggs and made the toast.

I ate my eggs and smiled at him across the table. "I think I'm going to like being married to you, Connor McNeil. Are you going to make me breakfast every morning?"

"No. I expect you to wait on me hand and foot like a devoted wife should."

I laughed. "You keep on expecting that."

Charles leapt onto the table in front of Connor and hissed. Connor jerked back and lifted his hands in protection. "Whoa there. I didn't mean it."

"Do you want Charles to come and live with us?" I asked.

Connor eyed the big cat. "Do you want to come and live with us, buddy?"

Charles turned his head and looked at me.

"If you do," Connor said, "you can't be jumping onto the table."

Charles leapt down.

Connor and I stared at him.

"I think he answered you," I said at last.

"I think he did."

Charles washed his whiskers.

* * *

The police had left no evidence of their presence at the library last night, and I was glad of it. I didn't want to be pestered with questions as to what was going on.

As Connor had noticed, I'd slept well. Which wasn't what I would have expected would happen. Someone had threatened me, warned me to back off. I didn't like that, and I had to ask myself why they'd done so. I wasn't doing much active investigating in this case, such as going around to people's houses or confronting them with hard-hitting questions about where they'd been at certain times. I simply knew most of the people involved, and we talked about the death of Rich Lewiston and considered possible motives when we were together. Wasn't that a natural thing to do? I'd asked questions some might consider nosy, and I'd talked about the case with the police. Did Rich's killer think I knew more than I did?

As a regular Saturday morning at the library swirled around me, I thought about all that had happened over the past few days, trying to remember what I'd said to whom when. I'd told James Dalrymple I was good at finding things out. Had that been a mistake? I'd been warning him to be careful around Charlene, but had he thought I'd meant something else?

I'd have had no reason at all to think that James, a visiting professor from England here to do academic research, had anything to do with the death of a Boston lawyer if not for Evangeline's reaction to seeing him. He hadn't reacted to her in return, but maybe he was better at concealing his feelings than she was. Or maybe he'd expected to run into her at some point in time and had prepared himself for when it happened.

It was time for me to talk to Charlene. Enough of doors slamming in faces and surreptitious meetings anyone else would call dates. Charlene and I were friends, and if she was falling for James, and if James was mixed up in any way in the killing of Rich Lewiston, Charlene had to be told.

Before I could do anything about that, Louise Jane came into the library, a bounce in her step and a huge smile on her face. "I have fabulous news, Lucy," she declared.

I didn't say, *You're running away to sea?*—but I thought it. Charles left his post on the wingback chair near the magazine rack and climbed onto my desk to hear this fabulous news.

"What?" I said.

"Are you always so suspicious, Lucy? It does you no credit."

"I'm not in the mood for guessing games this morning, Louise Jane."

"You will be when I tell you." She stood in front of the desk, beaming at me.

"Mrs. Covington," I called to a passing patron. "How nice to see you this morning."

"And you as well, Lucy. How are the wedding plans going?"

"Slow but steady," I said. "We're thinking of late next year, once hurricane season has passed, or maybe the following spring."

"I was hoping you wouldn't go to Boston for the wedding. You're an Outer Banks girl now."

Louise Jane cleared her throat.

"I'm sorry," Mrs. Covington said, glancing between us. "Am I interrupting anything?"

"No," I said.

"Yes," Louise Jane said.

Mrs. Covington slipped away, leaving me no one to chat to. Except for Louise Jane, who let out a heavy sigh. "Really, Lucy."

"I can't talk about my upcoming wedding with patrons and friends?"

She couldn't restrain herself any longer and blurted out, "I've found you a house."

I hadn't been expecting that. "You've what?"

"I've found you and Connor a house to buy. You said you don't mind a fixer-upper if it's at a reasonable price. Well, it's at a reasonable price, and it's in Nags Head. Awful good location, right on the beach. A nail here, a screw there, and it'll be as good as new."

"Louise Jane, Connor and I can't afford a collapsing garden shed on the beach in Nags Head."

"You can afford this one. When do you want to come and see it? This afternoon would be good."

"You're not kidding, are you? This isn't a practical joke?"

"When have you ever known me to joke?"

"Never," I admitted.

"Call me when you've spoken to Connor, and I'll take you around to see the house. It needs to be in daytime, though; the atmosphere at night isn't . . . conducive to a proper inspection."

"Uh. Okay."

She turned and had started to walk away when I remembered what I'd been thinking about. "Louise Jane, one thing. Did you and Daisy go into the marsh last night?"

"No. We had dinner and then went to a movie in town. I like Daisy a lot. I'm going to miss her when they go back to England."

"Just you and Daisy went to this movie?"

Her eyes narrowed. "Why are you asking?"

"No reason."

"Of course there's a reason, Lucy. You never cared before about my social arrangements."

"Sure I have." I smiled at her.

"Whatever. Yes, just Daisy and I went to the movie. James was doing something with Charlene. I don't know what. Don't forget to call Connor, now."

"I won't."

Louise Jane headed for the bookshelves, and I leaned back in my chair and thought about what she'd said. James hadn't been with his wife yesterday evening. Did that mean he'd been sending texts to me and nailing warnings to the library door? Not necessarily, but it was time to find out what was going on. James had been spending a lot of his time in the library, working in the rare-books room—easy enough for him to find my phone number. I picked up the desk phone, but before I could make the call, Daisy and James arrived.

"Hi." The rows of bangles on Daisy's arms tinkled cheerfully as she lifted a hand in greeting.

" 'Morning," James said.

I studied his face, searching for a sign of . . . what? Guilt? Disappointment to find me still here?

I saw nothing but polite disinterest.

"Have a nice evening?" I asked.

I'd been talking to James, but Daisy answered. "Great. Louise Jane and I went to the cinema."

"What about you, James?" I said nonchalantly. "What did you do?"

"Nothing special." He walked away.

Daisy called, "Cheerio!" clattered her bangles once more, and followed James up the back stairs to the rare-books-and-maps room. Louise Jane's arm popped out from the stacks, and she gave them a wave as they passed.

The next person through the doors was my aunt Ellen accompanied by one of her friends. "Good morning, Lucy," they called.

" 'Morning."

"We're here to help with Saturday activities," Aunt Ellen said. "The marsh walk the other day was such an enormous success, Ronald wants to carry what the children learned out there inside with activities to do with Eastern North Carolina wildlife."

"He's got the school-aged children keeping a diary of sightings," the other woman said. "We're going to help them with that today."

They headed for the stairs. *Curses.* Saturday is always the busiest day at the library. Ronald had children's programs all day, and that meant parents would be in too, needing help or wanting to chat, and the volunteers, such as Aunt Ellen, would be needed in the children's library. Bertie didn't usually come in on Saturdays, and she wasn't expected today.

Meaning, I was trapped here until closing time.

Maybe not. "Louise Jane!" I called.

Her head appeared around a shelf. "Yes?"

Louise Jane was a regular volunteer at the library. She knew her way around the place and how we did things. All I needed was someone to staff the circulation desk for an hour or two, and she'd done that before. Charlene and Ronald were in the building if anything came up.

I'd take an early lunch hour. In the past, Bertie had given me permission to take the time I needed when I was helping the police. I'd assume she'd do the same this time. It shouldn't matter that this case didn't directly involve the library community, should it?

Better, as they say, to ask forgiveness than seek permission.

"I'm taking my lunch break early, and I have to go into town," I said. "Do you mind watching the desk for an hour or so?"

"Not at all. I need to start getting more familiar with how things work around here anyway."

"Why?"

"No reason." Louise Jane gave me a wink. "No reason at all."

"Thanks. I guess. I'll call you in half an hour. If you don't hear from me, call Connor and tell him I decided not to take his advice."

Her eyebrows rose. "What does that mean?"

"He'll know." I checked my watch. "It's five to ten now. I'll call at ten thirty, and then every half hour until I get back." I set the timer on my phone to remind me.

Louise Jane's intense eyes studied my face. "Are you in some sort of trouble, Lucy?"

"No. It's another beautiful summer's day on the Outer Banks; what sort of trouble could I get myself into?"

* * *

I phoned Evangeline to let her know I was coming, and I found her and Leon Lions relaxing by the hotel pool. Not as calm as I'd been last night; my nerves were on edge, and I'd kept my eye on the traffic around me all the way into town. No one seemed to be following me. Would I have been able to tell if they were? Still, as I'd said to Louise Jane, it was daytime. I'd be sure to stay in public places, surrounded by people.

Josie'd called this morning when I was still at Connor's, wanting to make sure I was okay. Jake told her what happened, although either Butch hadn't told him about the note left on the door or he hadn't shared that with Josie, and I decided not to tell her that she'd been threatened as well as me.

The threat had been intended to scare me off investigating the death of Rich Lewiston. Instead, now, more than ever, I was determined to get to the bottom of things. Suppose they never found out who did it? The threat would hang over me for a long time.

Evangeline looked terribly glamorous relaxing in the sun beside the pool in a black one-piece bathing suit, huge sunglasses, long dangling earrings, and an enormous straw hat adorned with a black ribbon. Her dark hair was pinned up on top of her head, and a glass of orange juice rested on the table next to *Paris Is Always a Good Idea* by Jenn McKinlay. Leon did not look the least bit glamorous in orange-and-purple swim shorts collapsing under the weight of his big round white belly and a tow truck company's orange ball cap protecting his balding head from the sun. He also had an orange juice, and his choice of reading material was a political biography.

The juice, I couldn't help but notice, was extremely pale. Meaning it had been watered down with sparkling wine to make a mimosa.

"Good morning," I said cheerfully.

Evangeline lifted her sunglasses and peered at me. "What's this about, Lucy?"

"Where's Ricky?"

"I haven't seen him this morning. He and Stephen went out last night after dinner."

"Hungover, probably," Leon said. "Oh, to be young again."

"Can I speak to you, Evangeline?" I asked. "Privately, I mean."

"What about?"

"That's the private part."

Leon lumbered to his feet. "Don't mind me. I'll get us another round of drinks." He took his cap off, rubbed idly at his bald head, and dropped the hat onto the table next to him. "Lucy?"

"Nothing for me, thank you," I said.

He went into the main building, and I pulled over a chair. The area was busy with children splashing in the cool water of the pool and parents soaking up the hot sun, but no one was sitting near enough to overhear us. I kept my voice low. "Let's not waste time. Leon will soon be back. I'm going to ask you a question, Evangeline, and you're going to tell me it's none of my business, and I'm going to insist. Let's go directly to the answer part, shall we? Why did you lie to the police about never visiting Nags Head?"

She lowered her sunglasses and looked at me for a long time. "You've changed, Lucy."

"That falls under the none-of-my-business category, which we're not bothering about."

"I never knew you to be so forthright."

"I've always been forthright. Perhaps I hid it behind a veneer of polite disinterest. The difference between me and you and my mother and the rest of your social set is I don't disguise my forthrightness as gossip."

Rather than getting directly to the point, we were now discussing the habits of the Boston country club set. Not where I wanted this to go. "The cops know you lied. So I'm asking why."

Evangeline sighed. She put her sunglasses back on. "I've discussed this with your Detective Watson, so I suppose it's not a secret worth keeping any longer. My husband visited Nags Head every one or two years for more than thirty years, almost the entirely of our married life. He did not go fishing, and he did not meet with clients."

"I didn't think so."

"I didn't come every year to keep tabs on him, and I never came when he was here. I did, however, drop by on a few occasions to check as to how his visit had gone. The fact is, Lucy, Rich has a child who lives on the Outer Banks."

I wasn't expecting that. "Really?"

"A child conceived with and born to another woman after Rich and I were married. Rich never acted as a father to the child, and as far as I know the child, now an adult, never knew him as their father. The mother is still alive, and . . ." Her composure momentarily broke. She glanced away and swallowed deeply. Then she turned back to me. The sunglasses were large and dark and I couldn't see her eyes. "Rich kept yearly contact. He assured me they no longer had a . . . relationship, but as he was sending money for the child's support, he wanted to ensure it was being handled properly."

"Was that true?"

"Yes. I visited on occasion to make sure it was true. The affair was over, but Rich wanted to see his child occasionally. It was always done discreetly."

"James Dalrymple."

She pulled down her glasses and peered at me over the top. "Who?"

"James Dalrymple. I could tell that you knew him and you were surprised to see him in the library." James was the right age to be a son of Rich. He'd told me his mother lived in England. Maybe she came once a year to meet with her former lover. James had also told me he hadn't been back to America since he was a child. I pushed the conflicting accounts aside. I'd worry about all that later.

Evangeline shook her head. "I don't know anyone named Dalrymple, and Rich's illegitimate child is not named James. Your mother might think you're some sort of a private detective, Lucy, but if you are, you're not very good. Now, if you'll excuse me, I think that's enough true confessions for one day." Up the sunglasses went, and Evangeline picked up her book.

I struggled to recover my wits. "Okay, so I was wrong about that, but I wasn't wrong about you visiting the Outer Banks. What's the relationship between you and Leon?"

Down came the glasses. "Leon? I hope you're not about to accuse Leon of killing my husband. Leon and I were close years ago when he spent much of his time in Boston. We were very close. Do you understand what I mean by that, Lucy?"

"Yes." From deep inside my pocket, the timer on my phone rang. Time to check in with Louise Jane and let her know I was still alive. I didn't like the interruption, but I didn't want Connor and half the Nags Head Police out looking for me either.

"Sorry. I have to take this." I sent Louise Jane a text: *All okay here.*

This is weird.

I set the timer for another half an hour and turned my attention back to Evangeline.

"The matter is closed," she said. "Leon and I have not had personal contact for a long time, and before you ask, we did not get together when I was visiting the Outer Banks on that other matter. When he heard via mutual friends I was in Nags Head following the sudden death of my husband, he wanted to be of support to me, as old friends do. Once again, this is none of your business, but you are being very persistent. If I had wanted to leave Rich and marry Leon, I would have done so long ago. Leon is more than comfortable financially, and he's never been married."

"Careful there!"

Evangeline and I looked up as Leon yelled at a child running across the pool deck. Leon did a series of stumbling steps and almost dropped the two glasses he was carrying. The child cannonballed into the pool with a shout of triumph and a spray of water, and Leon kept his footing and his grip on the drinks. The flash of irritation on his face was replaced by a look of sheer joy when he realized we were watching. I should say when he realized Evangeline was watching. I highly doubt I had anything at all to do with his reaction. The bit of hair he had left on the top of his head fluttered in the wind, and his round face turned red with pleasure.

That round face. The thinning hair. The average height and the big round belly.

I sucked in a breath. "Leon's Ricky's father."

"Perhaps you're more observant than I've given you credit for," Evangeline said. "I trust you'll keep that to yourself."

"Does Ricky know?"

"No. He does not, and he will not. Do you understand me, Lucille?"

"He won't hear it from me. The resemblance isn't that strong. It was the way Leon looked when that kid almost tripped him. And the hair. Or lack thereof."

"Oh yes, the hair. Rich was always so proud of his thick hair. Fortunately, my father went bald early in life. Rich had no reason to ever wonder."

"Does Leon know?"

"We've never discussed it. He might suspect, but he doesn't know anything." She patted the table next to her and gave the man under discussion a huge smile. "Thank you, Leon. You're always such a dear."

He basked in the praise.

"So, Leon," I said. "What were you doing Monday night around nine?"

"Lucy!" Evangeline said.

Leon chuckled. "Oh yes. Your mother told us you like to play girl detective." He sat down and stretched out his legs. "Let me think. What was I doing? Oh yes. I was at my aunt's house for her eighty-fifth birthday party. She never married and never had children, and she and I are close. I arrived at six to help with the setup. The last of the guests left at eleven, and I waved them good-bye. I spent the night at Aunt Joan's and came home the following morning after a late breakfast. Before you ask, my aunt lives in Elizabeth City, so I did not slip out between serving rounds of cake and canapés and drive to Nags Head to kill a man I'd never met."

"Just asking."

"The police asked the same. I've since had calls from Aunt Joan and my brother asking why I need an alibi."

"Satisfied, Lucy?" Evangeline asked.

"Yes. Thank you. But I am wondering about one more thing . . ."

She leaned back in her chair with a sigh. "Go ahead."

"You and Gordon Frankland recognized each other at Jake's on Monday night. It was obvious you didn't care for the man. How do you know him?"

"Odious man," Evangeline said. "I told the police they should be concentrating on him as the killer of my husband, but they were not interested in my suggestions. He was a client of Rich. He came around to the house one weekend, barged in uninvited and unwelcome, demanding to speak to Rich. I told him Rich did not conduct business at home. He was very rude, and so persistent Rich finally emerged from his study, and I went back to the garden. Mr. Frankland did not stay long, and I did not care enough to ask what he wanted. Now, I ask you again, are you satisfied, Lucy? This is all getting quite tedious."

I stood up. "Thank you."

"I will not be returning to Nags Head. Have a nice life." She picked up her book and started to read.

" 'Bye," Leon said.

I walked away, my tail tucked between my legs, but I didn't go back to my car. I reminded myself that sometimes people need to be eliminated as suspects before one can concentrate on finding the guilty party.

Rather than waiting for the elevator, I ran lightly up the stairs. I approached room 220. I lifted my hand to knock. Then I dropped it. Was I really going to accuse Ricky of killing the man he'd always believed was his own father?

I walked away.

Chapter Nineteen

I was in line at Josie's Cozy Bakery when the timer on my phone trilled once again. Once again I texted Louise Jane. Once again she replied, *This is so weird.* Once again I set the timer for another half hour. I ordered a latte and ham and Swiss on a baguette and found a table. All around me espresso machines hissed and people chatted and laughed and placed orders. I unwrapped my sandwich and bit into it. As long as I was on my lunch break, I might as well have lunch.

"What brings you here this early, sweetie?" I looked up to see my cousin standing over me.

I chewed and swallowed. "Having an early lunch. Do you have time to sit?"

Josie dropped into a chair. She waved to Alison behind the counter. "Bring me an Americano, will you, please." She pulled off her hairnet, untied her ponytail, combed her long blonde hair with her fingers, and retied it with a quick twist of her wrist. "I'm under orders not to leave the bakery unless I'm under guard."

"Jake told you what happened?"

"Yes, he did. You were lured out of the library, and my name was used to do so. We're all worried about you, and Jake is worried about me too. Why are you unguarded?"

"Because I didn't tell anyone I was leaving the library except Louise Jane, and I'm checking in with her regularly. Besides, what can happen in the middle of the day in the middle of town?" I swept my arms around me to take in the busy bakery and the crowded streets outside.

"That's what I said to Jake. He said he doesn't want to find out what can happen."

"Fair enough. Thing is, Josie, I have no intention of living that way, so I've stepped up my so-called investigating. I'm determined to get to the bottom of this. The best way to do that, I've decided, is to eliminate suspects one by one and see who I end up with."

"How's that going?"

"Not well," I admitted. "I'm eliminating suspects and being left with no one." I took another bite of my sandwich. "This is good."

"Did you doubt it would be?" Josie said.

I grinned. "Nope."

"Here you go." Blair put a mug in front of Josie. "Can I get you anything else?"

"No thanks."

He left, and I leaned forward and kept my voice down. Josie leaned toward me. "Neither Evangeline nor Ricky has an alibi, but no matter how much I try to imagine it, I simply can't believe either one of them killed Rich. If Evangeline wanted to kill him, as his wife she'd have had plenty of better opportunities to make it look like an accident or a random act. And Ricky . . ." I shook my head. "Not the Ricky I know. Frankly, he's just too laid-back to do anything that drastic and dramatic. Ricky prefers to wait for things to fall into his lap. Which they usually do. Eventually."

241

"You never know what people will do when they're desperate."

"That's true. Maybe I'm wrong, but I don't think so. And, if I may be so immodest, I don't believe Ricky would have deliberately tried to frighten me as happened last night. I sense he still has a certain fondness for me."

"More than that, sweetie."

"Meaning what?"

"He looks at you, when you're not looking, as though a hole has opened up in his life and you're the only thing that can fill it."

"Nonsense. You're imagining that. Heavens, the man asked Grace out. Anyway, back to the subject at hand—the only person left on my list as a viable suspect is Gordon Frankland, and I can't go around and start questioning him. If he thinks I'm accusing him, he'll sue me. I don't mind that so much, but Connor wouldn't be happy."

"Gordon Frankland wouldn't have killed anyone, Lucy. He gets his jollies out of suing people. He craves the attention. He comes in here sometimes, and I absolutely dread the very sight of him. I'm terrified one of my staff is going to spill a hot drink on him or he's going to slip on something, have a fall, and sue me. Every business owner in town's the same, and that's the way he likes it. We live in fear of him, but we don't fear he's going to kill us. Killing takes place in the shadows. Gordon Frankland lives in the limelight. A rather putrid limelight, but not the shadows."

"That's a good point, Josie."

"Plus, it's not his style to make anonymous threats. If he did kill that man and he thought you were getting close, he'd think of some reason to sue you so as to occupy all your attention. You might think you've done nothing he can sue you over, but believe me, if he put his mind to it, he'd come up with something."

"That might have already happened." I told Josie about the Charles-versus-Frankland incident at the library yesterday.

"That'll do it," she said.

I mentally called up my list and drew a line through Gordon Frankland's name. "If I dismiss him as a suspect, then the way I see it, Rich's death must have something to do with inheritances. Rich was losing money, and fast. The killer needed to stop that. Yes, killing for the inheritance appears to suggest it had to have been Evangeline or Ricky. I assume Evangeline will inherit everything, but maybe not. At book club the other night, Butch said something about previously unknown relatives coming out of the woodwork at will-reading time. Not only unknown relatives but former lovers, maybe even . . . uh . . . illegitimate children. If there are any. Even a shelter for homeless cats."

"Charles would be in favor of the latter."

"More than once I've thought Charles would be a good murder suspect. If he could drive a getaway vehicle and wield a weapon. I'd like to get a look at Rich's will. Dad probably can, but it's unlikely to the point of inconceivable that he'll share the information with me. Before the reading, anyway."

"Can a married man disinherit his wife?"

"In Massachusetts, not completely, no. A spouse has some rights. He or she can seek to void such a will and take an appropriate share of the estate for themselves. 'Appropriate share' is open to legal debate. If Rich did try to cut out Evangeline, and if she knew about it, she would have had no reason to kill her husband." I thought about Rich's illegitimate child. Who was, it would seem, not James Dalrymple. Might this child—now an adult—have realized that Rich was running through his money fast and decided to put a stop to it? This person was a native of the Outer Banks. It might therefore be someone who knew of my past involvement in police cases and knew I lived and worked at the library. They might even know my phone number. That was not a comforting thought.

I folded up the remaining half sandwich and stuffed it into my bag to finish later. "Gotta run. Thanks."

"Your phone's beeping."

Once again I pulled it out. Not the timer this time, but a text from Louise Jane: *How much longer are you going to be? I have yoga class at noon.*

Louise Jane took yoga?

I replied: *At Josie's. Leaving now.*

I stood up, and Josie did also. She reached for me, and we hugged each other tightly. "You take care," she said to me.

"You too," I replied.

"If anything at all odd happens, don't be afraid to call for help."

"I won't. That goes for you too."

I got in my car and headed back to the lighthouse, keeping my attention on my surroundings all the way. Not my full attention, though—I called Sam Watson as I drove. "Hi," I said when he answered. "It's Lucy. I'm calling to see if you figured anything out about what happened last night."

"I'm sorry to say, no. The intruder didn't leave any prints on the paper or the nail or drop whatever they used to hammer the nail in. It hasn't rained for a few days, so the ground around the lighthouse and in the parking area is dry—no usable footprints or tire tracks. I'm sorry, Lucy, but I want you to know I won't be letting this go. I don't like it, don't like it at all."

I felt a nice warm ball in my tummy and spoke around a lump in my throat. "While I have you on the line . . . I had a chat with Evangeline this morning. She told me something shocking. It shocked me, anyway. Rich Lewiston had a child out of wedlock, and that child, now grown up, lives near here."

"I know. She finally admitted to me that she's been visiting Nags Head over the years to keep an eye on her husband and the child's mother, as well as the child itself."

"Do you know who this child is?"

"I do."

"And—"

"And I'm not going to tell you or anyone else their identity, Lucy."

"I don't want to know. I'm wondering if you thought to check that person's whereabouts on Monday night."

"I paid a call on the mother of the person in question. She was not, understandably, happy to know that I know her secret, but she assured me the child is not aware of his or her parentage and has never expressed any interest whatsoever in Rich Lewiston, his family, or his whereabouts. I've left it at that, and I expect you to do the same."

"That doesn't mean they don't know. Maybe—"

"Lucy, I said I expect you to do the same."

"Okay. Have you seen Rich's will?"

"Lucy! You've been warned to stay out of it. I'm adding my voice to that. Stay out of it."

"But—"

Detective Watson hung up.

* * *

The library was hopping when I got back. "Thank you so much, Louise Jane," I said. "I appreciate your help."

"Anytime, Lucy. Did you call Connor?"

"No. Why should I?"

"About the house."

"Oh, the house. Right. I'll let you know what he says. Anything happen while I was out?"

"Nothing memorable. We've been busy. You really do need more help around here." Louise Jane got up from behind the desk and smiled at me.

"Thanks again," I said. "What brings you here today, anyway? Don't you work at the beach supply store on Saturdays?"

"I quit."

"You quit?"

"Working at Uncle Dennis's branch of Beach Blanket Disco Mart isn't a job I want to do, but I've been helping him out when he needs it. I've found something else, so he'll have to manage without me."

"You mean you got a new job? Where?"

She smirked. "You'll find out. 'Bye, Lucy."

I watched her leave, a decided swing to her step, but I didn't have time to wonder what she'd meant, as a young man came to ask for my help filling in job applications on the computer.

* * *

The final children's program of the day ended at four thirty, and Ronald came downstairs to wave off his excited little charges, who were clutching their homemade scrapbooks and telling their parents to be on the lookout for wildlife.

"Good day?" I asked him.

Ronald rubbed his curly gray hair. Today's tie featured the Simpsons.

"A very good day. I'm looking forward to seeing what wildlife sightings they record in their books over the week. I'm expecting lots of dogs, outdoor cats, and squirrels."

"Would you mind watching the desk for a few minutes?" I asked Ronald. "I need to talk to Charlene."

"Happy to," he said.

I'd been ordered off the Lewiston case by Sam Watson. I might be able to ignore the threat from anonymous, but I couldn't ignore Watson. I had to think about something, and at slow times during the day I'd tried not to think about who might have killed my father's law partner. Instead I'd found myself thinking about Charlene and her English visitors. As long as I was sticking my nose into other people's secret relationships, I might as well keep at it. I climbed the stairs to the third floor. Charlene's office door was open, and I knocked lightly.

She turned to me with a smile, which I was pleased to see. "Hi, Lucy." She took the earbuds out of her ears, and the pounding beat flowed around me. She pushed a button on her phone to stop it. "I want to apologize for snapping at you the other day."

"Not a problem."

"I'm sorry. Truly sorry. All I can say in my defense is I've had a lot on my mind." She smiled again. She looked different somehow, I thought. She looked like a woman in love.

And I was here to burst her balloon. I took a deep breath and spoke quickly before my nerve failed me and I fled. "I know something's been going on with you, Charlene, and I'm hoping we can talk frankly. As friends. We are friends, right?"

"Yes, we are. You're right that something's been going on. Bertie's going to tell you and Ronald on Monday, but as long as you're here—"

"Bertie? What's this got to do with Bertie?"

"It's got everything to do with Bertie. With you and Ronald too. I quit."

"You what?"

"I quit. I'm leaving the Lighthouse Library at the end of the month."

"But . . . Charlene, why?"

She beamed at me and clapped her hands. "It's so sudden and so exciting! I'm going to England. I've got a job offer at Oxford. To my considerable surprise, they remember me there and would like to have me back. I told Bertie yesterday."

"James and Daisy are at Oxford, aren't they?"

"Yes, Lucy. That's sort of the point. It's all happened so dreadfully fast, but I know this is the right thing for me to do." Her eyes glowed with sheer happiness. "James and I want to be together, and neither of us wants a long-distance relationship. Those things never work out. I have job opportunities in England, and he doesn't have any here. Thus I'm going to England. I'm so excited!"

I took a deep breath. "But, but . . . Charlene, what does Daisy have to say about this?"

"Daisy? What about Daisy? She's happy for us. I like her a lot, and I'm glad we're going to be close."

"Uh. Okay. If that's what you want. I guess. What about your mom?"

"Mom's well enough to travel these days, and she'll live with us."

"She's okay with that?"

"Lucy, are you feeling all right? Of course my mom's okay with it. She's looking forward to the change of scenery, although she'll miss all her friends in Nags Head. She wants me to be happy. I want me to be happy. Don't you? I know it means changes here, at the library, but that's no reason for you to look so glum."

"I want you to be happy, Charlene, I do. Forgive me, please, but I don't see that this is the right way to go about it. I mean, James and Daisy . . . I mean, Charlene, he's married already! This can't end well, and you're giving up your job and moving halfway across the world."

Charlene fell back against her chair and started to cry. I took a step forward, ready to wrap her in my arms and comfort her. Then I realized she wasn't weeping. She was crying with laughter. "Oh, Lucy. Dear, sweet Lucy. You didn't think— James isn't Daisy's husband. He's her brother."

"But . . . but . . . he can't be her brother. They don't look at all alike."

"Half brother. They have the same mother but different fathers. They both completely take after their fathers. They sometimes joke about how neither of them bears the slightest resemblance to their mother. Except that their mother's a professor emerita at Cambridge and because of her they grew up immersed in history books."

"James told me his American father died when he was a baby and his mother brought him back to England. But . . . he and Daisy have the same last name. Daisy wears a wedding ring." Although James did not.

"James grew up close to his stepfather, so as a way of honoring him when James was old enough, he took his stepfather's name." Charlene wiped tears away. "Daisy's husband's back home in Oxford, caring for their baby daughter. She kept her own name when she married for professional reasons. Some women do these days, you know, Lucy."

"Uh. Yeah. I guess." *Don't I feel the fool?*

"You weren't here when they first arrived. I introduced them to everyone and mentioned the relationship. I think it's sweet that a brother and sister work so closely together. I never thought to . . . to mention it again." She fell back with another round of laughter.

"But . . . but . . . why did you run out of the Dockside Lounge Bar the other night when you saw me?"

"You were at Dockside? I didn't see you, Lucy. If I had, I would have suggested James and I join you. The place was too crowded and we didn't want to wait for a table."

"That's good, then," I said. "Not good that you're leaving, but good that you and James are going to be together. Congratulations."

"Thank you, Lucy."

I leaned over and gave her a hug. She reached up and hugged me tightly in return, and I could feel her body shuddering with more laughter.

"Can you, uh, not mention this to anyone?" I asked, when we'd separated and Charlene was drying her eyes. "It's kind of embarrassing. What I thought, I mean."

"Your secret is safe with me, Lucy."

"Has Bertie any thoughts about who's going to replace you? Not that you can be replaced, Charlene. You're irreplaceable."

"It's nice of you to say so. I have a candidate in mind and I made the suggestion, and she seems to approve of it. I'll leave it up to Bertie to tell you and Ronald on Monday, okay?"

"That'll have to be okay. I'm happy for you, Charlene, very happy. Now that I know James isn't a dastardly cad out to do you and Daisy both wrong, I'd like to get to know him better."

"He'd like that too, Lucy. He told me he found you very cold, and I was surprised to hear that. I guess I now know why." And she burst into another round of laughter.

Chapter Twenty

Once again I escaped with my tail between my legs. My mother might have bragged that I have investigative skills, but these days I was turning out to be wrong every single time.

My mother might have bragged . . .

When I got back downstairs, it was almost five o'clock. Closing time on Saturday. "Ladies and gentlemen, boys and girls," I announced. "The library's about to close. Please take your books to the desk. We'll be open again on Monday morning."

Ronald went upstairs to lock up the children's library. Only one patron was still in the building, and she brought me one book and left without trying to engage me in conversation. Once I was alone, I placed a call. "I need you to try to remember something, Mom. It's important."

"If I can," she said.

"A couple of people said something to me lately about you telling them I'm a detective. I'm nothing of the sort, but that doesn't matter now. Can you remember what you said to whom and when?"

"I didn't say you were a detective, Lucy. Why would I do that?"

"I don't know, Mom. Maybe you were making conversation. Perhaps you didn't use those exact words, but can you remember saying something like that? It's important."

Silence came down the line, and I let her think.

"Didn't we talk about this on Wednesday," she said at last, "when we were at the hotel when the police spoke to Evangeline?"

"That's right," I said. "You said I had people to interview."

"I was providing you with an excuse to get out of spending the day with Evangeline and her crowd of hangers-on. I didn't mean it."

"Doesn't matter if you meant it or not. Not if people thought you did."

"Then again, I believe I also said something to that effect yesterday evening. We were in the hotel bar, and you called me and mentioned that the police were going to release Rich's body. Evangeline asked what we'd been talking about, and I told her you were investigating again. I might have said that once you get an idea in your head, you never give up."

"Do you remember who was there? Evangeline. Anyone else?"

Silence again. "Ricky, Evangeline's friend Leon, and the lawyer your father sent to keep an eye on things down here—Stephen."

"Thanks, Mom."

"What's this about, dear?"

"Nothing."

"Obviously not nothing. Go ahead and keep your secrets. Are you coming for dinner tomorrow? Ellen's going to invite you and Connor. I'm planning to go home on Monday with Evangeline."

"Dinner tomorrow. We'll be there."

I thought back to my list. I'd eliminated most of the suspects. Who remained?

I made two phone calls. Neither was answered. I left messages to call me back.

Ronald clattered down the stairs, briefcase in hand. "Any plans for tomorrow, Lucy?"

"I'll probably see my mom before she leaves. Connor and I were hoping to have a beach day, but now we have a house to look at, so we'll see how it goes."

"Good luck with that." He waved good-night and left.

Daisy and James and Charlene came next. Charlene and James were holding hands.

"We're going to Rodanthe tomorrow for the day, Lucy," Charlene said. "Would you and Connor like to come?"

"Thanks, but I doubt I'll have time. My mom's leaving Monday, and I have a line on a house for Connor and me to see."

"Good luck with the house." She smiled at James, and he gave her a look of such adoration I felt awful all over again at distrusting him. Daisy punched her brother in the arm. "Let's go. I missed lunch, and I'm absolutely starving."

They left, and I remembered I was supposed to have called Connor about Louise Jane's supposed house find. I doubted very much it would be worth looking at, but it couldn't hurt.

"Louise Jane wants to show us a house?" he said.

"That's what she said."

"It's not my birthday. It's not your birthday. We've had our engagement party. Is she planning a surprise shower and using this as a pretext?"

"I might have suspected something like that too, except she didn't specify a time. She asked me to let her know when we were free. Not at night."

"Might as well do it tomorrow. Get it over with."

"Okay. I'll tell her ten?"

"That'll work. About what happened last night . . . I assume there were no more strange happenings today?"

"A perfectly normal day at the Lighthouse Library. I haven't forgotten about it, and I kept myself on alert all day."

"Good. I wish I could see you tonight, but—"

"But this mayoral meeting's been arranged for a long time and you have to go. It's okay, Connor. I have no plans for tonight except to stay in. I'll be safe as lighthouses. Once the front door's locked, no one can get to me without a battering ram. I have a can of soup in the cupboard and half a sandwich from Josie's for dinner. Charles and Fluffy are here to protect me from any intruders."

Hearing his name, Charles leapt onto the desk and lay down for a belly rub. I obliged.

"Why does that not make me feel better?" Connor said.

"It should. Charles has protected me before."

Connor chuckled.

Charles nodded.

Chapter Twenty-One

Ricky was the first person to return my call. As I'd told Connor I planned to do, I'd made myself an impromptu dinner of a bowl of soup and a leftover sandwich before curling up on the bed with Charles on one side of me, Fluffy on the other, and my iPad on my lap, watching a movie on Netflix.

"Mom and I will be leaving on Monday," Ricky said. "The police are going to release Dad's body, and the arrangements have been made to take him home. I'd like to see you before I go."

I hesitated. "I don't think I'll have the time."

"What about now? Tonight. I know you're home. You're the only person I know who still has a landline, so I know you're in the lighthouse."

I hadn't thought Ricky had lured me out of the lighthouse the other night. I couldn't believe he'd want to frighten me. Maybe I was naïve, but he still seemed to have feelings for me. His comment confirmed my instinct: if it had been him, he would have called me on the landline.

Rather than answering his question about coming over, I explained. "The cell reception's poor to nonexistent here, so we still need a physical connection."

"That's what I thought. It's not late, and you're off work tomorrow. How about I come and get you and we can go into town? Find a nice lounge somewhere, have a couple of drinks, listen to some music, talk about the good old days. About us in the good old days. I can be there in fifteen minutes. Please say yes, Lucy. We did have some good days, didn't we?"

Despite my assurances to myself about Ricky, my danger antenna pricked up. "Why would you come all this way to get me?"

"So I can ply you with liquor, of course. For old times' sake, Lucy?" His voice was playful, trying to make light of the issues—*no big deal*—but I could hear the seriousness beneath.

I felt guilty about even thinking that Ricky, a man I'd known for so long and been close to once, could possibly have meant me harm. "I'm comfortably settled for a night in."

"Then I'll join you. I haven't seen your apartment yet."

"Ricky. No. That's not why I called you. This is important. I have a question, and I need you to answer without asking why I'm asking."

He chuckled. "Detecting again, Lucy?"

"No. I'm just curious. Your mom said you and Stephen went out for a couple of drinks after dinner last night. Is that right?"

"You don't want me to ask why you're asking?"

"Please."

"Only for you, Lucy, only for you. Yeah, that's right. To be honest, I'm getting mighty tired of my mother's company. Her and that Leon. Geez, he's in for a mighty big disappointment."

"Why do you say that?"

"He's hanging all over her, all the time. They dated a long time ago, before she met my dad, and he seems to want to pick up where they left off. He's trying to impress her by being buddies with me. As if."

"Back to what I asked you. You were with Stephen for how long?"

"Not long. We had one drink, and he moved in on a table of women. I wasn't interested, so I left him to it. I walked back to the hotel; it wasn't far. I probably shouldn't have left him with the rental car, not if he was going to keep on drinking, but he gave me a wink—just between us guys, you know."

"Yeah," I said dryly. "I know. What time was this?"

"Ten, ten thirty or so? Not much later than that. I can't persuade you to let me in?"

"No, you cannot. And . . . good night, Ricky."

As I hung up the phone, I might have heard him say, "Good night, my love."

I leaned back with a sigh. I tried my dad again, and he answered this time.

"Sorry I didn't return your call, honey. It's a Saturday night, but I've been in meetings all day trying to sort out Rich's affairs, and I can tell you, it's not going to be easy. The guy's practice was a mess, giant gaps in his records, unexplained expenditures, dodgy income. Not to mention that the police are showing a lot of interest. I should never have allowed things to get this far. Have you spoken to Ricky today?"

"Ricky? Yes. I was just on the phone with him. He and Evangeline are bringing Rich home on Monday."

"Monday's too late. I need Ricky here. Now. He needs to start explaining this mess. Sorry, honey. I'm sure you didn't call to hear about the firm's problems. What's up?"

"Actually, I did call to talk to you about something to do with the firm. Stephen Livingstone. Can you—"

Dad cut me off. "He's another one who needs to be here explaining himself, not gallivanting around the beaches of the Outer Banks."

"Gallivanting? Didn't you send him here to act as Evangeline's attorney in case she needs one?"

"Stephen? No. Can't stand the little—uh, guy. He's Rich's lapdog, not mine."

"He told me you sent him here."

"I wouldn't send him across the street for a bagel." I heard Dad take a deep breath. Someone had been coaching him on calming techniques.

"You told Mom you were sending someone down here to represent Evangeline if she needed it, and to keep an eye on the firm's interests. Not Stephen?"

"When I say I'm sending someone to do something, Lucy, I mean I tell someone to tell someone to send someone. I don't pick a junior attorney out of the pack."

"Oh."

"Maybe I should. I would never have involved Stephen Livingstone. Never mind that, honey. My problems to deal with. Why did you call?"

"Just to say hi."

"Hi," he said, and I was pleased to hear the warmth creep into his voice.

"When all this is over, Dad, you and Mom need to come down for a real visit. A vacation. You know, the beach, swimming, seeing the sights, nice dinners out."

"That," he said, "sounds like a great idea. Good night, honey."

" 'Night Dad."

I hung up. Charles was sitting up, watching me. "You know what I'm going to do now, Charles?" I said. "I'm going to do what everyone is always telling me to do and hand it over to the police."

I made another call, and it was answered immediately.

"Sorry to bother you at home on a Saturday evening, Detective." In the background I could hear the muted sounds of a TV. "I've learned two pieces of information about the Rich Lewiston case, and I thought you'd want to know."

"You're not bothering me, Lucy. CeeCee's waving hi. Hold on a sec." A door slammed and the TV sound died. "What's up?"

"You met Stephen Livingstone."

"Yeah. Lawyer guy from Boston; your dad sent him down to act as Mrs. Lewiston's attorney."

"I've just learned that my dad didn't send him. My dad doesn't like him—doesn't think much of him anyway—but he worked for Rich. If anything, Dad's angry that he's here rather than back at the office helping sort out what he calls Rich's mess."

"You think that significant because?"

"I'd dismiss it as an eager young associate trying to curry favor with the late boss's wife and son, but you've taught me that when people lie to the police, even about insignificant matters, it's worth wondering why."

"Particularly about insignificant matters. I hate to think I've taught you anything about policing, Lucy."

"Nevertheless, you have. That's one piece of the puzzle. For the second piece: did anyone ask Ricky and Stephen where they were last night when I was being lured out of the lighthouse?"

"Officers questioned the lot of them. I can't recall precisely what everyone said, which means I didn't regard it as significant."

"I bet Ricky and Steven said they went to a bar after having dinner with Evangeline and Leon Lions and your officers left it at that. According to Ricky, they had one drink together and then Ricky went back to the hotel, leaving Stephen at the bar. With the car."

"What time was this?"

"Around ten thirty, Ricky says. I'm guessing, and it is just a guess, that not long after Ricky left, Stephen abandoned the table of women he was trying to charm, got the car, and went in search of me." Conveniently for him, I'd been at Jake's—a place Rich's killer would know I hang out at. "Maybe he wanted to talk to me, to find out what I know, or maybe his intention all along was to threaten me." I remembered a car following us out of the parking lot of Jake's and out of town, then continuing on up the highway when we turned into the lighthouse laneway. Easy enough to turn around, switch off the headlights, follow us and watch us. "He saw Josie drop me off and drive away and me go inside. So he had the bright idea of trying to scare me. Did you locate the owner of the phone that called me?"

"A burner. Probably at the bottom of the Sound by now. This is good, Lucy. Very good. You've given me something to work with. I'm going to call your father and ask for more information about this Stephen Livingstone and then pay him a call myself to ask about his activities last night. Sometimes all I need is to make a small chink in the wall of artifice, and the whole case comes tumbling down."

"I assume you mean the case is built *up*, but never mind, I get the point. Glad to be of help, Detective."

"Where are you now, Lucy?"

"I'm home. I have no plans to go anywhere tonight. Safe as lighthouses."

"Glad to hear it. Thanks again."

We hung up, and I settled back with my movie while Charles snoozed on one side of me and Fluffy dreamt she was chasing rabbits on the other side. The movie was a murder mystery story with Daniel Craig as a private detective, and I found it unrealistic compared to my own experiences. About halfway through I switched it off, disturbed the animals, and got up to microwave a bag of popcorn. I then settled back on the bed, resettled the dog and cat, turned the movie back on, and made my way through the entire bowl while Daniel continued his investigation.

I was licking my fingers clean when Daniel Craig solved the mystery and the movie ended. "As if that ever happens," I said to Charles and Fluffy.

Fluffy jumped off the bed and ran for the door. Charles went into the kitchen to check out the contents of the food bowl. I yawned and stretched. I was ready for bed, but dog duties needed to be attended to.

When I last spoke to Evangeline, she'd said nothing about coming for Fluffy and pretty much said she hoped never to see me again. The little creature was growing on me—I was becoming fond of her, and she and Charles had made friends, but I didn't want to be stuck with Fluffy if Evangeline went home without her. I'd have to call her in the morning and arrange a time for Evangeline to pick up the dog.

I took the pink leash down from the hook by the door. Fluffy's ears perked up, and she did a joyful little dance at my feet. I fastened the leash to her collar, told Charles we'd be right back, and let us out of the Lighthouse Aerie.

We descended the stairs, round and round and round, in the dim light from the fourth-floor landing above and the library alcove below. The library snoozed peacefully around me, and I imagined I could hear the soft breathing of the characters as they prepared for another busy day of being read on Monday.

When I moved, I'd miss this place at night. The peace. The quiet. Maybe I could convince Connor to come occasionally for a sleepover. Provided no one moved in, that is. Which reminded me that Charlene had quit and Bertie would have news to give us on Monday. Would the new academic librarian be young and single and wanting to live ten miles outside of town and four stories above the marsh? Never mind being pestered by library patrons when trying to sneak in and out of their own home. It wasn't the life for everyone.

I opened the door to be greeted by a wall of fog so thick the lamp over the door scarcely illuminated the bottom of the steps. I switched on the small flashlight I keep fastened to my key chain. "We won't go far tonight, Fluffy. It's easy to get lost in this muck."

High above us the thousand-watt bulb flashed, but the illumination barely reached the ground.

I'd take Fluffy down to the parking area and then we'd turn around and come back, sticking strictly to the path so as not to get lost in the fog and end up wandering in circles. A long walk could wait until tomorrow. Fluffy didn't seem to mind. She did what she had to do on a patch of grass and then sniffed her way down the path next to me. We reached the parking lot and were about to turn around when her head shot up, her ears lifted, and she let out a growl, deep in her throat. I glanced at her in alarm. She pulled at the leash, continuing to growl, staring intently into the dark. The hairs along her back were standing on end. I have to admit, the hair on the back of my neck was doing the same. She growled again, the sound low and menacing and unlike anything I'd heard from the tiny lapdog before.

I tugged at the leash. She didn't come but growled once more. "Come on, Fluffy. Nothing's out there. Let's go in, why don't we?"

"Don't hurry away on my account," came a voice from inside the swirling mist.

Chapter
Twenty-Two

S tephen Livingstone stepped into the dim light thrown by
my little flashlight. He held a solid Maglite in his right
hand, but he'd switched it off.

My heart rate did not settle, and the hairs on the back of
my neck did not relax. Fluffy lunged for him, snapping and
snarling. I gripped the leash tightly. I swallowed. "Hi!" I said,
trying to sound cheerful. "Goodness. You scared me there. Out
for a walk in the marsh, are you? Not a good night for it." I
pulled at the leash. Fluffy resisted, but I was bigger and stron-
ger. I dragged her away, inch by protesting inch. "Still, some
people like the atmosphere, or so they say. Spooky, right? Like
in *The Hound of the Baskervilles*. I saw corpse candles in the
marsh one night last October, around Halloween. It was a
night much like this one, come to think of it, although a bit
colder." I shoved my free hand into my pocket. It came up
empty, and I stifled a curse. I'd put my phone on the table
when I got in from work.

Stephen said nothing. He simply stared at me, his eyes
dark, unemotional pools in the shadows of his face.

"I'd invite you in," I said, "but it's late, and I'm tired. "Come
on, Fluffy."

265

He spoke at last, his voice low and threatening. "You really don't know to mind your own business, do you?"

"Sure I do. I'm minding my own business right now. I'm going inside. Me and the dog. Straight to bed. This is where I live, believe it or not."

"I know you do. I saw you at the hotel this morning, talking to Evangeline and her fat friend."

"Yup. That was me. Evangeline's a good friend of my mom's."

As I talked, I edged slowly backward. Stephen matched me, step for step. The fog shifted constantly. One moment I could see him clearly, and the next he faded into tendrils of mist. He might disappear, but I could hear his voice and feel the sheer menace emanating from him.

Fluffy continued barking. I continued backing up. I continued chatting inanely. The back of my foot touched the bottom of the stairs. I held the leash in one hand and my flashlight, focused on the ground, in the other. The mist swirled around us, but I could make out Stephen in the flash of light from high above us. The light went out, and then it came on again. I braced myself. I breathed. I was ready the moment the light went into its 22.5 second dormancy, and I turned and ran up the stairs. I grabbed for the doorknob, but at that moment Fluffy dashed for safety between, of all places, my legs. The leash wrapped around my right ankle. I stumbled and then Stephen was on me, grabbing my shoulders, pulling me away from the door. I dropped the leash and kicked, but my flailing foot met nothing but air. I screamed. Fluffy barked. Stephen's arms were tight around my chest as he dragged me away.

"What are you doing!" I yelled. "Let me go. You're making a mistake."

"No," he breathed in my ear. "You're the one who's made a mistake. A fatal one, I'm sorry to say."

I kept kicking and struggling. His grip around my upper chest was so tight I was having trouble breathing.

And then, suddenly, Stephen cried out in surprise and shock, and I was propelled forward. I managed, thank heavens, to keep my footing as well as my senses and whirled around. He'd slipped on the bottom step, damp from the mist, and fallen.

He wasn't, unfortunately, knocked out, and he recovered quickly. His hand shot out and grabbed at my leg. I kicked as hard as I could, and I felt a satisfying jolt and heard him grunt. He started to stand up, and I knew I wouldn't be able to get the door open and shut behind me before he was on me again. I leapt off the steps and ran for the marsh. Fast, light footsteps pounded the ground behind me. Fluffy.

I switched off my flashlight. The dog barked. I tried to hush her without making any noise. It was a warm summer's night, and I knew my way around out here. If I had to, I could stay hidden; I'd be fine until daylight, when people began to arrive. Otherwise I could try to make my way through the marsh to the highway and flag down a passing car.

But I didn't have much chance of staying hidden with a small hysterical dog next to me.

"Lucy!" A disembodied voice drifted toward me. "I want to talk to you, that's all. I didn't mean to frighten you. I couldn't see in the dark, so I stumbled, and then I grabbed you inappropriately. I'm sorry about that."

As the mist shifted, I could see Stephen's light moving away from the bulk of the lighthouse, coming toward me. I tried to wave Fluffy away. She would not be discouraged, so I bent down and scooped her up. I put my hand around her muzzle, and she fell quiet. She whimpered, and I stroked the back of her neck softly. I could feel the rapid beating of her small heart. Mine was going just as fast.

"I can't stand yappy little dogs myself," Stephen said. "I went around to Rich's house one day to bring him some papers to sign. Evangeline was away, and I told Rich I'd strangle the miserable mutt if he wanted me to. He said thanks but no thanks."

I slipped to my right, keeping to the soft marsh grasses. The Maglite focused straight ahead. Fluffy yipped, and the light swung around.

"My dad told Detective Watson about you," I called into the dark. "He knows you've been helping Rich embezzle money from the firm. Dad's opening the books to the police. They'll have all the proof they need soon. You should make a run for it while you can."

"What can I say? I'll admit, I fell under Rich Lewiston's influence. I mean, he was a powerful man, right? Knows all the right people, belongs to all the right clubs, has the right politicians in his pocket. I let him convince me to help him out of a couple of jams. Poor me, boy from the wrong side of the tracks, impressed by the rich and powerful. I thought I was helping the firm. If I'd known what Rich was truly up to, I would have told the senior partners. Right away."

"You can try that story on the police, but they won't believe you. And even if they do, that's not much of an excuse for killing him."

"Me? Kill Rich? Why would I do that? I was nowhere near Nags Head on Monday night. Why would I be? I called the office and told them I'd come down with a sudden cold on the weekend so I had to stay home Monday. Rich didn't come around to my apartment Sunday evening, drunk out of his tiny, very tiny, mind to say he was going to tell Millar everything and he wasn't going to wait until Millar got back from his daughter's engagement party. I didn't try to convince him not to do anything rash. I didn't follow him when he left my place and wait outside his house to see if he really was going to go through with it."

Now that I was no longer panicking and Stephen was no longer threatening, Fluffy had settled down. She tried to wiggle out of my arms, but when I wouldn't let go, she let out a contented sigh and snuggled close.

"I knew Millar was in Nags Head. That was no secret. Ricky told me his mother was determined to barge in uninvited on Millar's daughter's engagement party and try to get her to leave her intended and marry Ricky. You might want to know, Lucy, Ricky didn't think that was such a great idea. He came down here with his mom to try to keep her from doing anything stupid. I wasn't watching the Lewiston house Sunday night, and I didn't see Rich stagger out in the early hours of Monday morning, throw his suitcase into his car, and drive out of town, heading south. And, because I didn't see that, I didn't head for Nags Head myself. Are you still out there, Lucy? You're probably thinking of making your way to the highway. That's a lot of ground to cover. In the dark. Trying to be quiet. The dog's finally stopped barking. That can't last much longer."

Holding Fluffy, not daring to turn on my flashlight, I picked my way carefully through the marsh grasses. The fog covered all traces of moon and stars, and I couldn't see a blasted thing. On the other hand, that meant Stephen couldn't see me either.

I stepped on a dead branch. It snapped with a sound as loud and sharp as a gunshot.

"Oh, you're over there," Stephen said, in a voice calmer and far closer than was good for me. Still, as long as he was talking, he wasn't killing me. Clearly, he was so impressed with his own cleverness that he had to tell someone all about it.

"You're wondering why I might have wanted Rich to die, as that would inevitably lead to an examination of his records, which would in turn incriminate me. Truth be told, Lucy, I didn't much care if Rich lived or died, but his timing wasn't good for me. I was taking my own time, being careful, scrubbing any traces of my involvement in some of his schemes out of the records, moving my money slowly and carefully so it couldn't be traced. The records are mostly clean now, but I didn't need Rich blabbing the whole story to Millar before I'm ready to take my leave of them all.

"You're also wondering how I might have gotten Rich to the restaurant that night, if I'd wanted to that is. If I wanted to, I'd have sent him a note, asking him to meet me. No one ever said Richard Lewiston Junior was smart. I wouldn't have been able to use my phone, didn't want anyone tracing it. I couldn't use a burner; he wouldn't answer a number he didn't recognize. I didn't tuck the note under his windshield wipers when he was paying for gas. No need to sign it; he'd know who it was from."

Stephen was right about one thing: it was a long way to the highway. Was the mist thinning? I feared it was. I'd soon be dreadfully exposed out here in the marsh. I needed to get to the shelter of the trees before the light of the moon broke through.

"You might be thinking it was a coincidence that I asked— didn't ask, I mean—Rich to meet me at the same restaurant you were having dinner at. I never trust to coincidence, Lucy. I checked online to see which were the nicest restaurants near Evangeline's hotel. The sort of places she would go to. The name *Jake's* rang a bell. Ricky had said something several months ago about Millar and Suzanne going to her niece's wedding in Nags Head. Did you know Evangeline tried to wrangle an invitation, but Suzanne was having none of it? It was a small family celebration with the reception at the fiancé's restaurant, a place called Jake's. Ricky got quite a hoot out of his mom being snubbed like that.

"You never know what apparently insignificant bits of information are going to be useful someday, Lucy. That's why I never forget anything. Rich appreciated that about me. Anyway, if I wanted to kill Rich, which I didn't, that's the way I would have gone about it. I'd have arranged to meet him at the restaurant where his family and associates were dining. A bunch of rich, entitled people, some of them lawyers, no less, being questioned by small-town hick cops confuses the waters. If I had been involved in Rich's nasty little schemes, I would have had a tough decision to make while I finished moving my money. Stay at the Boston office and help Millar sort through the accounts, or come back here to keep an eye on things knowing that Rich's records are such a mess even Millar would need time to trace anything back to me. Enough idle chatter. Got you!"

A bright light shone directly into my face, blinding me. A hand reached out of the fog and seized my arm. I screamed and dropped Fluffy. The dog fell in a chorus of frightened barks, and I was thrown to the ground next to her.

Stephen was on me, his hands around my throat, his weight pressing me down. I scratched at his arms and tried to reach his face. He grinned down at me, his face a horrific mask in the harsh light thrown by his flashlight. I kicked and thrashed, but he didn't let go. The pressure increased.

Connor.

I would never see the house Louise Jane had found for us.

Stephen let out a howl of pain, and his eyes opened wide in shock. I felt his body move as he kicked out at something behind him and the pressure on my throat relaxed. I sucked in a breath, gathered all the strength I could, and shoved at him. He fell to one side, and I rolled away. He didn't try to stop me, and I scrambled to my feet.

I looked down to see Stephen lying on his back, screaming, his pant leg torn, his leg bleeding, his hands up to protect his face as Fluffy, sweet little Fluffy, lunged for his throat.

Chapter Twenty-Three

I hesitated. Should I make a run for it, save myself while I had the chance, or take precious time to grab Fluffy? Stephen would soon get the upper hand, and he would kill the sharp-toothed but tiny dog in his fury.

Fortunately, I didn't have to decide. The quiet (aside from the screaming of the man and the snarling of the dog) of the marsh was shattered by blaring sirens. Red and blue flashing lights cut through the night and the fog. Doors slammed. Men and women shouted. Flashlight beams blinded me.

I held my hands in front of my eyes and yelled, "I'm okay. I'm okay! It's him. He killed Rich Lewiston."

"Get it off me!" Stephen screamed. "Shoot it!"

"No! Don't shoot. The dog saved me. Fluffy! Fluffy. Here." I grabbed the little dog, still having a go at Stephen's throat, by the back of her collar and pulled her away. She came without resistance, and I scooped her up.

Powerful flashlights shone on Stephen and the area around him. He lay on his back, gasping for breath. His lower pant leg was covered in blood, and more blood leaked from scratches on his throat and arms. He stared up at me, his glasses hanging off one ear, his small, dark eyes full of rage. The expression disappeared, and he said, "Thank heavens you got here in time, Officer. That dog must be rabid. It attacked me out of nowhere."

"She was defending me," I yelled. "He tried to kill me. He killed Rich Lewiston."

"Cuff him." Sam Watson stepped into the circle of light. "Then have the medics check him out. He's yelling loud enough, the bites can't be that deep." He turned to me. "You okay, Lucy?"

I clutched the squirming Fluffy to my chest. She wanted to get down and say hello to all these new arrivals. "The dog saved me. Don't let them hurt her."

"I won't." He held out his hand. Fluffy sniffed at it and then gave Watson a lick of approval. "Let's go inside. You need to sit down."

"That woman's a lunatic," Stephen yelled as Watson and I, still holding Fluffy, walked away. "She lured me into the marsh. She threatened to tell the cops I killed Rich if I didn't pay her off. When I said no, she put her dog on me."

"Save it for the judge," Butch Greenblatt said. "I'm not interested, but I have to say, buddy, if I was going to get an attack dog, I'd go for something a bit bigger."

Beside me, Watson chuckled. "I wouldn't have thought this little girl had it in her." The mist was lessening, the tendrils of fog thinning. I could see the vague shape of the lighthouse looming ahead.

"I guess we all have it in us," I said, "if we have to. To defend ourselves and those we care about."

"The skin on Stephen's throat's bitten, but I didn't see any outright puncture wounds, although it looks like she did get a nice chomp out of his leg." Watson rubbed between Fluffy's ears. "She wouldn't have been able to keep him down for much longer."

"In *The Hound of the Baskervilles*, the spectral hound, nothing but an ordinary dog painted with phosphorus, kills the villain Stapleton when he runs onto the moor in confusion in the fog, and Holmes has to shoot the dog. Thanks for not doing that to Fluffy."

Watson chuckled. Fluffy woofed.

"What brings you here?" I asked. "In such a timely fashion?"

"After you and I talked, I went around to the Ocean Side to speak to Stephen. Ricky and Evangeline said they hadn't seen him for hours. I called his number and got no answer. So I started getting worried that he'd try and come after you. I might not have worried too much, knowing you'd be perfectly safe inside the lighthouse, but I then remembered the dog. And that dogs have to be walked. I called to tell you to stay inside but got no answer. So I decided I'd better check things out for myself and bring backup in case Livingstone was hanging around."

"Thank you for that," I said.

Connor sprinted across the lawn toward us, mist curling at his feet. "Lucy! What's going on? Are you okay?" He grabbed my arms and peered into my face.

"I'm fine. Thanks to Fluffy."

The dog wiggled happily between us.

"What happened? Butch called me to say there was an incident—another incident—at the lighthouse."

"Let's go inside," Watson said. "I need Lucy to make a full statement, and she can tell you at the same time."

I wanted to fall into Connor's arms, but I didn't dare put Fluffy down.

"We can't say anything about this in front of Charles," I said. "If he finds out that Fluffy saved the day while he was inside sleeping, there will be no living with him."

Sam Watson and Connor McNeil laughed.

Chapter Twenty-Four

S unday morning as arranged, Connor and I went to Josie's Cozy Bakery to meet Louise Jane.

"Don't get your hopes up," I said as the lineup edged toward the counter. "Louise Jane's enthusiasms have a way of not turning out exactly as advertised."

"She hasn't told you anything more about this supposed beach house?"

"No. She likes to play her cards close to her chest, as we well know. Makes her seem mysterious, she thinks. A large low-fat latte and a blueberry muffin, please."

Connor ordered black coffee and a Danish, and we found seats at a table for two in the bustling bakery. We were supposed to be meeting Louise Jane at ten, and now it was quarter to.

Connor and I had had a long night and an early morning. In the main room of the library, I'd given Sam Watson my statement about what had happened out on the marsh, saying, "Stephen pretty much told me, step by step, how it all happened, but he covered it up by saying if he wanted to do it, this is how he'd have gone about it. That won't stand up as a confession, will it?"

"No," Watson said, "but it gives us a darn good place to start. And we'll start with the attempted murder of you tonight. He'll deny any ill intent, of course, but he didn't sneak up on you in the dark and knock you to the ground—"

Connor growled, sounding much like Fluffy had earlier.

"—for a lark. He drove down to the Outer Banks on Monday and then drove straight back to Boston after, allegedly, killing Rich. We'll find proof of that. A search of his phone history should show that he looked up Jake's address Monday night. Anything your father finds in Rich's files proving Stephen was in on whatever was going on will give us motive."

"He told me he's scrubbed the records where they showed any involvement on his part."

"Something always remains," Watson said. "These guys are never as clever as they think they are."

"He wasn't on my radar at all for killing Rich," I said, "even when we considered that it might have had something to do with what was happening at Richardson Lewiston. I'd been overly influenced, I fear, by *The Hound of the Baskervilles*. I kept coming back to the inheritance angle."

"He wasn't on anyone's radar," Watson assured me. "Until you figured it out."

A woman came into the lighthouse. She was dressed in white coveralls, a hairnet, and white boots and carried a small case. "I need samples off the dog," she said.

We looked at Fluffy, the hero of the hour, snoozing happily at my feet.

"She's not as dangerous as she looks," Connor said.

The woman didn't laugh. I dropped to the floor next to Fluffy and rubbed her belly while the woman took swabs from her nails. I then scratched under Fluffy's chin while tissue samples were taken from inside her cheek.

Evidence given, Fluffy returned to her nap.

When the police had left, I turned to Connor. "I'll have to call Mom and let her know what's going on."

"Yup," he said.

We were awoken early the next morning by a phone call from my dad. "You're up early," I said when I answered.

"Haven't been to bed. Your mother called me after you spoke to her, and I knew I'd be hearing from the police soon. Which I have. I've been at the office all night, going through Rich's papers, trying to sort out what will help the cops with the case against Stephen. I always knew I didn't like the man. Never would have thought he was a killer, though. Your mother tells me he attacked you. Are you . . . okay?"

"I'm fine, Dad. The local equivalent of the Hound of the Baskervilles saved me."

"Whatever that means. I've been checking up on Livingstone's recent activities. I was able to tell the police he called in sick on Monday."

"The day Rich died."

"He was, it would seem, driving to Nags Head. He looked none too well, I've been told, when he came into the office late on Tuesday morning. Which would be because he hadn't slept for days."

"The drive from Boston to Nags Head takes about twelve hours each way, and that's with no stops or traffic snarls. A lot to cover in two days."

"On Tuesday afternoon, when I sent word that I wanted someone to go down to North Carolina to be with Evangeline, Livingstone was aggressive about putting himself forward."

"That was a foolish thing to do. If he'd stayed in Boston, he could have kept himself out of the picture."

"He couldn't stand not knowing what was going on and thought he needed to keep an eye on things. More than one criminal's been caught because they simply can't stop themselves hanging around the police investigation. And because they're nowhere near as clever as they think they are." Dad chuckled. "Keeps us in business. This might sound harsh of me, but I've ordered Ricky to get back to Boston. Today. I want him on the first flight he can get. He needs to come clean, and fast, about what he did and did not know about what his father and Livingstone were up to. Your mother will accompany Evangeline and Rich's body tomorrow."

"That's good of her."

"You take care of yourself, honey."

"I will, Dad."

We hung up. "As long as we're awake," I said to Connor, "might as well get a start on the day."

He reached for me. "As long as we're awake . . ."

Fluffy had run to the door in agreement, and Charles had leapt off the bed and headed for his food bowl.

"Here she is now."

Louise Jane came into the bakery, and I gave her a wave. She nodded before joining the line. A few minutes later, coffee in hand, she approached our table. "Big happenings last night at the lighthouse, I heard."

"Big enough," I said.

"They say Mrs. Lewiston's dog brought down your attacker, Lucy."

"Yes."

"Seems hard to believe. A little thing like that against a grown man."

"She—"

"I've told you many, many times, Lucy, that the spirits of the marsh are not to be trifled with. Haven't I told her that, Connor?"

"More than once," Connor agreed.

"Fluffy—"

"Fluffy," she snorted. "Ridiculous name for a dog. Fluffy might have bitten the man, but we have to ask what made her do that. What forces beyond our understanding caused that miniature ball of fluff not to run away, as you'd expect, but to turn into a killer beast?"

"She didn't—"

"When we've finished seeing the house and you've put in an offer, I have to get straight home. I have lot of research to do on paranormal influences on animals."

"I don't—"

"Aren't you jumping the gun, Louise Jane?" Connor said. "We don't know that we'll be putting in an offer on anything."

"You will," she said, with typical Louise Jane confidence. "Ready to go?"

Connor downed the last mouthful of his coffee, stood up, and took his keys out of his pocket.

"I'll drive," Louise Jane said. "My uncle will meet us there."

The front seat of Louise Jane's rusty old van was covered in books, maps, and papers, so Connor and I climbed into the back. She threw the van into gear, and we lurched out of the parking lot.

"I feel like I'm being kidnapped," I whispered to Connor. "Being driven through the streets with no idea of where my captors are taking me."

"At least she didn't put hoods over our heads."

"I heard that," Louise Jane said. "I want you to relax and enjoy the scenery."

"I'm thoroughly acquainted with the scenery of Nags Head, thank you," Connor said.

We drove south, heading in the direction of the lighthouse. Connor and I exchanged looks. Despite Louise Jane saying the property was "on the beach," I'd expected to be going toward what passes as inland on this narrow spit of sand. Rather than taking the wide turn into Whalebone Junction, she continued straight onto South Old Oregon Inlet Road. Tall, colorful beach houses passed us on either side, and I could see the open ocean between the properties to our left. The road was perfectly flat, with a wide swath of neatly mowed grass on both sides. A culvert ran along our right, a sidewalk to our left. The houses lining the beach were large, new, and expensive. This road led out of town, nothing but the National Seashore and the Bodie Island Lighthouse beyond.

"I was down this way only yesterday," Connor said. "I didn't see any house for sale."

"Because you don't know the right people," Louise Jane replied.

"Should we have brought drinks and snacks for the trip?" I asked. "We're almost at the end of the road, and there's nothing else out here." Up ahead I could see the back of the blue sign welcoming visitors to Nags Head.

Louise Jane flicked her turn indicator and slowed. She glided to a halt at the side of the road and said, "Ta da."

Connor and I stared out the window.

"This place?" Connor said. "First of all, Louise Jane, it isn't for sale, and second of all, we couldn't afford it even if it was, not a lot this size sitting right on the beach. Never mind the house, which is, you might have noticed, falling down."

"All it needs is a bit of TLC," Louise Jane said. "It's owned by my uncle Ralph, and even though he doesn't live in it, he's kept it up all these years."

The house stood at the end of the street, on the last lot in Nags Head. It was unpainted, the wood brown and worn, scoured by decades of salt and wind. Large and multistoried, it stood on stilts, with balconies and gabled windows sticking out all over and a wide porch wrapping around the entire second floor.

"There's Uncle Ralph," Louise Jane said.

A man was standing next to a car parked in the weed- and sand-choked driveway. "That's your uncle?" I said to Louise Jane.

"Yup."

We hurried to get out of the van.

He rolled toward us, his gait that of a man more accustomed to being on the water than on land. His gray hair curled around the back of his neck, and most of his face was covered by an unkempt gray beard and bushy eyebrows. His oatmeal fisherman's sweater, which I would have thought too hot for the day, was dotted with holes and strands of unraveling thread. His warm blue eyes were the color of the sea, his hand was outstretched, and he was smiling.

" 'Mornin', Lucy," he said to me in a thick Outer Banks drawl. "Mr. Mayor." He and Connor shook hands.

"Mr. Harper," I said. "How nice to see you. I didn't know you were related to Louise Jane."

"Related to just about everyone in these parts," he said. "Everyone who matters, anyway. And some what don't." I'd met Ralph Harper when he'd been a suspect in a police investigation. A local fisherman from a long line of fishermen, he was reclusive and very, very suspicious of outsiders. For some reason, he didn't consider me to be an outsider. He'd called me a water woman—high praise indeed. I'm from Boston, but I don't think that's what he meant. I never had found out what he meant.

"Like 'er, Mr. Mayor?" he asked Connor.

"I love her." Connor threw his arms wide. "Every Banker's dream is to own a member of the unpainted aristocracy. But she needs a lot of work."

"Which," Louise Jane said, "is why it's going cheap."

"How cheap?" I asked.

Louise Jane looked at her uncle. He named a sum.

Connor laughed. "At that price, you're going to tell me the property's been condemned or a toxic waste dump is going in next door."

"You didn't tell 'em, Louise Jane?"

"Tell us what?" I asked.

"Let's have a look around first, shall we?" Louise Jane quickly led the way to the house. "Over the years Uncle Ralph has done what he can to keep the house in some sort of shape, but without anyone living here, things do get out of control." We climbed the steps, the old boards protesting at our weight.

"Why don't you live here?" I asked Ralph as he unlocked the door. It creaked as it opened, and we stepped into the light-filled interior.

"Jo won't have it," he said.

"Why not?"

"Never mind that now," Louise Jane said. "Look at that view."

And we did. The main floor was completely open—no internal walls. Sunlight streamed into the room, reflecting off spiders' webs and illuminating the dust mites dancing in the air. The large, empty room was bathed in golden morning light, and the open expanse of the sea sparkled in the distance. I could hear the faint sound of waves rushing to shore. I took a step forward, but Ralph's arm shot out and he grabbed mine. "Better not walk around willy-nilly. Some of the floorboards need replacing."

"There's damp in that ceiling," Connor said. "I don't like the look of it."

"Needs work," Ralph said. "I won't deny that. But the bones are good. Darn good. This house has stood for most of a hundred years. Gonna stand a hundred more, iffen it finds someone to love it like my mamma and granddaddy did."

"How long has it been for sale?" I asked.

Ralph and Louise Jane exchanged glances.

"Okay," Connor said. "What are you not telling us? Why is the price so reasonable, and why is this beautiful old house being allowed to fall into disrepair?"

"Uncle Ralph would like to live in it," Louise Jane said. "But Aunt Jo doesn't want to."

"Why hasn't it sold then?" I asked.

"Because it's haunted," Louise Jane said.

Chapter
Twenty-Five

"We put in a conditional offer. Conditional on the inspection not turning up anything Ralph neglected to tell us. Anything structural, I mean."

"Are you sure that's wise, Lucy?" Ronald said. "Old houses have a way of drinking money."

"Connor loved it on first sight. He says he's often driven past and thought it a shame such a magnificent old house was simply abandoned."

"Unpainted aristocracy doesn't come up for sale very often," Charlene said.

It was Monday afternoon, and the library was about to close for the day. Louise Jane and Bertie were having a private meeting in Bertie's office, and we'd gathered to hear Bertie formally tell us Charlene was leaving and what would happen next. James had his arm thrown casually over Charlene's shoulders, and Daisy, who had not the least bit of interest in talk of a house a mere century old, was flipping through a fashion magazine.

Historic homes and cottages of Nags Head, like the one we'd just—*gulp*—bought, are known as the unpainted aristocracy for the simple reason that the original cedar shakes are unpainted, the wood allowed to deepen and darken with age so the buildings now blend with the shoreline. The majority of the houses have been passed down through the generations, and each generation has made as little as possible in the way of improvements or modernizations in order to preserve the property's historic charm. A beloved and important part of Nags Head history and heritage, the majority of them cluster in a group close to town.

"We know that," I said. "But Connor thinks the work will be manageable."

Connor had crawled over just about every inch of the house yesterday and decided that the house did, as Ralph had said, have good bones. "It needs a lot of cosmetic work, Lucy, and some updating in the kitchen and bathroom, but the structure is sound," he'd told me. "Other than that, I wouldn't want to modernize it much at all. It deserves to be left largely as it is."

I'd read the glow in his eyes and realized he was already head over heels in love.

"Connor and his dad can do a lot of the work themselves, and what they can't do or what they don't have time to do, the price of the house itself is good enough we can afford to hire a contractor."

"You'll be close to work and right on the beach," Charlene said. "I think it's an excellent choice."

"Except for the haunting bit," James said.

"Yes, there is that," I admitted. "The supposed haunting bit. I've spent a lot of time listening to Louise Jane try to convince me the lighthouse is haunted, to no avail, so I'm inclined not to believe anything she says about that. Ralph Harper never married, but he lives with his sister Jo, who's refused to so much as set foot in the house since she ran out of it one night when she was seventeen years old."

"Why?" Ronald asked.

"Louise Jane was cagey about that." So cagey I'd been immediately suspicious. If her aunt Jo had seen an actual ghost, Louise Jane would have delighted in telling me all about it. I suspected a teenage prank gone wrong. "The main reason the house hasn't sold isn't because it's supposedly haunted but because Ralph won't sell it to just anyone. His grandparents built it, and his parents lived in it until his mother died. Peacefully in her sleep, I might add. It's never been on the open market, because Ralph doesn't want casual tourists wandering through. He's been waiting fifteen years, since his mother's death, for the right buyer to come along. And, it would seem, Connor and I are the right buyers."

"When do you move in?" Charlene asked.

"Soon, I hope. Once the water and electricity are connected, we can live in one or two rooms while much of the work's being done. It's going to take a long time."

"Are you happy about this?" Ronald asked.

I thought of Connor's beaming dust- and spider-web-covered face as he finished his inspection. Ralph Harper's kind eyes as he told me he wanted me to live in the house his grandparents had built. The sound of the surf at my door, the scent of salt in my hair, the cry of gulls circling overhead, the quiet creak of old floorboards.

"Yes. I am. It's perfect. It's time for me to leave the Lighthouse Aerie and start my new life, and I can't think of a better place in which to do that."

"Good afternoon, all!" Theodore joined us. "I hear you had some excitement recently, Lucy." Ronald hurried to lock the door behind the new arrival before anyone else could wander in.

"Connor and I have put an offer in on a house," I said.

"You did? That's all fine and good, but I meant excitement of a criminal nature."

"Oh yes, that. The police made an arrest in the death of Rich Lewiston."

"Glad to hear it. We can all rest easier tonight knowing Nags Head's finest are up to the job."

"With Lucy's help, as usual," Charlene said.

Theodore tilted his head to one side. I sucked in a breath. I know Teddy well, but I'd never before quite noticed the shape of his eyes, the smaller-than-average teeth, the plump lips . . . the full head of hair.

And I understood. Evangeline hadn't been reacting to James when she saw him the first time but to Theodore, who'd come in with the group. Theodore's as much a feature of the library as the table in the alcove and the books on the shelves, so I hadn't even considered that seeing him was what had so shocked Evangeline. She'd reacted much the same way at book club, when James hadn't been there. Theodore had.

I've met Mrs. Kowalski, Theodore's mother, but I'd never heard mention of a Mr. Kowalski. I'd simply assumed he was dead or Theodore's parents were long divorced.

I remembered back to the night Mom and I waited at the police station with Evangeline. I'd tried to question Evangeline as to what she knew about James Dalrymple, but she'd turned the conversation to Theodore. At the time I thought it a clever diversion, but it wasn't that at all. What had she said about Theodore? She was surprised he'd be able to afford to make a substantial contribution to the library restoration fund. The only way she'd know that would be if she had some knowledge of his financial situation.

Which meant she not only knew of him, but she knew many of the details of his life.

Theodore Kowalski was Rich Lewiston's son.

"Lucy?" He peered intently at me. "Is something wrong?"

I mentally shook my head. Then I physically shook it. "Wrong? No, nothing at all. It's nice to see you this afternoon, Theodore."

"Okay. If you're sure. It's nice to see you too, Lucy."

"Although we are closed," Ronald pointed out.

"I just popped in for a book. Won't take long. Don't mind me. What's going to happen to your apartment when you move, Lucy?"

"Speaking of the Lighthouse Aerie." Bertie's head popped around the corner. "My office please. Lucy, Charlene, Ronald."

James gave Charlene's shoulder a light squeeze, and she smiled at him. "I'll wait out here," he said.

Theodore went in search of the book he was after.

Ronald and I fell into step behind Charlene. "Do you know what this is about, Lucy?" he whispered to me.

"I know some of it, but I suspect not all," I replied. That Louise Jane had spent so long in Bertie's office, behind closed doors, had to mean something.

Louise Jane nodded at us as we came in, her face folded into serious lines. She couldn't quite hide the twinkle in her eyes or the air of self-satisfaction that hung over her. I gave her a questioning look, and she turned away from me, the edges of her mouth curling up. Charles perched on top of the filing cabinet. He, on the other hand, didn't look at all pleased. Charles doesn't care for change.

"Lucy," Bertie said, as she settled herself behind her desk. "Did your mother get away all right?"

"Yes, thanks." I'd gone to Aunt Ellen's this morning to say good-bye. Mom and Evangeline had hired a limo to take them to the airport, where they'd meet Rich's body for the flight home. I'd taken Fluffy with me, and she'd be on the plane with Evangeline and Mom. To my surprise, I'd been sorry to see Fluffy go. I'd grown fond of the little thing. Maybe once we were settled, Connor and I could get a dog. As Fluffy and I walked out of the lighthouse, I'd turned back to see Charles watching us. I swear, he might have lifted one paw in farewell to his new friend.

I hadn't spoken to Evangeline, and that suited me perfectly well. Ricky had left on Sunday, in answer to Dad's summons. He hadn't called me to say good-bye.

Bertie cleared her throat. She announced what I already knew: Charlene had handed in her resignation in order to take up a new position at Oxford University. Ronald hugged her and wished her the best, and I joined in. When we separated, Charlene wiped tears from her eyes.

"As for Charlene's position here," Bertie said, "she will be almost impossible to replace, but I think we've hit on a good solution. Charlene?"

"My friend Denise Robarts works at North Carolina at Chapel Hill," Charlene said. "She's an Outer Banks girl, and she's past sixty. She's been wanting to retire and move back to Nags Head, but she loves her job and is worried about keeping herself busy. She's a widow and her children live in Manhattan, which she detests. I've convinced her to work part-time here. She gets to come back to the Outer Banks, she keeps working, and she can ease into her retirement at her own pace."

"That sounds like a good fit," Ronald said. "But you're always so busy, Charlene. Will a part-timer be enough?"

Louise Jane shifted in her seat.

"I've decided," Bertie said, "to split the job of academic librarian into two. Denise will do the archiving and most of the work with our own rare documents and those we get on loan. The actual interaction with visiting scholars and researchers, and searching secondary sources, will be the job of—" She cleared her throat.

"Me!" Louise Jane couldn't contain herself any longer, and she leapt out of her chair, punching her fists into the air. "Me! I'm going to be the new academic librarian assistant. You won't regret this, Bertie, I promise you that." She grabbed Ronald's hands and pumped them. "I start tomorrow so Charlene has time to show me some of the ropes." She dropped Ronald's hands and lunged at me. She wrapped me in a hug so tight it brought back the uncomfortable memory of being strangled by Stephen Livingstone. "We're going to be colleagues, Lucy! Isn't that wonderful? Now, don't worry about a thing. I'm starting work tomorrow, but I'll wait until you move out before I move in."

"Move in?" I asked.

"To the Lighthouse Aerie! At last! You won't mind if I run up now and measure the space, do you?"

Charles put his paws over his eyes.

I briefly considered putting my paws over my own eyes, but instead I threw my hands into the air. "That is so great. You love this place, Louise Jane, and it's a perfect fit. Like the members of the unpainted aristocracy, the Lighthouse Aerie needs to be lived in."

"You think so, Lucy?" she said.

"I do. I do." Louise Jane truly loved the library, and the library, I believed, loved her in return. If she wanted to tiptoe around at night, hunting for ghosts, what was the harm? Bertie and our new librarian, Denise, would make sure she didn't confuse fact and legend in her job.

As for me . . . time to move on. I loved living in the Lighthouse Aerie, but I'd always known it wouldn't be forever. Connor and I had an exciting future waiting for us in our new house, and I couldn't wait to get it started.

Even if I had to learn how to wield a hammer.

Author's Note

The Bodie Island Lighthouse is a real historic lighthouse, located in Cape Hatteras National Seashore on the Outer Banks of North Carolina. It is still a working lighthouse, protecting ships from the Graveyard of the Atlantic, and the public is invited to tour it and climb the 214 steps to the top. The view from up there is well worth the trip. But the lighthouse does not contain a library, nor is it large enough to house a collection of books, offices, staff rooms, two staircases, and even an apartment.

Within these books, the interior of the lighthouse is the product of my imagination. I like to think of it as my version of the TARDIS, from the TV show *Doctor Who*, or Hermione Granger's beaded handbag: far larger inside than it appears from the outside.

I hope it is large enough for your imagination also.

Read an excerpt from

DEATH BY BEACH READ

the next

LIGHTHOUSE LIBRARY MYSTERY

by EVA GATES

available soon in hardcover from
Crooked Lane Books

CROOKED
LANE

NEW YORK

Chapter One

How hard can it be?

As it turns out, it can be very hard.

When Connor McNeil and I began searching for a house in which to begin our lives together, we realized almost immediately that our options were severely limited. The Outer Banks of North Carolina is a hugely popular tourist area, so it can be hard for local people to find a property that fits their budget. Connor's the mayor of Nags Head, and as long as he's in that role, he wants to live within the city limits. I want to be as close as possible to my own workplace, the Bodie Island Lighthouse Library. I'll admit I was spoiled by my previous commute—the hundred steps of the spiral iron staircase leading to the tiny, perfect apartment on the fourth floor I called my Lighthouse Aerie.

In a stroke of exceptionally good luck, we were offered a great deal on an old house that hadn't been lived in for many years. It hadn't been put up for sale, as the owner was waiting for the "right" buyers to come along. Connor and I suited his idea of the right buyers. The house sits on the beach, at the southern limit of Nags Head, almost within sight of the lighthouse. Built in 1923, it's one of what are known as the "unpainted aristocracy." These Nags Head landmarks are so called because they're unpainted, the siding made of cedar shingles that can withstand the effects of being so close to the ocean. Most of the unpainted aristocracy are located in a cluster nearer to the center of town, but this one stands proudly alone as a testament to the eccentricity of its original owner.

A lover of Outer Banks history, Connor had always dreamed of owning one of those magnificent old places, but they were well out of his budget, even if one did come up for sale. Which almost never happens.

Because this house hadn't been occupied since the death of the owners' mother some fifteen years ago, it was slowly falling into genteel disrepair. Connor's dad, Fred McNeil, had made his living as a carpenter, and Connor had grown up wielding a hammer. So, as long as the bones of the house were sound, which they proved to be, Connor decided he and his dad could do much of the work themselves as time and our budget allowed.

My handyperson skills end at changing a lightbulb. *But*, I thought, as I watched the huge smile spread across the face of the man I loved when he inspected the house, *how hard can it be to learn?*

Very hard, it turned out. For me, anyway. I fell off the stepladder when I tried to put in a fresh lightbulb over the back door and twisted my ankle. Later, in one of my first attempts at wielding a hammer, I managed to hammer my thumb rather than the nail. That incident ended in another trip to the hospital and a couple of weeks of thumb immobility. Fortunately, it was my left thumb, not the right, so I was still able to function. Moderately.

After that, Connor decided I was better suited to fetching mugs of coffee and glasses of tea for him and his dad, planning the furnishings and decor, and maybe thinking about what to do with the patch of weedy sand we optimistically hoped to turn into a beachside garden. I also needed to plan our wedding, scheduled for a year from now.

As its name suggests, the house is made of unpainted cedar shakes, darkened over time and through countless winter storms. As is customary for beach houses in these parts, stilts hold the entire building above the sand and two staircases lead from the ground level up to the entrances. The house is one and a half stories tall, with a peaked roof and numerous white-framed windows. A wide, covered deck stretches across the front and partway down both sides of the house. At the front, a third staircase leads directly to the beach. The house has kept some of its historical features, but it wasn't entirely untouched. The previous owners had modernized it by laying carpeting over the wide-plank boards, removing the traditional sloped benches on the porch and the hinged shutters over the upper windows, and filling in the gaps in the wooden walls that allowed fresh ocean breezes to blow through. The last was probably a good thing, as the gaps also allowed in a great deal of sand in summer and icy ocean winter breezes in winter.

Slowly, slowly, over the fall and winter, the house was hammered into livable shape. Connor's not only the mayor but he also maintains a part-time schedule at his dental practice to keep his hand in. He spent every spare minute he could find hammering and sawing—and muttering and cursing—while I spent every spare minute making tea or coffee and poring through decor and wedding magazines. Fred McNeil was originally supposed to "help out," but as could have been expected, he threw himself into the project wholeheartedly. Connor's mom, Marie, confided in me that Fred wasn't taking well to retirement and this venture was exactly what he needed to feel useful again. For any jobs that were too heavy or complicated for Connor and his dad to do, we called on some of our legion of friends to pitch in, which they did gladly and cheerfully while I ran back and forth with drinks and snacks and our cat Charles howled from the closet where he'd been confined because of so many people coming and going. The roof was repaired first and then the water and electricity reconnected and lines replaced where needed. The previous owner had closed off the second floor and it was in by far the worst shape, but we had plenty of room on the main floor, so Connor blocked off the staircase and said we'd get around to it eventually. The main bathroom, kitchen, and master bedroom were renovated and updated, and last week Connor and I moved into our new home.

I love it here—the quiet at the end of town, the sound of the surf rolling to shore outside our window, the morning sun rising over the ocean and pouring into our bedroom. Connor was born and raised in Nags Head, scion of generations of fishing families, but I'm from Boston. The history of the Outer Banks isn't mine the way it is Connor's, but it's becoming important to me, and I love this charming old house. There wasn't a lot I could do to decorate it yet, but I didn't have many things to bring with me from the Lighthouse Aerie in any event. I'd arrived in North Carolina two years ago with nothing but what would fit into the trunk and back seat of my small teal Yaris, and I'd never sent home for more stuff.

I love living full-time with Connor too. Of which I need say no more.

In North Carolina, the sun rises over the ocean, and we leave the slats of the blinds partially open so we can be woken when the first rays of the new day creep into the bedroom. This morning I stretched luxuriously in my soft bed, wiggled my toes, and extended my arms. I opened my eyes and said, "Good morning."

My bed partner stretched every fiber of his body, rolled over to face me, and said, "Meow."

I laid my hand on the thick, soft fur. "Don't make a habit of taking up that space, buddy."

Charles leapt off the bed and headed into the kitchen, no doubt hoping his food bowl had miraculously been refilled overnight. He is always disappointed, but he never gives up hope. I admire that in him.

I didn't leap off the bed, but I did roll over and sort of fall out. It was Tuesday and I had to get to work. Connor had left in the wee hours of the morning for a dental convention in Raleigh. He'd be home Thursday. Charles had wasted no time in taking Connor's place.

I showered and dressed and caught up on the news from back home in Boston over my cup of coffee and bowl of muesli and yogurt. My mom was showing enormous restraint in not constantly phoning or texting demanding to know what was happening with my wedding plans. We'd set the date, booked the church, and arranged to have the reception at my cousin-in-law's restaurant, Jake's Seafood Bar. I figured that was enough planning for now, but my friends were hinting that I needed to draw up the guest list and wanting to know if I'd chosen my dress or the bridesmaids' dresses (or the bridesmaids), never mind what I wanted for table settings or our first dance. I glanced around the kitchen. This room was almost finished, but it was obvious that the entire house was still a construction site. A drill rested on the counter next to the sink; a stack of ceramic tiles left over from the ones that replaced the linoleum in the bathroom were propped next to the side door. The microwave that would be installed over the stove was still in its box on the counter. It was important to Connor, and thus to me, that the original charm of the house be maintained as much as possible while still allowing for modern upgrades. Such as a microwave in the kitchen and a shower stall in the master bathroom and good lighting throughout. He'd done the kitchen in shades of cream and pale blue, with a granite-topped island and four sleek white-and-chrome stools, a blue glass backsplash and glass-fronted cabinets above the deep double sink, and open shelving along one wall. Pot lights were fitted in the ceiling, the flooring was pale wood, and we'd modernized the appliances with a black ceramic-topped stove and steel fridge. The wall separating the kitchen from the living and dining rooms (and thus cutting off the view) had been mostly removed, except for a couple of load-bearing pillars, leaving the space open and full of light.

Before starting my own breakfast, I'd fed Charles and refreshed his water bowl. Meal over, he was standing by the kitchen door, glaring at me to hurry up, and almost tapping his foot.

I sent Connor a quick text full of heart emojis before closing my iPad. "I don't need a watch when you're around," I said to the impatient cat. I put my dishes in the dishwasher, gathered my things, scooped up the big cat, and stuffed him into the cat carrier by the door, under the thin leash hanging on the hook next to our raincoats and sun hats. He hissed at me, just so I knew he wasn't happy about going into the carrier, but he didn't resist. Not too much, anyway.

Charles isn't my cat. He's the library cat, named in honor of Mr. Charles Dickens. He lived at the library when I started working there and simply followed me upstairs one night to the Lighthouse Aerie and settled in. When I moved, I'd been unsure of what to do with him, but as I carried my last cardboard box down the twisting iron staircase, I found Charles waiting for me by the front door. I put him in the box and carried him to the car.

He might live with Connor and me, but he's still the library cat, and he still has to go to work. After my first several attempts to stuff him into the cat carrier for the short drive to the library (almost requiring another trip to the hospital, this time to have the scratches on my arms attended to), we came to an understanding. If Charles agreed to stop fighting me and get quietly into his carrier, he could come to the library. If not—no library for Charles. Charles never does anything quietly, but my threats to leave him behind seemed to have worked, and the short journey now passed uneventfully.

* * *

It had been a long, cold, damp winter, and now that spring was in the air, everyone seemed to have an extra bounce in their step or wider smile on their face. Our children's librarian, Ronald Burkowski, was off today, and our academic librarian's assistant took the circulation desk while Bertie James, the library director, and I shut ourselves in her office and struggled with the quarterly budget.

Several miserable hours later I staggered out of her office (doing the budget is not my favorite thing) to hear a burst of female laughter and the deep, rolling chuckle of an older man coming from the main room.

We'd had a couple of staff changes here recently when our academic librarian, Charlene Clayton, fell in love with a visiting researcher and moved to England to be with him. Charlene was virtually irreplaceable, but we'd been lucky to find Denise Robarts, an older woman looking to move back to her beloved Nags Head to ease into her retirement. Denise wanted to work part-time, so Bertie hired Louise Jane McKaughnan, an enthusiastic (to say the least) amateur historian and library patron, to be a part-time academic assistant. Louise Jane had moved into the Lighthouse Aerie so quickly that when I left, I'd passed her hurrying up the steps laden with her own possessions.

I'd been wary, very wary, of Bertie's decision to give Louise Jane a formal position at the library. Her deep family roots and love of Outer Banks history could get a bit, shall we say, out of hand. Along with her propensity to embellish facts to make them more interesting, she specialized in what she saw as the paranormal history of the area in general and the lighthouse in particular.

To my surprise, and delight, the arrangement was working out splendidly. Louise Jane and Denise functioned well together, and between them Denise and Bertie had been able to convince Louise Jane that her paranormal investigations were not part of the job. Personally, I was getting on better with Louise Jane. She'd always envied me working at the library and living in the Lighthouse Aerie, and now that she'd achieved her dream, she didn't try quite as much to get under my skin.

I emerged from the budget meeting to find Louise Jane, Denise, and several of our patrons huddled around the table in the alcove—where this week's display centered around the Puritan history of New England—laughing uproariously.

Ralph Harper, Louise Jane's uncle and the previous owner of what was now Connor's and my house, gave me a smile. "Here's Lucy now," he said.

"What's so funny?" I asked.

"Ralph and his stories," Denise said. "I'd tell him to write them down for posterity except that I never know what part of them is true."

Ralph crossed his arms over his barrel chest and said, "Every word, Miss Robarts, every word. The sea's a hard mistress, and her stories don't need no embellishing."

A snort came from the wingback chair next to the magazine rack. Mr. Snyder took that seat regularly, three times a week. He sat there for two hours, browsing magazines, listening to the conversation swirling around him but rarely participating, and stroking Charles, who liked to curl up on his lap. Mr. Snyder was in his early eighties and widowed. He'd been a popular high school teacher for many years, I'd been told, but he was finding life very lonely since the death of his wife. A modern library is many things to many people, and if the elderly gentleman came here for some human companionship and feline affection, he was more than welcome. I gave him a private smile and he winked at me. Ralph Harper could get carried away sometimes.

Denise swung her purse over her shoulder, and the patrons dispersed. "I'm off home. Louise Jane, I've prepared that letter to go to the people in Halifax and emailed the draft to you. If you can tidy it up, check all the links are correct, fill in some of the blanks, and then send it off, I'd appreciate it."

"Sure," Louise Jane said. "I'll do that now. Lucy?"

"Go ahead. I'll take the desk. Nice to see you, Ralph. How are you today?"

"Better now that the ocean's calming down. Been bad out there these past weeks."

I settled myself behind the desk. Ralph was a fisherman from a long line of fishermen. What showed of his face behind the enormous white beard and matching eyebrows was as weathered as ancient leather and as wrinkled as crumbled paper. He walked with a rolling gait, as if the land was not his natural environment, and his voice was always pitched as though he were bellowing orders to seamen in the face of a tempest. He didn't have a lot of time for "city people," meaning just about everyone who didn't make their living from the water, but for some reason he'd decided he liked me. He called me a "water-woman." High praise indeed, although I had absolutely no idea what I'd done to deserve the designation. Ralph had held on to the home his grandparents had built, in which he'd grown up and in which his parents had died, for fifteen years after his mother's death, waiting for a "water-woman" and "Outer Banks boy" to come along.

Ralph himself had not lived in the house since his youth, and it stood empty until Connor and I moved in. Ralph had never married and lived with his younger sister, Joanna, whom everyone called Jo. After an incident when she was seventeen, Joanna had refused to step foot in the house again. She was sixty now and she'd kept her vow all these years. No one really knew what had happened that night that frightened her so much. Louise Jane insisted the house was haunted and Joanna had disturbed something she shouldn't. Most other people thought she'd been the victim of a teenage prank gone wrong.

I never pay any attention to Louise Jane's stories of the paranormal, and I didn't concerning our house. When I first arrived at the library, she'd tried to frighten me out of the

Lighthouse Aerie by spinning stories of the hauntings of the lighthouse in general and my apartment in particular. If the building did have any ghosts, they were friendly ones. I'd never felt anything but good vibes here.

"What brings you in today?" I asked. Ralph wasn't normally a visitor to the library.

He pointed to the alcove. "That does."

"You mean the history of New England?"

"Mr. Nathaniel Hawthorne. Favorite of my mother's, he was. Louise Jane said you're reading *The House of the Seven Gables* for your little club."

I smiled at him. "That's right. And thus we prepared that exhibit to accompany the book and Hawthorne's other works. Do you want to come to book club? You're very welcome. We meet next Thursday at seven. Will that give you enough time to read it?"

He shrugged. "Don't need to read it. I remember it well enough. My mother talked about it all the time." His brilliant blue eyes, the color of the ocean on a sunny summer's day, slid to one side. "I . . . uh . . . figured long as I was here, I'd check as to how the house is doing."

I thought I understood. He wasn't really interested in coming to the next meeting of the Bodie Island Lighthouse Library Classic Novel Reading Club. He'd come in today wanting to ask me how I was finding living in the house. Natural enough. That house had been built by his grandparents. He'd grown up there, and his mother had lived in it her entire life. He had to have a strong attachment to it. He hadn't come around since Connor and I took possession in the fall and work had begun. He'd been respecting our boundaries, which was thoughtful of him.

"We love it," I said. "We truly do. You know Connor's determined to do the best by it and preserve what he can of what your grandparents built."

"Wouldn'ta sold it to you otherwise," he said.

"The next thing Connor and his dad are going to do is put new windows in the downstairs guest bedrooms, stripping the wallpaper and painting. When summer arrives, we'd like to be able to have guests to stay. Did your family entertain much?"

"Not when I was a boy. My grandparents, so my mother told me, put on grand parties in those early days. Parties that were the talk o' the town." Something dark moved across his face, and a winter storm began building behind the blue eyes.

"Ralph?"

"Louise Jane and some other folks say the house is haunted."

"I know that. You were honest about telling us that. I can assure you we've sensed nothing. More importantly, Charles has sensed nothing."

As usual, Charles seemed to know when he was being discussed, and his black nose peered out from behind Mr. Snyder's magazine. He leapt onto the floor and from there to a high shelf, the better to hear the conversation.

"That's good, then," Ralph said. "Animals have powerful senses. Stories grow and spread in the telling. Bad enough in my day, but I hear it's even worse with this Tweety thing."

"Tweety?"

"What they call the social media?"

"Oh. Twitter. Yes. Although I have to say, I've found the Lighthouse Library word-of-mouth grapevine to be just as efficient."

Mr. Snyder chuckled, but he didn't lower his magazine.

Ralph turned and walked away without another word. On his way out, he passed the shelf on which Charles was perched. The two of them looked at each other, and I'd swear they exchanged identical nods.

I laughed out loud. Two curmudgeons.

A woman put a stack of books on the desk. "Guess what I'm doing when I get home, Lucy," she said.

"I can't. What?"

"I'm putting all my winter clothes away and getting out the summer ones." She spread her arms. "I've decided to declare that spring is here, and not a moment too soon."

"I'm with you on that," I said.

Spring. New beginnings. Everything in my life was absolutely perfect. My love for Connor and his for me was strong. Our wedding was approaching, even if I hadn't managed to get the matter of the table settings sorted out.

As I did several times a day, I lifted my left hand to admire the ring on my finger. The perfectly cut two-caret diamond flashed pure clear light. Connor hadn't bought the diamond; it had been a gift from a friend in thanks for a favor we'd done her, and he'd had the gorgeous stone set into a band to make my ring.

We had a house, which we were making into exactly the home we wanted. A place to grow old together, surrounded by our family. My friends and family were all well. Peace and comradery reigned in the library community.

Fall and winter had been cold and wet but peaceful: no murder or high drama at the Lighthouse Library.

I was a happy woman. Charles landed on the desk and rubbed himself against my arm. Charles was a happy cat.

The door flew open and a woman walked in. She was in her midsixties, dressed in a baby-blue knockoff designer suit over a blouse with a blue-and-pink polka dot bow tied at the neck. Her makeup was heavy but well applied, and her hair cut in a perfect line at her chin and dyed an unnatural blond. Her deep-red lips broke into a huge smile at the sight of me sitting behind the desk, but the smile didn't reach her eyes. Her high heels tapped on the black-and-white tile floor as she crossed the room, arms outstretched. "Lucy! How marvelous to see you." She leaned across the desk, and instinctively I half rose to meet her. She brushed my cheek with her lips, and I caught a wave of Chanel No. 5.

"Diane," I said. "What brings you here?"

"I'm back in town, Lucy, and so happy to be here. I've taken a darling apartment in Nags Head. At first I worried it would be too small, but it's so much nicer than that drafty old house, which was such a dreadful chore to keep clean, and I'm finding it absolutely delightful to be near the shops and restaurants in town. I've missed you all so much. I hear congratulations are in order. I'm so happy for you and Connor. I always knew you were meant for each other."

"Thank you. It's . . . uh . . . nice to see you," I lied.

Not as polite as me, Charles arched his back and hissed.

"You still have that cat, I see. How . . . nice." Diane showed Charles her teeth. He hissed again. "Is Bertie in? Don't get up; I can find my way. I haven't forgotten how important my dear late husband Jonathan was to this library, and I've come to once again offer my services, now that that . . . minor unpleasantness with Curtis is over and done with." She laughed lightly, and her freshly manicured fingers fluttered.

"You mean when you suspected a person of being a killer and also knew they were out to get me but you kept that detail to yourself?" I said.

Death by Beach Read

"All misunderstandings. Water under the bridge. Don't let me keep you from your work, Lucy dear. I'm so delighted to be back. I'm sure we'll be seeing a great deal more of each other." She tottered away, waving cheerfully to library patrons like the queen on parade.

I picked up the phone to warn Bertie that Diane Uppiton was heading her way. I was no longer a happy woman.

Charles hissed one more time at the retreating figure.

Charles was no longer a happy cat.

Chapter Two

When I got home, I found Fred McNeil's truck parked on the road and the hardware store delivery van filling the driveway. Connor's father gave me a wave as I hustled Charles into the house.

"What's up?" I said, when the cat had been freed from his carrier and shut inside the house and I'd come out to join Fred.

"Wood for the deck. We're planning to get that started this weekend."

"I thought the main floor guest bedrooms were next on the list."

"Connor wants the deck ready soon as the weather's warm enough to sit outside of an evening. Spring arrived fast this year, and the forecast for the weekend is good outdoor working weather."

Two men carried loads of lumber past us and around the house. The scent of fresh sawdust trailed behind them and mingled with traces of salt coming off the ocean.

"You know Connor's away for a few days, right?" I asked.

"Back Thursday."

"Are you planning to do any work here tonight?"

"No. I have to wait for him. I hate to say it, Lucy, but my back's been acting up." His face twisted. "Not quite as young as I used to be."

I smiled at him fondly. I liked Connor's parents a great deal, and they seemed to like me. Connor took more after his mother than his father. From her he got the dark hair, the blue eyes framed by long black lashes, the sharp cheekbones and strong jaw. He'd inherited his lean frame from his father and his height from both his parents. The McNeils towered over five-foot-three me, and no one ever called me lean. This close to the ocean, I could almost feel my always-out-of-control black curls curling even more. "Pop in for a cup of coffee or a beer before you leave," I said.

"Thanks, honey, but no. It's my poker night, so I gotta get home for an early dinner."

Connor's father had been almost as thrilled as Connor at getting the chance to fix up a member of the unpainted aristocracy. The first time he'd come into the house, he'd looked around with eyes so full of memory, I could tell he'd spent some time in a house much like this one in his youth. But his eyes had been dark, and he hadn't smiled or fondly run his fingers over the cracked and aging wood, so I didn't think the memories were necessarily good ones. But then he'd almost physically shaken off the ghosts of the past and said, "She's a beauty, all right, and scarcely changed a bit."

I waved to him and went inside.

* * *

I jerked awake. I'd closed the blinds tonight, and only a tiny sliver of light leaked into the bedroom from the night-light in the master bathroom; otherwise, all was completely dark.

Charles was standing next to me, his ears up and his tail sweeping slowly back and forth, back and forth. His eyes were focused on the doorway, and the hair along his back stood on end. I laid my hand on his side. Every muscle was stiff with tension.

This was an old house undergoing much-needed repairs. It creaked and it moaned and it sighed. It stood on pillars, and the open ocean was steps from those pillars, and the surf rushed to shore throughout the night. The beach was public, and although not many people walked along it late at night, some did on occasion. I reminded myself of all of that and told myself to go back to sleep.

A floorboard creaked.

I stiffened and sucked in a breath. Charles sailed off the bed and ran out of the bedroom. I threw off the covers, swept my phone off the night table, and went after him. I hit the switch, and the room flooded with welcome light. I stopped in the hallway and strained my ears, listening for another sound.

All was quiet. So quiet, I feared that if we did have an intruder, they'd be able to hear the beating of my heart.

"Charles," I said, more to myself than to him. "It's nothing but a mouse in the walls. Come back to bed."

Nothing. I hesitated, wondering which way to go. The ocean-facing living room was in front of me and the dining area beyond that. Down the hall to my left were the kitchen, two guest bedrooms, and the back (i.e., street-facing) entrance to the house. I peered into the living room. Moonlight streamed through the uncurtained windows. The yellowing shag carpeting had been pulled up and loose and rotting floor-boards replaced, but the final flooring wouldn't be laid until work is finished on the more important rooms of the house. At the rear of the living room, adjoining the kitchen, a staircase leads to the upper level, where we plan to eventually put in a games room or den and another bathroom and guest room. The staircase is guarded by a six-foot-high block of wood firmly attached by hinges to the wall. The upper level, Connor said, is not safe, and he wants to ensure no one goes up there. I crossed the living room in a few steps and shook the makeshift door. It held firm.

A wall separates the living and dining areas. Connor plans to eventually remove the wall, opening up the space to the flow of light and conversation. The door was open and I peeked into the dining room, where I'd happily envisioned laughing friends and family crowded around a huge wooden table groaning under the weight of food and drink. This room was also empty.

I turned back to the living room, preparing to have a quick check of the rest of the house and then go back to bed, when I saw Charles at the windows, caught in a beam of moonlight.

I blinked and slowly came to realize that Charles was not in the living room. He was on the crumbling deck itself, on the far side of the sliding door. Which meant the door was open. I ran across the room, heedless of the old wood creaking under my weight. The open gap between the door and the wall was not much wider than a cat's width. I pulled and pushed at the door as I called to the cat, but it wouldn't open any farther, and I finally realized the rusty sliders were clogged with sand and debris.

"Charles! Get in here." I clapped my hands and made summoning noises. Charles was not an outdoor cat. If he decided to do some nocturnal exploring, I worried he wouldn't be able to find his way home. Ignoring me, he leapt onto the railing and gazed out to sea.

I sucked in my stomach and managed to edge myself sideways through the gap between the door and the wall. The wooden planks of the deck were soft with age and the effects of constant sea spray, which was why they needed to be replaced. "Charles," I said. "Get in here."

He didn't move. I held my breath, as though that would make me weigh less, and cautiously took a step forward. The wood shifted beneath me, but nothing cracked apart, so I crossed as rapidly and lightly as I could. I reached out, grabbed the cat, and hurried back inside. It was a tight fit, getting us both through the door, but I finally managed. I wrenched the door shut and put Charles down. "Don't do that again," I said in my sternest voice.

He flicked his tail and strolled away. "Silly ca—" The words died in my throat. This room had no working lights. A tangle of wires, ending in nothing, hung from the ceiling where a chandelier had once held pride of place. Moonlight streamed through the ocean-facing door and windows, illuminating dust mites swirling in the air, disturbed by my passing. The room had no furniture, and the floor was thick with accumulated sand and dust. I watched Charles leave a faint trail of paw prints behind him, next to the marks laid down by my own bare feet. I could see something else, something that had my heart leaping into my throat. Shoe prints. The indistinct outline of a pair of shoes, crossing the room from the kitchen to the sliding door.

At that moment a cloud moved across the moon and the light died, and I was plunged into semidarkness. I switched my phone's flashlight on, but in the beam of that bright light all I could see was a dirty floor with a few indistinct marks on it. How long had those prints been there? I hadn't been in this room for weeks at least. Not since I'd admired the view from the sliding door and calculated what size couch and coffee table would fit.

Could the prints have been left by Connor or his dad? Entirely possible. I was in bare feet at the moment, but Connor had told me that with all the loose old boards and rusty nails around and the chance of fresh nails being dropped, I should always wear my shoes.

The prints had seemed too small to be Connor's, but they weren't a clear outline. Perhaps the deliverymen had come in here earlier to drop off some of their supplies. I'd seen them taking the finished planks around the front of the house, but they might have come inside with smaller items before I got home.

My fingers hovered over the phone. Should I call the police? I know several people on the force. One of my closest friends was dating a cop, and he was my friend also. I'd more than once been able to help Detective Sam Watson with his cases.

I hesitated. I'd lived in the Lighthouse Aerie for two years, comfortably and happily alone at night in that old building as it creaked and swayed in the wind. But the lighthouse has one entrance and windows set into four-foot-thick stone walls. The apartment has a locked door, and the window is a hundred feet above the ground. In there I was as safe as lighthouses.

This house has three sets of external stairs, numerous windows, several doors, and access to the deck directly off the beach.

This was the first night I'd been alone here. I planned to live in this house for many long years to come. If I called for help already, would that cast a pall over the way I felt about the house? I couldn't allow myself to be frightened here.

I returned to the sliding door and yanked at it to ensure it was firmly shut. I flicked the latch and verified that it was locked. The deliverymen had been on the deck, and they hadn't bothered to make sure the door was shut and locked behind them when they left. Perhaps it had gotten stuck and they'd decided it wasn't worth bothering about. I made a mental note to check every door before retiring for the night from now on. That wasn't being nervous—it was only practical.

Just to be safe, I decided to check the rest of the house now. I gripped my phone in my hand and left the flashlight app on, although I switched on what lights were working as I passed through the house. The north side of the kitchen opens into the dining room, and a door in the western wall leads down the outside steps to the path to the garage and the street. I tested the door and found it satisfyingly locked. The bathroom and bedroom doors on either side of the narrow hallway were closed. The hallway's used regularly, as it ends at another door to the outside, so no dust and sand had accumulated on the floor that could capture footprints. I put my hand on the bedroom door nearest the entrance to the house, gathered my courage around me, took a deep breath, and threw the door open with enough strength to have it bouncing off the wall. We hadn't put any furniture in here yet, pending the stripping of the peeling yellowing wallpaper, and the smaller bedrooms don't have closets, as was the custom in older houses. Not even a mouse could find a place to hide from me in here. The other bedroom was the same, as was the sleeping porch tucked next to the deck at the south side of the house.

Lastly, I went back to the kitchen, where I found Charles batting his empty water bowl around the room. A puddle next to the sink indicated that he'd knocked the bowl over. I had one last place to check and, now feeling slightly foolish, opened the door to the pantry and shined my light in. A big bag of kibble, a few cans of cat food, some tomato sauce, packages of rice and dried pasta, cleaning products, and wicker baskets containing potatoes and onions. In here there were places for mice to hide, but nothing any larger. I shut the door behind me and grabbed a dish towel off the oven handle, wiped up the spilled water, and refreshed the bowl.

"That's enough excitement for tonight," I said to Charles in a loud, firm voice. "I'm going back to bed. You can come or not."

He ran on ahead, and by the time I'd rechecked every door and all the windows, he was curled in the center of the bed, snoozing contentedly. I crawled in next to him, but I didn't get much sleep. I'd left every light in the house on.

* * *

The sunlight didn't wake me, and it was only the sound of an incoming text that had me jerking awake. I fumbled for the phone and peered at the screen.

> Connor: *Good morning. Most boring conference I've ever been to. Missing you lots*
>
> Me: *Missing you too*
>
> Connor: *Everything okay at the house?*

I thought. Was everything okay? Of course it was. Perfectly okay.

> Me: *All good. Wood for deck delivered*
>
> Connor: *Dad told me. Xxxxx.*
>
> Me: ♥

As I showered, I thought about last night. Standing under the hot, steaming water, in the full light of day, I decided I'd overreacted. Frightened by the creak of an old house in the night. I'd better get my nerves under control, and fast. I told myself I was simply getting used to this big old house, particularly being in it by myself.

Except for Charles, of course. I tried to shove aside the image of Charles when we'd first woken up, but it refused to be shoved. *Something* had alerted Charles, and he'd never before been one to be spooked by anything. If he'd heard a mouse, he would simply have jumped off the bed and chased it away.

Some say this house is haunted. Ralph's sister refused to cross the threshold even to visit her parents. What sort of teenage prank gone wrong would result in behavior so extreme? Maybe, I told myself, Jo Harper simply didn't like her parents and eagerly latched on to a good excuse not to visit them. Maybe she was a drama queen who relished the attention. Maybe she'd made up a story and it got out of control and she didn't know how to call it back.

I walked through the house, switching off lights I'd left on all night. Outside, the tide was coming in and the sea rushed to shore. I carried my coffee into the sun-filled living room. The sliding door was shut and locked, as I'd left it. Of course it was. What had I been expecting? I sipped my coffee and watched the activity outside. A few neighbors walked along the sand while their dogs chased sandpipers through the surf or sent sea gulls flying high. Charter fishing boats headed out to the open sea and closer to a handful of poles arched over the beach into the water. I turned. The sun streaming into the room caught traces of marks in the sand and dust. Cat's paws, bare feet. And shoes. Just in case . . . I took pictures of the prints but when I examined them they didn't look like anything at all.

"House," I said, my voice echoing off the walls in the empty room. "I love you already. We'll take care of you, and I know you'll love us in return."

Back in the kitchen, I found Charles waiting for me by the door. If Charles wasn't bothered by the events of last night, neither would I be.